Like Doves

of the Valleys

Like Doves of the Valleys

A Novel

David Herington

REDHAWK
PUBLICATIONS

Redhawk Publications
The Catawba Valley Community College Press
2550 US Hwy 70 SE
Hickory NC 28602

ISBN: 978-1-959346-04-3

Library of Congress Number: 2023931988

Layout and edit by Robert Canipe

Cover by Shelly and Robert

Cover photo credits: Inset photograph, front cover right--NPS.gov--public domain, usage unrestricted.

All other cover photos are from the author's personal collection.

Printed in the United States of America

redhawkpublications.com

Main Characters

Enslaved people:

Sarah: personal servant of Carrie, mother of Brock and others, b. 1797

Emma: personal servant of Carrie Adams, mother of Kee and others, b. 1797

Brock: son of Sarah, husband of Kee, Father of Cat b. 1818

Kee: daughter of Emma, wife of Brock, mother of Cat, b. 1820

Cat: daughter of Brock and Kee, b. 1839

Non-enslaved people:

George Morgan Adams: husband of Carrie, b. 1794

Carrie Adams: wife of George, b. 1797

Thomas Jefferson Adams: "Thomas," son of George and Carrie, b. 1817

Felicia Frazier Adams: wife of Thomas, b. 1820

Thomas Jefferson Adams, Jr: "Jefferson," son of Thomas and Felicia, b. 1839

Philip Parker: pastor, and overseer for George and Carrie

Evangeline Parker: wife of Philip

Table of Contents

Author's Note

"That cheerful eye, under the influence of slavery, soon became red with rage; that voice, made all of sweet accord, changed to one of harsh and horrid discord; and that angelic face gave place to that of a demon."

Frederick Douglass wrote those words about the woman whose home he entered as an eight-year-old enslaved boy in 1826. Douglass, and many other writers of the day, pointed out how the owning of enslaved people poisoned the souls of the enslavers, and how slavery corrupted society at large.

I used this passage as a jumping-off point for my effort to imagine what that process would look like for the millions of Americans who chose the enslavement of others as a pathway to their own comfort and prosperity. Instead of what Douglass saw happen over the period of a few years of his first period of enslavement in Baltimore, I tried to imagine how the corruption of heart and soul might play out over three generations of an enslaving family and the enslaved people.

A few comments. First, some may recognize that Chapter 14 is familiar. I tried to make that passage an homage to *The Grapes of Wrath*, John Steinbeck's masterful depiction of callous exploitation. I used his descriptions of the Oklahoma used-car dealers (Chapter 7 in *The Grapes of Wrath*) as an inspiration for my descriptions of the slave traders of Shockoe Bottom. I would like to imagine that what I write carries a faint echo of his great work.

Second, I intentionally chose to minimize the use of place-names, except to use those that were needed to tell the story. My intent is to broaden the story, and to make the themes applicable to a wider time and place.

Third, it is not my goal to bestow feelings of guilt on any folks whose ancestors enslaved people. Many Americans have ancestors who enslaved people, myself included. The enslavers are, of course, long dead, and whatever injustices they committed belong to them, not to today's generation. But the institutions they built, before and after emancipation, have consequences that have come down to us through the generations. The systemic racism of our generation is a legacy to us from the enslaving generations of the past. Our task is to acknowledge that legacy, and address it for the benefit of our children and grand-children.

D.H., 11/2022

Dedication

To Karen, With All My Love

Like Doves of the Valleys

"My new mistress proved to be all she appeared when I first met her at the door—a woman of the kindest heart and finest feelings...But, alas! this kind heart had but a short time to remain such. The fatal poison of irresponsible power was already in her hands, and soon commenced its infernal work. That cheerful eye, under the influence of slavery, soon became red with rage; that voice, made all of sweet accord, changed to one of harsh and horrid discord; and that angelic face gave place to that of a demon."

—Narrative of the Life of Frederick Douglass

But they that escape...shall be on the mountains like doves of the valleys, all of them mourning, every one for his iniquity.

—Ezekiel 7:16, KJV

Chapter 1 —1861—Regrets

Carrie Adams lay in bed, her head resting on a feather pillow. Soft moonlight filtered through the curtains at the window, casting patterns of light and dark on the wall. She lay with her eyes closed, but she knew from many nights past that sleep would not come, not for hours.

She sipped down her dram of laudanum, the little bit the doctor granted for her pain hours before. On top of that, she took two long swallows from her bottle of brandy, hoping the mingling of the two would grant her respite of sleep. So the burning pain was a bit lessened, and her head swam with the intoxicating effect of the opium and alcohol. But slumber had not come. Not yet.

She opened her eyes and lifted her hands, dimly illuminated in the moonlight. The twisted fingers and misshapen joints appeared in front of her, a legacy from years, decades now, of ravaging by rheumatism. It plundered her body, stealing away her youth and beauty, and now, at age 64, was stealing everything else, leaving her crippled and useless. Worse than useless, a burden.

She dropped her hands down and closed her eyes but, still, she knew that she would linger in wakefulness for hours yet. In these quiet hours of the night, before sleep granted her a brief measure of oblivion, memories would come flooding into her, regrets piling one on top of another. Her mind would roll through, one by one, the choices made that brought her to this bitter ending.

She thought back to Richmond, where she was born and grew up, rich and privileged in a huge brick mansion. She could never have stayed in Richmond. Even now, decades later, the man who hurt her, who seemed ready to kill her, was there, living his life in freedom. She could still smell the tobacco on his breath, still taste the sour taste of whisky on his tongue. More than 40 years later, she still saw his name in the newspapers, risen high in politics, a venomous man full of hate, thunderously proclaiming the justness, the righteousness of the Southern cause.

Her thoughts turned to her beloved George, so strong and full of fire. George had been the answer to all of her desperate wishes. He defied her family, taking her in marriage, then taking her away from Richmond, building a home for them here, on this very land.

When they wed, George cared nothing about slaves or money. All he wanted, besides Carrie herself, was land. Land to own, to build a home for them, to pour himself into. But Carrie was fearful—wanted security—something more than uncertain promises in an unknown country. So when the time came to claim her inheritance, she asked for slaves, insisted on them. Because of that, years later, George was murdered. Carrie did not strike the blow that killed him, but the fault for it was hers. She bore the guilt.

She was left alone with Thomas, the only child to come from her marriage to George. Sadly, none of George's strength or drive was passed to his son. Now past forty, Thomas was still a child, an angry boy grown up in a man's body. He never forgave an insult, never forgot a slight, no matter how small. Yet they lived here together, mother and son, in this falling-down farm house. Both of them widowed for years now, both lonely, her regrets matched only by his dark rages.

Her thoughts turned to her grandson Jefferson, born out of Thomas's brief marriage. Jefferson came into the world in a tempest of suffering and pain, damaged and barely alive. His poor mother Felicia died when he was just three days old, wracked with fevers, her chills shaking the whole house. Jefferson survived, a slender reed whipped about by his father's black moods. Now he was off at University, set to receive his diploma in a few months. Would he come back here? In her heart, she wanted him back for the sweet solace of his companionship. In her mind, she hoped he would stay away and not be taken in, not be deceived by this beautiful cursed land.

She lay in her bed, watching as the track of the moonlight moved slowly across her wall, hour by hour. It was the same every night. Again and again, the same melancholic phrase would course through her mind: my wasted, wasted life.

Why couldn't she and George have gone somewhere else, used her inheritance to buy land in the north or out west? The money would've allowed them to go anywhere. Instead, she chose the slaves. So they stayed in the South, on this wild patch of land. But the wild land was fickle, mocking them, taking all that they put into it but returning less than half. Their money drained away. So they sold the slaves, one or two at a time, just to keep their heads above water until the slaves were gone, or nearly so.

Her memories turned to Sarah and Emma, her two slave half-sisters, the only true friends she ever had. She promised them a home, and they trusted her, served her faithfully. But she betrayed them, sending their precious children back to Richmond, to the slave market there. The money saved the farm and saved them from going bankrupt. She longed for them every day, mourned her loss of them. She wondered where they might have been sold, if they were even still alive. In the most secret place in her heart, though she knew that, if faced once more with the same choice, she would sell them again. For the money. To save her life here.

§

Well after midnight, as she drifted toward sleep, she startled awake, sensing a dark form at her door. The moon was now set, and a deep shadow filled the room. She saw the tip of a cigarette glowing and smelled corn liquor. She called out to her son, "Thomas, what is it? Are you ill?"

She received no answer. She called out again, but again there was nothing, only silence. She saw the form move in toward her. It moved to the side of her bed, next to her head.

"Thomas, answer me. I know it's you. What's wrong?"

Instead of hearing Thomas' voice, she suddenly felt fingers pushed down against her face, covering her nose and mouth. She felt panic as her breath was cut off. She flailed her frail arms and crippled hands about, striking them against the strong forearms pressing down across her face. This time, though, she was no match for her assailant. She felt herself sinking into darkness, much darker than her room. Her last thought, just before fading into total oblivion, came to her in a rush: My wasted, wasted life.

Chapter 2—1817—Coming to the Land— Carrie

In an instant, Carrie Adams felt free. The sudden awareness of liberation came to her all at once, surging through her and lifting her like a wave lifting a ship on the ocean. Even as she sat still on the rough wooden wagon seat, she felt the crushing weight of memories, of rages and fears, held for so long inside her, falling away. It was so sudden that her breath caught for a moment as she adjusted herself to the new sense of emancipation.

She looked up at the sky ahead of her, framed by a curtain of trees on either side of the road. Dusk was coming on, and the clouds on the western horizon were a glowing palette of purples and reds. Rising from below, the mountains stood out in a dark silhouette. The beauty of the moment seemed to perfectly reflect the new feeling, the new lightness in her heart.

She shifted her gaze over to George, her husband for the past four months, seated next to her, holding the reins as the wagon bounced along on the road, and the feeling of peace surged into her again, lifting her to new heights.

She took in a deep breath of air, savoring the scent, the taste of her freedom. It was almost beyond belief. A year ago, she wouldn't have dared to contemplate being here, sitting on this wagon, traveling miles and miles away from Richmond. A year ago, she hadn't known George and could scarcely have imagined that a man like George could exist. Now, George filled her up to overflowing. George was the one who let her believe in herself, helped her to find her courage, then to act, to put herself on this path.

Without George, she would still be in the grasp of her family, still being slowly suffocated by her mother, her two older sisters, and most especially by Frederick, her pompous older brother. All of them, even her married sisters and their husbands, still lived together in the huge brick mansion in Richmond, where Carrie was born, where she lived her whole life until now.

Her father, dead the last ten years, had set the family on this course. Born poor, he amassed a vast fortune, buying up land along Virginia's rivers, turning the land into plantations worked by an army of slaves, growing tobacco, and transporting it around the world in his fleet of ships. He built the mansion, a massive edifice of red bricks and stones, as a monument to himself and his genius and imprisoned his family within it. He was killed when Carrie was ten, and Frederick ascended onto the throne, imperiously ruling over the family and its empire of wealth.

Carrie's mother was only 50 when her husband died, an attractive widow in possession of a towering mountain of wealth. She could have remarried, built a new life for herself, found happiness. She could have traveled to Europe or anywhere in the world, wherever she wished. Instead, she devoted herself to preserving her husband's memory. She left the mansion untouched, year after year, a shrine to the Great Man frozen in time. Carrie had resigned herself to playing her role in the family drama, living her life in the dark shadow of her dead father.

Now Carrie was liberated from all of that. She had escaped, brought back to life, emerging from the mansion like Lazarus walking out of his tomb. George had done that for her.

That was not all of it, though, not even the largest part of her liberation. There was someone else, someone whose very presence in Richmond cast a darker and much more painful shadow over Carrie than any of the people in her stupid family. Carrie acknowledged the person, even as she tried to keep her mind averted away from him. She was liberated, forever, she hoped, from seeing the face or hearing the name of a man, a certain man who still freely walked the streets of Richmond. The man who raped her. The man who, if she had not struck back at him, would have killed her.

It was four years past now, but the memories remained sharp. Carrie just turned sixteen. A scant two months before, she and her mother traveled to Charleston, attending concerts and balls, announcing to the upper levels of society that she would receive callers. A steady stream of boys came to call, youngsters scrubbed and dressed up by their mothers, awkwardly making feeble efforts at small talk. Some of the boys would try to hold her hand, their palms moist with perspiration.

The man who came to call that day was different. A scion of one of Virginia's founding families, he recently returned to Richmond after travels in the West and overseas. Carrie secretly peeked at him through a window as he stepped out from his carriage, confidently climbing the steps to the mansion.

He stepped into the mansion's library and, catching sight of Carrie waiting there for him, greeted her with a broad smile.

"Enchanted," he said to her, a single word, yet his rich, sonorous voice seemed to carry so much more meaning. He presented her with expensive gifts, then showered more sweet words on her. Flattered by his attention, Carrie walked with him onto the mansion's wooded grounds, out of sight of the house. As they strolled among the trees, Carrie was unable to hide her smile, feeling her heart warming toward the man. He moved in more closely to her, and Carrie expected to feel his lips brush against her cheek. Instead, he seized her with powerful hands and pushed her roughly against the trunk of a tree, smirking and laughing at her fearful expression.

Summoning her voice, she called out, "Help, help me," but as quickly as the words left her, she felt a shock of pain as the man drove his fist into her face. Pressing down onto her chest with his shoulder, he hiked up her petticoats and loosened his trousers, prying her legs apart and thrusting between them, forcing himself into her. As his grunting and snorting died away, he opened his eyes, looking into hers with spiteful contempt. He moved his hands up to her throat, running his thumbs across her windpipe. As the man's face twisted more deeply into rage and hate, his hands compressed harder, cutting off Carrie's breath.

Either God or good luck intervened in the form of her half-sisters, Sarah and Emma. They called out loudly from the small cottage nearby, yelling Carrie's name. The man turned toward the noise, releasing for a moment the pressure that had held Carrie fast against the tree trunk. Sensing her chance, Carrie arched her back upward, pushed herself away from the tree, and drove her naked knee forward with all her strength into the space between the man's legs. The man screamed and buckled, crumpling onto the ground, his curses filling the air. Carrie, her vision blurry from tears and perspiration, nearly tripped over his writhing form but managed to leap over him and run to the arms of her sisters.

Carrie never spoke a word about the man to anyone, not her mother, not her sisters. Certainly not Frederick. Only Sarah and Emma knew.

Years passed. The man gained stature in the growing city, moving up in Richmond society, taking a wife, and becoming a business success.

Carrie would inevitably run into him on the streets, at the theater, and even in church. He would stare at her with a cutting sneer and hateful eyes. She would turn away, forcing down her sense of helpless panic.

Now, she believed, she would never see him again, never hear his name again. Ever.

She gazed again at George, huddled by her side on the wagon seat. How ironic that her freedom, her escape from that man still in Richmond, came from a vow she had taken, a marriage vow binding her for life to a different man, to George. But George was nothing like that other man. She squeezed his hand and leaned her head against him.

George was like a lost puppy when she first met him, literally wandering onto the mansion grounds from the street. She remembered him calling out, "Hey now... is anybody around? Anybody? A poor fellow needs some help here..." She had walked over toward the sound of his voice and caught sight of him, his rough clothes, and his worried face. Despite herself, before uttering a word, she burst into laughter. George looked shocked at first, then began laughing as well, laughing loud and long. And Carrie began to fall in love.

That happened less than a year ago, in June. After that, he would come by the mansion nearly every day, as often as he could slip away from his apprenticeship. She would always be there to meet him. By the end of November, they were wed.

Returning to Richmond from their honeymoon, the two of them bent to their task, planning their escape from Richmond together.

They approached Frederick, consulting him about their plans. Dealing with Frederick was distasteful, but they had no choice. The reason was simple. Carrie was married now and entitled to claim her inheritance, but Frederick controlled the family's money, every cent of it. It was Frederick who would give final approval over what Carrie would receive. So they sat down with him and gave him their list. First of all, they wanted land for a farm far from Richmond. Money to buy supplies, to help them get there and make a start. And slaves. Carrie wanted slaves.

It turned out that the land was already available, just waiting to be claimed. The land was hundreds of miles away from Richmond, in the rugged hills of North Carolina. It had been bought by Carrie's father years before, sight unseen, and then left alone, mostly forgotten. But Frederick remembered the far-off little patch of property and offered it to the newlyweds.

Next came the slaves. Carrie sorted through them, picking and choosing the ones she wanted to take. The rest they took as money. It was all theirs now; a little golden crumb fallen away from the great pile of the family's wealth.

George made good use of the money. He bought a wagon and a team to pull it. He filled the wagon with supplies, food, and clothing for the journey, saws, axes, picks, and shovels for the land.

They left Richmond on the twenty-second day of March. George drove the wagon, filled to overflowing, away from the mansion, through the streets, and out of the city. Carrie sat beside him on the knobby wooden seat while a score of Black people, the people whom Carrie had chosen, trudged along behind.

Now it was late April. Carrie was keeping count; it was their thirty-second day on the road. Over a month now separated her from Richmond. Today she claimed her freedom. Whatever lay ahead, it would be better than what she left behind.

She turned her eyes again to George, tried to follow the path of his eyes, see what he was seeing, as the wagon swayed along in the rutted road.

"What are you thinking about, sweetheart?"

George started at the unexpected sound of her voice. He paused for a moment, his face betraying a hint of embarrassment at the question.

"Oh, nothing much, dear. Mostly just looking at the fences, there," motioning toward the rail fences lining the fields along the roadway. "I was just counting up the number of rails they have stacked up together to get the fence up that high from the ground and how each of those sections are laid out. Trying to figure how many trees they needed to take down and split up to get those rails. And wonderin' what kinda trees they use. Pine'll rot away too fast, I expect, and oak would be too stout, too hard to split. So, they must be usin' something else, cedar maybe, or chestnut, I'm thinkin'. Of course, you don't care much about all that, I don't expect, but I'm wantin' to be ready to make a start on the land as soon as we get there."

Carrie stared at her husband, a smile broadening on her face. Here she was, bumping up and down on the hard wagon seat, looking at the clouds and the mountains, thinking about Richmond. With just a word, she discovered that not only was George managing the team as it pulled the wagon along the road, but he was also studying the fences, the trees, everything that he saw, weighing it, putting it away somewhere in his memory like a page in a notebook. It would have shocked her except that the same thing happened over and over, nearly every day. Moreover, every jot, every tittle he put away somewhere in his memory was for them, for the land and the new home they would have there.

Carrie leaned over and snuggled herself against George, pulling him to her and kissed his cheek. She rubbed her hand across his shoulders, letting her touch linger on his supple muscles, tracing her finger across them through the padding of his jacket.

Carrie missed her monthly course two weeks before they left Richmond. She hadn't said anything to George about it, fearful that he would want to delay the departure or maybe even stay in Richmond until she delivered. She worried he might be disappointed or feel cheated somehow. But she was starting to show and would need to tell him about the baby. She would tell him. Soon. Not now, not today. George already had so much on his shoulders; it wouldn't be fair to add another burden. But soon. She promised herself she would tell him soon.

Carrie's thoughts traveled back again to Richmond, to the days and weeks before her wedding. Back then, as she contemplated her wedding night, Carrie was apprehensive, fearful that dark demons of memory, of that other man and how he hurt her, would come unbidden into her bed. So she steeled herself to her fears and forced herself to relive the day of the rape, sifting it, recalling every horrifying moment. Pushing through her panic, she scoured her memories, seeking out the smallest details. She plotted how to make her wedding night, her first night with George, the opposite of everything she remembered of that other man.

Carrie remembered the man was soft and pink, his face smooth and clean-shaven. She thought about how he smelled, odors of tobacco and whiskey blending with scents of lavender soap and rosewater.

George, thankfully, was darkly tanned and hard, his muscles tempered by years of labor. He looked nothing like the other man. That was a good place to start. But a good start would go only part of the way. The rest would take courage.

The wedding came, vows were recited, rings exchanged. They were married. That night, in their wedding chamber, Carrie waited for an opening for what she resolved to do. George headed to the wash basin to shave and wash.

Carrie spoke softly to him, "George, wait. Don't use the wash basin." He paused and looked back at her, his face questioning.

She walked over to him, pressing herself against him and pulling him tightly to herself. She felt the roughness of his cheek, took in the musky scent of his skin. She had been given a silk gown, a special gift from her sisters, but she left it, untouched. Instead, she shed her clothes all at once, standing in front of him naked, the firelight shining off her white skin. She moved quickly to remove his clothes, and they fell together onto the bed, kissing, touching, exploring.

Carrie refused to be passive. She moved her hands downward, surprising him with her touch. She offered her breasts to him, asking him to caress them, to let his tongue dance over their fullness, feeling herself become flushed in response. At length, as their desire was reaching its zenith, George began to turn, moving to lay on top of her. As she felt him, she felt as well a surge of fear, a remembrance of the other man. She breathed deeply, willing herself to be calm. She forced herself to rest her mind solely on this moment, on George and no one else, accepting him, opening herself up, and taking him into herself fully. She began to move, seeking to match his movements with her own until they climaxed together in a perfect duet of pleasure.

It worked. The demon, the dark shadow of memory, was stymied, blocked from coming between her and George. It was not gone, it was still there down deep, but she did not let it in.

Carrie said nothing to George about the man in Richmond. She didn't plan on telling him. She would keep it buried forever, she hoped. George didn't have to know everything.

§

Another week passed. Thirty-nine days since leaving Richmond. Carrie and George were back traveling on the road. But instead of the hard wooden seat of their wagon, Carrie sat next to George on the padded back seat of a carriage driven by the land agent who was helping them take title to the land.

Two days before, they rolled the wagon into the town where they were to meet the land agent, the Black people still plodding along in the dust. The agent had received letters from Frederick's lawyers in Richmond; it was he who would give them the title to the new land. Carrie knew nothing about the land except that it was far from Richmond. It belonged to her now, her and George. It was their new home.

Yesterday, they met with the agent, sat in his stuffy office, signed reams of papers, and shook hands with a line of grinning grey-haired men. The agent offered to drive them out to the land today, showing them the way. So they stowed away the wagon in the stable of their rooming house and boarded the Black people at the town's jail for safekeeping.

The land agent picked up Carrie and George at the rooming house early that morning, then drove his carriage westward away from town on a roadway wide and well-traveled. George and Carrie sat snugly in the back seat, huddling together closely for warmth as they gazed at the passing landscape.

There were cabins and small farms on both sides of the road, surrounded by acres of ochre-red soil freshly turned, ready for spring planting. In other areas, greening fields marked plantings of wheat or rye emerging from winter's sleep. Collections of pigs and horses and cows observed them impassively from behind split rail fences.

As they traveled along, mile by mile, Carrie noticed the fields becoming less extensive and the fenced-in pastures spaced farther apart until, finally, they were traveling through a land dominated by trees. Massive heavy trees with trunks 3 feet across cast shade onto the road, even as their branches and limbs put on the first of spring's burst of green and red buds. The sunlight flickered through the trees as they moved.

They forded many waterways. Most of them were little trickles crossing the road, but sometimes they traversed a substantial good-flowing creek. All coursed down from the hills ranging along on the southern side of the road, flowing toward the big river off to their right. Usually, the river was hidden from the road, but on occasion, it flashed into appearance through the trees, a brief shimmering sparkle of sunshine reflecting off ripples of river water.

Seven or eight miles along, they came to a sizable stream, the water splashing as it crossed the road. The land agent gave out a loud yell to the horses and pulled them to a stop. He twisted around in his seat and addressed his passengers. "Alright, folks, this is the place on the survey. This here is what was named in the land transfer from your brother, Mrs. Adams."

Carrie Adams looked toward George, but George's eyes were shifted away from her now, focused on the forest of oaks, gums, and beeches.

The land agent continued, "Actually, this creek here divides your property in two. We've been traveling beside your land the last half-mile, and it goes on another half-mile west along the road. And it goes back into the hills two miles, following the creek. All told, you folks got title to 1400 acres."

Carrie watched as George jumped out of the carriage and stepped tentatively onto his property. He walked a few steps off of the road. He turned his head and called back, "Carrie, come on, let's walk up there a bit and take a look."

Carrie sat on the carriage seat, regarding the back of her husband's hat, facing a dilemma. Traveling along in the carriage, despite huddling against George for warmth, she became chilled, nearly frozen through. And now, she realized, she needed to pee. But she couldn't say that in front of the land agent. Instead, she called to George, "That's all right darling, you go and take a look around; I think I'll stay right here for now. You go on."

George turned and looked back at her sheepishly. He walked back to the side of the carriage and spoke to her, "Alright, Carrie, yes, that's fine, just stay there. I'm just going to walk up through the woods and take a look. Be back in a few minutes." He turned and stepped back onto the land. She saw him striding away along the creek until he was lost from view.

Carrie sat in the back of the carriage, wondering how long George would be gone.

After a few minutes, the land agent murmured over his shoulder, "Just give him a minute out there, Mrs. Adams. I've seen plenty of men his age come out here, can't wait to get a first look at some piece of land, and all they want to do is climb around on it for a bit. Most men will do it once or twice, they see what the land looks like and how much needs to be done to farm it, and pretty quick they're on the horse back to the big city they came here from."

Carrie replied, "Well, sir, that may be true of some people, but you don't know my husband. And, sir, with respect, you do not know me. We did not come here to walk on the land once or twice and just ride away. No, sir, whatever happens to us here, this will be our home. We will not be going back to Richmond."

Carrie and the land agent lapsed into an uncomfortable silence.

After another quarter hour, Carrie decided she could not wait any longer; she was going to have to pee. She stood up, gathered up her skirts, swung her leg down over the side of the carriage onto the step, and stepped down onto the ground. She plunged off the side of the road, trailing her husband's pathway into the trees.

Carrie heard the voice of the land agent, tinged with surprise and concern, calling to her as she moved away from the road, "Mrs. Adams, I wouldn't want you going up into those woods. Them hillsides are covered with loose rock and dead branches; you could take a bad spill in there. Come on back here, Mrs. Adams, you get back in the carriage, and I'll go up and check on your husband."

Carrie turned and called back to him, "Don't fret; I'll be fine. George just gets lost in his thoughts sometimes, and I need to go and pull him back. Don't worry; I'll be careful, I promise."

Carrie walked quickly along the creek. As soon as she was out of sight of the agent, she lifted her skirts and her petticoats, leaned back against a tree for support, and emptied her bladder. She wondered what her mother would say if she knew her daughter was peeing in the woods. That made her think of Richmond and her old life there. And she felt, all over again, thankful for George and the escape they were making from there together. She stood up, straightened out the petticoats, and patted down her dress. She peered along the creek bottom, trying to determine where her sweet crazy George might have gone.

Carrie moved along through the trees, the creek on her right, a steep hillside to her left. Every few steps, she saw George's boot print in the mud. She came to a spot where a rocky ravine cut through the side of the hill, creating a natural staircase upward, and the boot prints stopped. She decided that George must have followed the rocky pathway upward, away from the creek. She began to climb up over the rocks and big boulders, ascending toward the top. After a few minutes of exertion, she came out onto a clearing at the top of the hill. Instead of trees, huge boulders, banded in black and white and flecked with patches of green moss, pushed up from the soil. She spied George on the far side of the clearing, looking off into the distance. She crept up as silently as she could, hoping to catch him by surprise. Finally, when she came within 15 feet of his back, she could see he was staring through a gap in the trees, away at the ridges of the distant mountains.

She continued her stealthy approach until she was only five feet away. She sang out to him in a sweet voice, "Oh George, dear George, did you forget about something? Remember, you have a wife now."

George spun around, startled out of his daydream, and Carrie saw the look of surprise on his face, which transformed into a broad smile. She walked closer to him, put her arms around his neck, and leaned against him. George wrapped his arms around her, squeezing her and holding her tightly to him and kissing her on the lips. She kissed him back, dropping her arms down around his waist and holding him close. She could feel the pressure of him against her and savored the flush of desire. They stood together, each enveloped in the other's embrace, for long moments. Finally, George separated his lips from Carrie's.

"How quick can we get back to the boarding house?" George asked thickly. Carrie laughed and pressed herself more firmly for a few more moments.

They climbed back down the ravine, sliding over stones and boulders, grabbing trees and stumps for balance. George folded his arms around his bride, protectively guiding her over the loose rocks and the broken branches. Finally, they got down to the flat ground and followed the creek bottom back to where the carriage was still on the road, waiting.

Carrie looked at George, who was looking back over his shoulder, back along the path beside the creek. She followed his eyes, saw what he saw, and looked back at his face, saw his joy. She understood and felt the same joy growing within her. The land was perfect, she decided, better than perfect. The ghosts of Richmond would not come here. There would be no going back.

Chapter 3—1817—Coming to the Land— George

The land agent's expression changed to relief when he saw Carrie and George emerging from the forest. "Thank goodness, Mr. and Mrs. Adams, I was just about ready to come in after you. You get into a wild area like that, and you can get yourself turned around, not even have a clue which direction to follow out of there."

George spoke to the land agent, "Yes, sir, I can see that. But the land is beautiful. It is just what I was hoping for."

George helped Carrie into the carriage, ascended the step himself, and snuggled onto the seat next to her. He wrapped his arms around Carrie and pulled her close to him. He felt suffused with happiness, warmth flowing through every part of his body, even in the cool air of spring. The driver got the carriage turned around, and they headed back, away from the land.

George turned his head, gazing at Carrie, fixing his eyes on her profile. The smile in his eyes expanded as he kept his eyes on her. Every day, George still found it shocking that this beautiful girl chose him and had persevered, holding tight to him even when so many others tried to tear them apart. A vast chasm of wealth and status lay between them. Carrie's family, her mother, brother, and sisters, were horrified at the idea of a man like George joining the family. Insults and abuse were heaped upon him long before they even laid eyes upon him. He was nothing but a fraud, a cheat, preying on the innocence of a young woman, hardly more than a girl. Richmond was full of men like George, common laboring men, rough and dirty.

George was born rough; that was true. He came into the world poor, the youngest child of an impoverished preacher. Orphaned at 8, he was tossed around among his older brothers and sisters like a runt puppy no one wanted. At 13, his oldest sister apprenticed him out to a drunken, dissipated cooper. A life of endless toil, building barrels destined to hold the wealth and treasure of the rich, stretched away in front of him.

Getting lost in the streets of Richmond turned his life around.

He went astray, missing a turn while driving a wagonload of barrels for a delivery, and suddenly he was in among great spreading trees and grand houses. He was lost, with no idea how to get out of there, back to his streets, the ones filled with workhouses and saloons. Searching around for help, he turned his wagon onto the grounds of a huge brick and stone mansion. Maybe a boy or an old gardener was around, someone who could show him the way back to the hard part of town. The one that met him, though, was not a boy or an old man. It was a girl, a beautiful girl with freckles.

The freckled girl laughed at him, and he laughed and smiled back at her. The next day he came back, and they laughed and smiled all over again. After that, every day, as often as he could get away, he came back, and she was always there. The smiles turned to looks of longing, then to touches, caresses, and kisses.

Word got back to the girl's family. Angry demands were issued, ordering him to stay away. When that didn't work, a bribe, a big one, was offered. All George would need to do was leave Richmond and never return.

The idea of leaving Richmond was fine with George. Richmond held nothing but bad memories for him. And, the girl, the beautiful freckled girl named Carrie, wanted to get away from Richmond as well. She told him so over and over. So he had a choice. He could leave Richmond with the bribe in his pocket or with Carrie. He decided he wanted Carrie far more than the money.

He ignored her brother Frederick and his pretend threats. He kept coming around, and she kept coming out to see him. Eventually, Frederick and her mother gave in. George and Carrie, his sweet, lovely Carrie, were married.

Only then did he learn that he would still get money, a lot of money, more than he had ever seen in his whole life. Carrie would receive her inheritance as soon as she married. So George found himself sitting across a desk from that arrogant little jackass Frederick, the very man who tried to bribe George to buy him off before the wedding. George remembered the look of Frederick, sitting at an ornate table, accompanied by his solicitors and clerks, disdainfulness etched on his face. George had done his best, trying to ensure that Carrie, who was herself barred from the room, received all that was due her in money and land.

And slaves. Carrie wanted her slaves. George could understand that. Carrie grew up with slaves her whole life. George would rather have done without. After all, he had been bound for seven years as an apprentice. George conceded that hadn't made him a slave, not by a long shot. But he knew bondage, having seen it from the other side, and he didn't like it, didn't trust it. He would rather work the land by himself or hire free labor. But Carrie insisted on keeping her slaves.

Now, by law, they were his slaves; he was the slave master. George found the whole thing distasteful. In truth, though, having been to the land, seen the hills and rocks and massive trees, he admitted that he could make good use of them. He needed their labor, their backs, arms, and legs. He imagined himself back on the land, working alongside the Black men and women, using axes and saws to fell trees to clear land for planting. It would work out fine having the slaves, he decided, and he would work hard to be a fair and just master.

Suddenly George's mind was snapped back into the present, sitting in the back of the land agent's carriage, bouncing on the road back toward town. He turned his head toward Carrie, who was looking up at him.

Carrie repeated her question. "I said, George, now that we have seen the land, and walked on it, what is next? What do you want to do?"

"Dear, I think it would be best to get right to work. You need to stay at the rooming house, of course, but I want to get the slaves out there as soon as I can and get them working on clearing some of that creek bottom. We can build some lean-to's for the slaves, and I can sleep in the wagon. I want to get started on this. And I want to look around the property for the best place to build a cabin for us. Someday, of course, we will build a proper house, but we may need to make do with a cabin for a year or two. Carrie, this is it; this is what we left Richmond to find."

George wrapped his arms around Carrie. "Carrie, I love you more than anything." And they sat enfolded together back to town.

As soon as they were back to the rooming house, alone in their room, they fell into each other's arms. At length, they arose, got dressed, and went downstairs to their supper.

That night, they made love again, each hungering for the touch of the other. Afterward, as Carrie slept, George lay awake all through the night, his mind like a river in flood, spilling over with ideas and plans for the land.

In the morning, George went to the rooming house's barn and hitched the horses to the wagon. The wagon bed was packed to overflowing, brimming with axes, saws, and other stock needed for the felling of great trees and converting the forested land into a farm. As well, locked in a strongbox were different tools. Cowhide whips. Iron shackles and chains. Pistols, powder, and ball.

He drove the heavy wagon to the county jail and settled the debt for the boarding of their enslaved people, twenty-five cents per head per day. He assembled the Black people behind the wagon, save for two light-skinned young women, Sarah and Emma, whom he ordered to go to the boarding house where Carrie was still sleeping. They would stay in town with Carrie while the rest headed to the land.

As he drove the wagon back out onto the road west, he felt a sense of lightness, like a weight taken off his back. The feeling surprised him. Here he was, more encumbered by property and obligations than ever before in his life. Yet he felt a feeling of relief, new since yesterday.

All at once, he realized why he felt that way. This was the first full day in the four months since the wedding that he would be wholly apart from Carrie. The realization came with a surge of guilt, even as he admitted that it was true.

He loved his wife, loved her with every part of his being. Loved her more than anything else in the world, his own life included. Even now, a part of him was pining for her, longing for her touch, her kiss. He knew as well that she returned his love, loved him just as much, probably more. The journey here, riding side-by-side in the wagon, spending nights together along the road, all of that was wonderful, a sensual feast of love. Truly it had been the best time of his life.

But there were other things, little things that became bigger with time. He didn't like explaining himself, and Carrie always wanted to know what he was doing and where he was going. She would sometimes even ask him, for no reason at all, what he was thinking. He would have to stop, pause his thoughts and come up with some sort of answer, something to satisfy her.

The time for all of that was passed. Now it was time to look to the future, to build, to begin taming this wild land.

He would be apart from her for a few weeks. She would stay at the rooming house with Sarah and Emma, and he would stay on the land, working there and sleeping there with the slaves. In a week, or maybe two, if things were progressing well on the land, he would take the wagon back into town and stay there for a bit. For now, though, he could breathe.

Chapter 4—1822— Five years on the land— Sarah and Emma

S arah advanced carefully down the hall toward the house's bare wooden staircase, which descended from the second-floor bedrooms. Balanced in her brown hands were a pair of earthen chamber pots stacked and held apart from her body. Even though she had them covered over with a thin towel, the sour odor rising from the pots was filling her nose. So she stepped gingerly onto the stairs, even as she tried to keep her face diverted away to the side, inhaling her breath through her mouth in tight short gasps. The stairs creaked with each footfall. At last, she stepped off the last step, her stinky smelly cargo still grasped in her hands.

Every morning she performed this task, collecting the chamber pots, entering the rooms quietly so as not to disturb her still-sleeping masters. Sometimes the pots were empty, or nearly so. Other times there was a collection of night soil and urine. And every once in a while the odor was like today, strong and sour like sulfur.

The masters of the farm, Master George, Missus Carrie, and little Master Thomas, nearly five years old, just moved into the house a year ago. Before that, the masters lived in the small cabin first built when all of them, the masters and the enslaved, arrived on the land five years before, when it was nothing but forest.

The first year was used to clear land for planting and build the rough cabin for the masters and shanties for the enslaved people. In the second year, Master George ordered the construction of the house to begin. Clay deposits discovered along the creek were mined, and the clay formed and fired into bricks. Loads of bricks, and many more loads of timbers hand cut from the forest, were carried to the home site in the wagon or on the backs of the Black people. Bricks and timbers, foundation stones, nails, shingles, everything was hauled up the low rise to the building site and fitted together according to the plan in Master George's head. Finally, the house was declared habitable, though there was still plenty of work awaiting the idle months of winter. The old cabin across the yard was now the kitchen.

Now, Sarah walked down the hallway from the staircase, passed through the dining room to the slave pantry, balancing the two pots ahead of her and trying to keep her head turned. She went out the back door and headed across the yard toward the kitchen cabin. "Damn, onions. They ate that stew last night; I bet Emma put onions in that damn stewpot." Emma and Sarah discovered over and over that whenever Master George ate onions, the next day, he would have smelly sour urine.

Sarah entered the door of the kitchen. Emma was there, working on breakfast. Sarah said, "Emma, girl, did you put onions in that stew last night? You oughtta' know better'n that, after all these years."

Emma looked up and smiled until she got a whiff of the urine smell. At that, her face turned into a nasty scowl as her nose wrinkled up. "Oh, my lord. Sorry. I was thinkin' maybe a few onions would be fine. Master George is all the time askin' for onions. He's always wantin' onions, so I slipped a few in. Those musta been strong ones."

Sarah walked back outside, calling back to her sister, "No onions, I don't care what he's askin' for." She headed down the path to the privy. When she got there, she set down the pots. She lifted the bucket of water that she hauled up from the creek earlier and poured water into both of the pots, swirling the thin mixture around before dumping the contents down the privy. She looked in the pots and noticed there were still brown bits of night soil clinging to the sides of one of them. She grimaced, picked up the rag hanging on the peg, wet it in the bucket, and used it to scrub out the brown residue. When it was clean, she rinsed out the rag, squeezed it, and put it back on the peg. She laid the chamber pots outside the privy to dry in the sun. She picked up the little scrap of soap, washed her hands, and rinsed them off with the last of the water in the bucket. She dried her hands on her apron and headed back up towards the kitchen cabin.

When she got back to the kitchen, Emma was hard at work, heating water on the stove for Missus Carrie's morning cup of tea. The frying pan was out on top of the stove, the sizzling sound of frying bacon filling the air. The rich aroma of white flour biscuits flowed from the oven.

Sarah looked over at her sister. By blood, they were only half-sisters. They were born of two different mothers, both owned by Missus Carrie's father, Old Master, at the big mansion up in Richmond. Sarah and Emma were born at nearly the same time, just months apart. Born in the little cottage, hidden away on the grounds of the big mansion, where their two mothers lived together, apart from the other slaves. It was there that Old Master came to visit the two Black women. And it was there, in the little cottage, that both Sarah and Emma were conceived, and were born, and grew up.

§

It was an easy childhood, Sarah knew, compared to most of the other Black children. Sarah and Emma, Mama and Auntie, and the other light-skinned children lived all together in the cottage. They were allowed to get most of their food from the big mansion. On most days, they spent their time playing together and exploring the mansion grounds. Mama and Auntie did some sewing and other handiwork for the people in the big mansion, but most of their time was spent together.

Two or three times a week, Old Master would appear at the cottage, walking down the short path from the mansion. Sometimes he came during the day, sometimes in the middle of the night. He always brought a bag of sweets for the children. The children got their sweets, then, even if it was the middle of the night, they had to go outside the cottage and wait while Old Master was in the cottage with Mama and Auntie. Finally, Old Master would leave, and the children were allowed to go back into the cottage. Mama and Auntie were always getting washed up. And there were always more sweets left by Old Master.

It was fun growing up in the cottage. Old Master and Old Missus, Old Master's wife up the mansion, had a little girl named Missus Carrie, the same age as Sarah and Emma. She came down to the cottage from the mansion whenever she could to play with Sarah and Emma. Missus Carrie always brought to the cottage lots of new things to play with, toys that she said her father, Old Master, brought home from far away, up North or across the ocean.

Missus Carrie was being taught by special teachers who came to the mansion every day, teaching her to read and write. After her lessons, Missus Carrie always came down to the cottage, bringing her slate and her chalk with her. Missus Carrie, Sarah, and Emma spent hours together tracing out letters on the slate. Pretty soon, they learned to write words, read words and started to read sentences, all three of them. That made

Mama and Auntie unhappy and worried, but they couldn't do anything about it because Missus Carrie was the one doing the teaching.

On Sundays, Mama, Auntie, Sarah, Emma, and all the Black people who lived on the grounds of the mansion, and worked there, put on their special clothes. They walked behind the carriage where Old Master, Old Missus, Missus Carrie, and Missus Carrie's older brother and sisters rode a mile to the big church. Old Master and Old Missus and the White children sat in the front. All the Black people sat in the Black part of the church. They sat on hard benches for two hours and weren't allowed to talk or even wiggle. There was some music and singing, but mostly it was just White men talking. Sarah hated it every single Sunday. And Emma loved it every single Sunday.

During the week, Emma wanted to talk about church every day, and she sang the songs over and over. Sarah remembered coming back from church one Sunday. Emma was smiling and singing more than ever. "Guess what, Sarah," she said excitedly.

"I don't know, what?"

"I asked Jesus into my heart."

Sarah looked at her blankly.

"You know, Sarah, the man at church said we should all ask Jesus to come into our hearts, so I did."

The next Sunday, Emma went up to the White man who was the preacher at church and said to him, "I asked Jesus into my heart." After that, every Sunday, there was always a group of White men and women at church who would gather around Emma and have her repeat it for them, and they would smile and clap.

When the three girls turned eight years old, Missus Carrie was given a birthday party up in the mansion, and a great crowd of White children came and brought Missus Carrie presents. Later, when Missus Carrie came to the cottage, she wanted to tell Sarah and Emma about all of her presents.

"And I got three different Bibles from three different children," Missus Carrie said as she ended reciting the list of gifts she received.

Emma smiled and shyly asked, "Missus Carrie, would it be all right if I had one of those Bibles?"

Missus Carrie had laughed and said, "Yes, of course, Emma," and she had run back up to the mansion right away. A few minutes later, she was back carrying one of the gift Bibles, still wrapped in paper. She handed it to Emma, "Here you go, Emma," and she put her arms around Emma and hugged her.

"Thank you, Missus Carrie, thank you." Emma pulled the wrapping paper off the Bible, opened it up, and began to read silently to herself.

After that, Emma always did her reading lessons with the Bible.

When the girls were about 10 years old, Mama and Auntie brought all the children together in the cottage. They were crying, both of them.

Mama said, "They tellin' us that Old Master has passed. Master Frederick is gonna be our master now."

Sarah asked, "Is Master Frederick nice?"

Mama replied, "Sarah, Master Frederick ain't gonna be like Old Master was. But he'll be fine. He'll be just fine."

After that, Mama and Auntie were ordered to go up to the big mansion every day and work in the kitchen preparing food and cleaning for Old Missus, who was still alive, and for Master Frederick and the other people that lived in the big mansion. A few years later, when they were about 12, Sarah and Emma were ordered to join them, going up to the kitchen every day, helping the other Black people to do the cooking and cleaning. They still got to live in the little cottage, all together, but they didn't get any more sweets, the ones that Old Master would bring to them before he died.

Missus Carrie still came to see them at the cottage, but not as much because she was going off to school a lot of the time. And when she was home, she had to sneak away to come down to the cottage because Master Frederick didn't like it. But still, they got to play together, and Missus Carrie still helped them with their reading and writing.

Missus Carrie came to the cottage one day and said she couldn't teach them any more writing or reading. Master Frederick somehow got wind of the teaching and ordered Missus Carrie not to do it anymore. He said they were breaking the law. But she didn't ask for Emma's Bible back, and Emma kept reading.

Things stayed like that. Master Frederick lived in the big mansion, but he never came down the path to the cottage, never came into the woods behind the mansion. Mama and Auntie and Sarah and Emma worked in the kitchen every day, but they still all lived in the little cottage. With Old Master dead, no one bothered to fix up the cottage anymore, and it started to fall apart. The roof leaked, and the floor sagged. After a few years, it was not much different than the other shanties scattered around the mansion grounds, where the other Black people lived. But Missus Carrie still came around, and the three girls still talked and laughed and were friends. The years passed along.

Around the time the three sisters were turning sixteen, Missus Carrie told Sarah and Emma that she was going to be presented, which meant she could start receiving suitors. A few weeks later, Missus Carrie and her mother went away to Charleston for a month. After she returned, Missus Carrie started having suitors come by. Mostly they were boys about the same age as Missus Carrie. The suitors brought Missus Carrie all sorts of pretty things as gifts. Missus Carrie always walked the suitors down through the gardens behind the big mansion and near the cottage, so Sarah and Emma could get an eyeful of them. Later, Missus Carrie would come down to the cottage so that Sarah and Emma could tell Missus Carrie what they thought about each of the young suitors.

One day, after the suitors had been coming around for a couple of months, Sarah saw Missus Carrie strolling down from the mansion with yet another well-dressed suitor. She called out, "Emma come over. Missus Carrie is comin' down with another boy. Have a look. Emma, he's ain't like the rest. Look at him; he looks like a grown-up man. Look at that."

But as the two sisters gazed out the window, they saw that this visit was going all wrong. Having guided Missus Carrie into a secluded spot, the man suddenly grabbed ahold of her and thrust her up against the trunk of a big oak, crushing his weight against her. Pinning her chest against the tree with his shoulder, he grabbed her flailing right hand with his left. With his right hand, he loosened his belt and trousers, then worked to pull up Missus Carrie's skirt and petticoat. Missus Carrie let out a cry for help, and the man balled his hand into a fist and punched Missus Carrie in the face, snapping her head backward.

Sarah and Emma looked at each other, each searching the other's face for guidance. They looked back at the awful scene.

Sarah moved away from the cottage window toward the door. "Come on, Emma," she called to her sister.

Emma followed. "What are we gonna do?"

"I don't know. Just yell, I guess," Sarah called back.

The two sisters burst through the cottage door and into the small yard. They both started screaming as loudly as they could.

"Oh my God, Missus Carrie, please, please, come quick! You gotta come, Missus Carrie, there's an emergency! Missus Carrie, we need you right now!"

Sarah looked over and could see that the man still had Missus

Carrie pinned up against the tree, his trousers falling around his boots, his backside shining brightly in the sunlight. Missus Carrie's skirts and petticoats were pulled up around her waist. At the sound of the yelling, he turned, releasing the pressure that had held Missus Carrie fast.

Sarah watched as Missus Carrie leaned forward, pushed herself up and away from the tree, and, with her skirts still up around her waist, thrust her bare knee with all of her might upward into the private parts of the suitor. To Sarah, the blow appeared to lift the man off the ground, leaving him suspended in the air for a moment before he collapsed onto the ground, screaming with the agony and surprise of the attack. Carrie leaped over his writhing form and ran to the arms of her two rescuers as the young man filled the air with curses and threats.

The three sisters ran into the cottage, slammed shut the door, and barricaded it with their bodies. In a minute, Sarah took a chance to peer out of the window. The man was gone, no trace of him left behind.

They sat Missus Carrie, sobbing and gasping, down on a stool. Emma held her tight while Sarah grabbed the bucket and a towel and bathed Missus Carrie's bruised and swollen cheek and throat, soothing her, trying to wash the man's presence away.

Emma looked out of the window again. The man had not returned. "Sarah, stay here with Missus Carrie." She began to walk toward the door.

"Where are you going?" Missus Carrie demanded.

"Up to the mansion; I got to go tell your mother about this."

"No, Emma, stay here. Don't tell my mother anything."

"But Missus Carrie, we got to tell, or that man will get away. Then he'll be doing this to other girls."

"I said no. You stay here. Don't go out that door, Emma. I'm giving you a warning, Emma. Don't tell my mother. Don't tell anyone. Ever. Do you understand me?"

Emma stood by the door, shock on her face. She was silent for a moment more, then said, "Yes, ma'am." She came back over and sat down on the stool next to Missus Carrie and began to brush through Missus Carrie's matted hair.

They sat like that for an hour. Finally, Missus Carrie said she was fine and forced a crooked smile onto her face. She stood up. "I'm going back up to the mansion." She turned and gave a hard look to Emma. "Don't tell anyone."

She began to walk back up the path to the mansion.

They never spoke about it. After that, though, no more suitors were coming to visit. Missus Carrie refused.

In a few months, Missus Carrie seemed to be like her old self, laughing and smiling. She came down to the cottage whenever she could. Everything seemed to be just like it was before.

Three more years passed.

One day, Missus Carrie was down at the cottage when a wagon loaded with barrels turned through the gate onto the big mansion grounds. The wagon was driven by a young White man. But he didn't look anything like the suitors. He wore rough clothes, rougher even than a slave. And he was not pink, he was brown, his skin tanned by sun and fire. Missus Carrie walked over and began talking to him.

The next day he came again, driving the same wagon, only this time it didn't have a load of barrels. Missus Carrie was there again and went out and talked to him for a long time. Sarah and Emma knew something was going on. Missus Carrie suddenly was putting on new dresses and tying ribbons in her hair. Sarah and Emma began to serve as lookouts in case one of the White people from the mansion might come down by the cottage and see Missus Carrie and the White man, who said his name was George, talking or holding hands or kissing.

Things went on like this for a few months. One day, Sarah and Emma were up at the mansion, cleaning and polishing in the kitchen. Without warning, angry shouts and screams rang out. The sound was coming from the library. The door was closed, and the words were muffled, but they could hear the voices of Old Missus and Master Frederick and Missus Carrie, each voice trying to drown out the other two. After half an hour, the library door opened, and Missus Carrie came out, slammed the door shut as hard as she could, and ran upstairs to her bedroom.

The next day, Missus Carrie came down to the cottage. Her eyes were rimmed in red, and her face was angry. Sarah spoke softly, "Missus Carrie, are you all right?"

"No, dammit, I'm not all right," Missus Carrie snapped back at Sarah. "My mother and my stupid ass of a brother told me I can't see George anymore. They forbid me from seeing him. It's so unfair. They don't even know him."

"What are you gonna do, Missus Carrie?"

Missus Carrie looked at Sarah. "I'm going to keep seeing him. They can't tell me who I can see and not see. I'm not their slave."

Carrie continued, "I wrote a note. You and Emma need to deliver it for me." She handed a folded-up piece of paper to Sarah.

"Yes, ma'am, Missus Carrie, but where do we take it?"

Missus Carrie told her the location.

"Missus Carrie, we never been over that way before. That's the bad side."

"Sarah, it'll be fine; you and Emma can go together. I'll give you a pass. That's where George works, just go over there and ask for George Adams and give him the note. Give it to him, don't give it to anybody else. Take it this evening before dark."

"Yes, ma'am, Missus Carrie."

A few hours later, Sarah and Emma walked together over to the part of Richmond where George was still an apprentice, building barrels for his master, and delivered the note. The next evening just before dark, Missus Carrie showed up at the cottage, her face etched with excitement and apprehension. An hour later, George arrived. He was walking this time, not driving the wagon. As he passed through the iron gate, Missus Carrie ran to meet him.

For the next month, nearly every day when Sarah and Emma were up working at the mansion, they would hear angry voices and yelling and screaming coming from the library. And nearly every evening, after Sarah and Emma had returned to the cottage, Missus Carrie would walk down from the mansion, and soon George would show up, and Missus Carrie and George would have their time together while Sarah and Emma stood by, looking out for Old Missus or Master Frederick.

Without warning, Missus Carrie came down to the cottage one day and was smiling again, and her face was glowing. She told Sarah and Emma that her mother and Master Frederick finally gave in to her, and she and George were going to get married.

Within a few months, there was the wedding, and Missus Carrie and George were married and went off for their honeymoon.

When Missus Carrie and Master George came back, all of the Black people that lived and labored at the big mansion were called together. When everyone was present, Master George stood up and spoke to them. "Alright, now, listen up, everyone. You all know that Missus Carrie and I are married now."

At that, a cheer went up, accompanied by some hoots of laughter from the Black people.

Master George held up his hand, then continued. "Now that means Missus Carrie is takin' her inheritance, and some of that inheritance is a portion of you all. Now I'm gonna read out a list of names, and when you hear your name, go over and gather underneath that big oak there, so Missus Carrie and I can come and talk to you."

Then Master George read out a list of twenty names. Now there was no laughter, not a sound at all. All was quiet except for the sound of the names being read. Sarah and Emma heard their names called. Mama, Auntie, and the children, who all still lived together in the cottage did not.

After the group of twenty was separated, Master George and Missus Carrie came over to them. Master George spoke again and explained to the group that he and Missus Carrie were now their masters and that they were leaving Richmond, all of them. They were going to travel a long way, to a new country where there were hills and mountains. The work there was going to be different and hard. They would leave at the very beginning of spring.

As he spoke, Missus Carrie came down into the group and stood between Sarah and Emma. After Master George finished, Missus Carrie turned to her two half-sisters, looking into their eyes and speaking softly, "I wanted the three of us to stay together, so I made sure your names were called. I promise you, this is going to be wonderful for all of us. We'll have a new home for Master George and me and you two. And for our children someday. It will be home for all of us forever, I promise you. Nothing will split us up, ever." Missus Carrie turned from them and moved through the group, smiling and speaking with each of the Black people in turn. In a few minutes, they were dismissed and told to return to their work.

By late winter, a wagon was packed with food and supplies for the trip. When the day finally arrived, everyone gathered together with hugs and kisses, and tears. The team of horses was hitched, and the wagon moved out through the gateway and began to move out into the street. Master George and Missus Carrie sat on the wagon seats, and the Black people fell in to walk behind.

That was the last time Sarah and Emma saw Mama or Auntie, or any of their light-skinned brothers and sisters that stayed behind in the little cottage, hidden away on the grounds of the big mansion in Richmond.

§

Sarah gazed over at her sister, standing at the stove. She observed

Emma's lips moving silently. Sarah knew that meant that Emma was singing a hymn silently to herself. Or maybe she was saying a prayer or repeating a Bible verse. Whenever she saw Emma like this, Sarah knew to stay silent. So she just got to work, preparing food for later in the day.

Here in North Carolina, in the summers, traveling preachers would come around and set up tents and have camp meetings that would stretch out over a week. Once or twice during the week, Black people would be invited to attend. Emma always asked Missus Carrie for permission to go and always begged Sarah to go with her. Sometimes Sarah went along. She would watch as Emma sang and prayed, and it would make her angry. She would scold Emma about it. "Emma, don't you see what these White preachers are doin'? All they tell us, over and over, is to obey our masters, and if we obey, someday, when we're dead, we get to go to heaven. But in the meantime, they treat us like we're nothin'. They buy and sell us like animals. Can't you see they're just tellin' us all this to help themselves, not us?"

Emma would respond, "Sarah, dear, yes, of course, I know that the preachers don't tell us everything, only the parts they want us to hear. But Sarah, there's so much more than what they tell us. I know because I read it all in Missus Carrie's Bible and because Jesus came into my heart just like He said He would. And He's there right now, givin' me peace." Sarah would see the look on Emma's face, and Sarah's heart would soften. She would still be a little bit angry but also filled with love for her sister.

A few times after Sarah and Emma attended the camp meetings, Sarah asked Emma to pray for her and prayed herself to have Jesus in her heart too. Sometimes, for a while, she seemed to feel the same peace that Emma felt. She would read the Bible and pray with Emma. But it never stuck. In a few weeks or a month, it always seeped away from her like it had never been there. After a few years, Sarah decided it just wasn't going to catch in her. So she quit getting angry when she saw Emma praying or singing; she just went on with her work. And Emma laughed at her sister and called her Martha. Sarah knew all about Mary and Martha; she heard the damn story a hundred times.

But Sarah knew that Emma was nothing like the Mary in the Bible story. Emma was up early every day, stirring the fire, gathering water and wood, and cooking ash cakes for the hands to take out to the fields, so they had something to eat at noontime. After that, the two of them would head up toward the kitchen together to begin their work preparing food and keeping the house clean.

Sarah and Emma both had husbands and families now. Barely a month after they all arrived on the land, one of the Black men, a man named Grover, asked Master George for his permission to marry Sarah. Master George gave his blessing, and Grover and Sarah jumped the broom the very same day. Nine months later, a boy was born. Master George gave the newborn boy the name Brock. Two years after that, Sarah gave birth to a girl.

Emma took a bit longer but was also married to a man named Julius now, and she now had a little girl. Master George named the baby girl Kee. Now, she was expecting again. The number of Black children on the farm was growing, adding to the wealth of Master George and Missus Carrie.

The months passed, turning into years. Every morning, Emma and Sarah walked from their shanties by the creek, up to the house, carrying along kindling wood and water buckets. Every evening, after the kitchen was clean and the fire in the stove banked, Emma turned to Sarah and say, "Let's go home," and they headed back down the hill to the shanties.

Some evenings, if Sarah felt prickly, she would chide Emma. "Why you call this old shack a home? This ain't no home, not for a dog, sure as hell not for our children."

Emma would answer back, "Sarah, I say home 'cause I got faith. I got faith that God didn't take us away from Richmond, from Mama and Aunty and the little ones, just to forget about us. And I got faith in Missus Carrie. She said this is gonna be home, for all of us. She ain't never gone back on her word to us, not once, never. I believe her, Sarah, and I believe Jesus; they both gonna take care of us. You, me, all of us."

Sarah would still have doubts, about Jesus, and about Missus Carrie, but she would keep silent until they arrived down at their shanties. Just before they separated, each to her own family, they always embraced. "Give 'em all hugs for me," one said.

"Yeah, sister, you too," said the other. "Love you."

Chapter 5—1824—7 years on the land— Visitors from Richmond

Carrie stood on the front porch of her home, the farmhouse, peering across the farm's fields. Her eye followed the muddy streak of the cart path, cutting its way through the green of the pastures, running from the house down to the main road. Her mouth set in a tight line; she imagined herself as a soldier, formed in line of battle, awaiting the cannons, the charging horses of an enemy army. She knew that was ridiculous since all she was waiting for was a stagecoach, bringing just three people for a visit to her home. Even so…

A letter arrived a month before. It was signed by her brother, Frederick, though it was written out by the hand of another. Some lowly scrivener had listened to Frederick's words and transcribed them onto the page. The letter informed Carrie to please make ready, Frederick and Carrie's two older sisters, Martha and Abigail, would be arriving by coach on a certain date, this very day, for a brief ten-day visit. Carrie had been speechless, staring at the letter. Seven years and barely a note, just a few lines at Christmas. Now a ten-day visit? What in God's name could they possibly want from her?

Now she stood, awaiting her fate on the front porch, hoping for a reprieve. Maybe the stagecoach was running late or would not come at all. A bridge could be fallen in, or a landslide could have blocked the road somewhere. But, as Carrie worked her way through all of the catastrophes that might delay the stagecoach, she saw it and heard the sound of the horse's hooves echoing across the fields from the road.

Without turning toward him, she spoke softly to George, standing next to her. "Hold on, sweetheart, we may be having a bumpy ride here."

George laughed softly. "You hold onto me, and I will hold onto you." He wrapped his arm around her and pulled her close.

The coach, traveling westbound towards Asheville, slackened speed as it approached the turnoff onto the farm's rutted cart path, where banners and flags waved in the breeze, placed there to give notice to the driver of his proper turn. The team of horses rounded effortlessly and gently propelled the coach up the cart path to the unfinished wooden front steps of the house.

Despite herself, despite her suspicions, distrust even, toward her brother and sisters and their motives, Carrie still felt a surge of pride as the stagecoach, propelled by a quartet of powerful horses, pulled up to her home.

The Black people, even the field hands who normally were out laboring until the day's last light, were permitted to come and watch for the coach. They stood in a group in the muddy rock-strewn yard, their animated voices filling the air.

The coach driver brought the horses and coach to a stop at the front steps. He turned and called out at the gathered Black people, "I need your mule driver. Show yourself."

Toby, a tall Black man, stepped out from the group, "Yes, sir, Master Driver, I'm the mule driver. What you needin'?"

The driver yelled back, "Just as soon as we get these passengers and baggage unloaded, we need to take the team down to the barn and get them watered and fed. I need to get back on the road quick as I can."

He shouted to the others, "Rest of you, get over here and help unload this baggage, quick now."

The driver clambered down from his seat, landing on the ground lightly. He moved around to the side and opened the coach door. He reached up his hand and called out, his voice silky now, "Miss, you be careful, those steps can get a bit of dust on them, traveling along the road. Just reach your hand, and I'll take it and help you down. We don't want to see anybody take a tumble here today."

A gloved hand extended tentatively from the inside of the coach and took the driver's hand. A foot clad in a silk slipper emerged and felt its way onto the top step. Finally, the whole rest of the woman emerged and came down the coach steps, leaning on the driver for balance. She descended carefully and stepped out from the last step onto the ground. With her feet firmly fixed, she cocked up her head. And Carrie saw, shaded beneath the silk hat, the face of her sister, Martha.

Next out, descending the steps right behind her, stepping gingerly, came her other sister, Abigail. Behind them was Frederick, Carrie's older brother. The three stood beside the coach, blinking in the bright sunlight. Carrie and George hurried down the steps, reaching out to the three of them, hugging and embracing. The little group ascended back onto the front porch, away from the driver, who began shouting orders again at the Black people, yelling at them to unload the mass of baggage.

In a few minutes, all of the baggage, boxes, chests, and trunks were hauled out of the coach and placed up on the steps of the house. The driver and Toby maneuvered the team of horses, still pulling the coach, toward the barn to provide them with water and fodder.

Quickly, though, Frederick gave orders to the gathered Black people. "You three, jump up here and shift this baggage into the house." And he turned to his sister, "Carrie, can you please have your servants show Martha and Abigail where they can go and get refreshed?"

Carrie called out to her house slaves, mingled in with the field hands, "Sarah and Emma, Grover and Robert, please come up here and help take the baggage up to the bedrooms." Carrie gave a sideways peek at her two sisters as she called out Sarah and Emma's names and saw both women's smiles turn hard and their bodies stiffen when she spoke the two names. And as Sarah and Emma walked towards them, Martha and Abigail separated themselves, taking refuge behind Carrie and Frederick.

Carrie took it in, and, despite her inner resolve, she felt her mood darken. But as the sour memories sought to find their way into her mind, she pushed them down and away. Her sisters, and Frederick, were her bridge back to her old life, to Richmond. Satisfying as it might be, in the moment, she was not yet ready to burn that bridge, to cut herself off from them completely. Some day she, George, and little Thomas might need these people and the wealth and power they commanded. She willed herself to push away the darkness. Forcing a smile back onto her face, she turned back to her sisters. "Abbie, Marty. Oh my gosh, I can't believe you're here. Goodness, it's hard to believe it's been seven years. You two look wonderful. You must be so happy there back in Richmond." Carrie went on and on, effusively complimenting her sisters.

Carrie heard running footsteps. She turned and caught sight of her son, seven-year-old Thomas, tearing up from the creek, mud-splattered over his boots, pants, and coat. Carrie winced. She had ordered Emma to dress him in his nicest clothes as a show for her sisters and brother, and had implored him not to get dirty. Somehow, though, he slipped out of sight, down to the slave shanties, and found Brock, his best friend, and they had been down to the creek, as usual. Now the two boys, having seen the coach and horses, were running up towards the house, mud caking both of them.

When they got close, Brock hung back and joined in with the other Black people, but Thomas scampered up the steps onto the porch and ran to his aunts. Carrie looked on, wryly amused, as her sisters navigated the offering of love from their dirty muddy nephew. To their credit, Carrie conceded, they both dove in, bending down and accepting wet, mud-splattered hugs from Thomas.

Thankfully, Thomas was never much of a hugger with anybody. He quickly broke free and ran into the house. As he ran, Carrie heard him yelling, "Sarah, Emma. Where are you? You gotta help me; you gotta get me cleaned up." As soon as Thomas was gone, Carrie saw her sisters begin to brush away the dirt from their traveling outfits, using silk handkerchiefs they each pulled out of their handbags. Carrie felt a sarcastic outburst building inside, but she pushed it down as well.

By this time, the stagecoach horses having been watered and rested, the driver was mounted on his seat and was driving the team up the path from the barn toward the house. As he proceeded past the people still milling about before the house, he checked the team briefly and gave a wave. He followed the dirty streak of the cart path back down to the main road, slowed again, and steered the team into a wide left-handed turn, headed west. The coach was empty of passengers now; the only remaining load consisted of mailbags, packages, and newspapers making their journey from Salisbury west up to Asheville.

The time of hugging and embracing was concluding. The field hands went back to their labors. The five White people stood on the porch, the conversation dying away. After a moment, Frederick suggested that he and George make a brief tour of the farm and fields. The two men stepped down off the porch and headed towards the barn.

That left Carrie marooned, alone with her sisters.

She guided them into the front room of the house, made up to be a small parlor. They found seats on the small settee and chairs. Carrie jumped in, hoping to steer the talk away from herself and George and the farm, "So, Abby, Marty, tell me about Richmond. Has it changed much?"

"Oh my gosh, Carrie," Abigail replied, "The whole city has gone mad. More people every day. Mama doesn't hardly want to go away from the mansion with all the different people. Half of them you can't even understand. Dutch and Irish, Carrie. And Jews. My goodness, the Jews are everywhere."

"Yes, Carrie," Martha agreed, "the Jews are all over. We can barely get the carriage down the street for all the Jews and their carts. And they call out to each other all the time. The Lord only knows what they are saying about us."

Abigail and Martha were off, detailing the declining character of Richmond brought about by the steady stream of immigrants. Carrie was content to let them run on with their sorrowful stories, keeping the focus away from herself and George.

The three sisters sat and chatted about old times. Carrie began to call to mind more and more details about her old life in Richmond. She remembered the parties, the food, and the other rich girls of her class at the Girls Academy. Remembrances came unbidden, things she had not recalled for years. Getting fitted for a new dress. The frenzy of anticipation as the social season approached when she and the other girls were put out to be seen by the eligible bachelors. The thrilled chatter of her young girlfriends as they announced, one after another, their engagements to the rich young sons of the Virginia aristocracy.

Without warning, dark feelings began to arise. They were not full memories, just pieces, horrifying bits of remembrance. Hot breath, the smell of whiskey and tobacco. Hard pressure of a shoulder against her chest. And the thrusting.

She sensed her rising panic, the taste of bile in her throat. She felt like screaming out in panic and anger. Instead, she willed it to go away, to go back down into the secret crevices of her heart where she kept it, unseen. She forced her mind back onto the here and now, back onto her two stupid silly sisters.

She tried to head the conversation in different directions. She asked Abigail about her suitors. Two years before, Abigail's husband lost a duel. In fairness, it was judged a draw since the other man was also killed. Abigail completed a year in mourning and was now being courted again. "Tell me about your beaus, Abby. You need to find one who will keep you happy, you know, under the blankets," said Carrie, a naughty note in her voice. Abigail smiled back, blushing like a schoolgirl, and began an extensive narrative about the crowds of ambitious young men seeking to court her.

Eventually, the conversation came to a pause, and Martha seized it, "So, Carrie, when are you coming for a visit? Mother wants to see you so badly, you and little Thomas. He needs to meet his grandmother, Carrie. He is her grandson, after all. She won't be with us forever."

Carrie nodded and looked down. A hint of terror and panic started to rise again as she thought about Richmond. "Yes, I know we need to come. It is just hard for George to get away, the farm is demanding, and there always seems to be one more job to do. But you are right, she deserves to see him, and he should meet his family and cousins."

"And Carrie, sweetheart, George could stay here, and you and Thomas could come," Abigail said. "Surely, dear, he could get along for a month or two without you. After all, you've given to him, that's the least he could do for you. We all know, Carrie darling, that George didn't bring a lot with him to your marriage. We all remember how Frederick had to lend him the clothes just to get married in."

Carrie's mood darkened at the insult to George. But she held back the impulse to lash back at her sisters, to match each of their cutting insults with one of her own. She forced it down, forced the smile to stay on her face.

"Abby, of course, you're right. We need to come. And Sarah and Emma could come with me to help with Thomas, and see their mothers and brothers and sisters. I'd like to see that little cottage again; we all had such fun there when we were little girls."

Martha and Abigail exchanged glances, their expression hardening. "Carrie, that old cottage is gone," Martha said.

Carrie's eyes widened, "Gone? What happened?"

"Burned to the ground," Martha said. "Mother told Frederick to have it burned. Right after you left."

"What about Mama and Auntie and all the children?"

"Well, of course they are all gone too," Abigail said. "Mother ordered them sold to a Georgia trader. She wanted them gone from Richmond. Gone from the state. Surely you can see why, can't you? She only let them stay after Father died because of you. Once you were gone, she wanted them gone too."

Carrie sat without speaking. As the three women sat silently, there was the sound of the door opening, and George and Frederick came back from their tour. Soon Sarah was calling out that supper would be ready soon.

For the following days, the pretense held, and the masks of comity stayed in place.

Carrie showed her guests all around the county. She shepherded them all to Sunday church services. She borrowed a carriage from someone in town and had Toby drive them west on the road all the way to the steep slopes of the Blue Ridge. And she even prevailed on them to put on boots and old clothes and led the way on a hike down to the creek and up the steep hill on the other side, climbing up through the ravine to the rocky clearing. She described how she and George climbed up here years before, climbing up through the ravine in the very same way, and saw their new home from this spot. But even as she spoke, she could see that her sisters and brother did not understand, would never understand, the depth of love she felt in her heart for this special place, just a rocky hillside in the woods.

The days passed. Abigail became increasingly shrill, longing for the fawning attention of her suitors in Richmond. Martha openly displayed her boredom and contempt. Frederick became increasingly dismissive and disinterested in the farm and all other subjects which did not involve himself.

The last full day of their visit arrived. The stagecoach was coming, by arrangement, the following morning, traveling back on its journey from Asheville toward Salisbury. The coach would pause in its journey east, come back up the cart path to the house and pick up the three visitors, and head on its way.

They gathered in the dining room, their last chance to converse together, dining on the bounty of the farm. After the meal, they stayed seated around the table, sipping coffee and sweet dessert wine and making small talk.

Thomas got restless as soon as the pie was finished. Carrie excused him, and he was up and out the back door in a second. Carrie was marking time, certain Frederick was going to make a speech, to announce the purpose behind this whole charade of a visit. The moment came.

"Well," Frederick began, "I must say, to both of you, that I didn't expect to see anything like what you have shown us these last days. I half expected that we might come here and be put up in shanties no better than the slaves. It is quite impressive, Carrie, and you too, George, what you've managed to do to this land in just a few years, considering what you started with."

"Thank you, Frederick," Carrie jumped into the conversation, "that means a lot. After all, it was only your generous consent to allow me to inherit this land and the slaves that made it all possible."

Frederick shot Carrie a look of irritation. Frederick was not intending to have a discussion, and he was not used to being interrupted.

He paused, then continued, "So, having said that and giving credit where credit is due, Carrie and George, it's clear to me that it's time for you to chart a different future for yourselves. The simple truth, plain to see, is that nothing will ever come from working on this land. The soil is too poor. The weather is too harsh. And even if you were to get a decent crop one year, you can't get it to market. The river can't be navigated here. Even if you could grow tobacco, cotton, or even a decent corn or wheat crop, you've got no way of getting it down the river to a port. You'd be stuck with it." He paused, waiting for his words to be taken in and appreciated by his audience. He resumed his narrative.

"Now, George, it's no secret that I suspected you and your intentions. I thought you were a fortune seeker. But I see now that you're a good man, a hardworking man. I believe you might make a decent manager for one of our plantations along the James. Tobacco is a difficult, demanding crop. You would make a fair and competent manager. Given the right circumstances, George, you could amass wealth, vastly more wealth than what you'll ever have here."

"You know, Carrie," Frederick continued, "When Father bought this land, it was no more than a joke. His friends were all buying up Western lands just so they could boast and brag about it to each other. Father just wanted to get in on it. He never expected to even come here, much less try to produce crops from it. The two of you, you've taken property that started as money wasted and made something mostly respectable out of it. But, Carrie, dear sister, you and George have proven yourselves to us. It's time to come home. Mother worries about you."

Abigail took up where Frederick left off. "Carrie, darling, it's just so painful to see you working so hard out here without any help. Why, most days, it's just the three of you, you and George and poor little Thomas, surrounded by these heathen slaves. They could just rise up and chop you to pieces, and no one would know. You might not be found for months, and then just a pile of bones. Just think what that would do to Mother. Carrie, it would kill her!"

At this, Carrie's dammed-up ire and annoyance at her sister burst through her restraints, "Oh good God, Abby, stop it with all this silly hysterical talk! Our slaves are not heathens any more than you are, and they are not going to chop us up in pieces. Emma's the most Christian person I know. I've never heard anything so stupid."

Abigail's mouth fell open, and her eyes widened in surprise at the sudden attack from her younger sister. "Fine, Carrie, I hardly care what you do. I didn't want to come here anyway, I just came because Mother asked me to. Just stay here and rot, for all I care. This place is halfway rotten already; we can all see that."

Martha intervened, "Please, Carrie, listen to us. Mother wants you back. She's forgiven you."

Despite her anger, Carrie was puzzled. "Forgiven me? For what?"

"For choosing George, and…and… this," she gestured with her arms, taking in the house and surroundings, "over your family, dear. We all forgive you, Carrie, sweetheart. You were young. You made mistakes. Mother understands. We all understand."

Frederick added, "And there's plenty of room at the mansion now. I know Mother is looking forward to having an energetic youngster like Thomas around the house again."

Carrie looked at each of her siblings. "So that's the whole point of this? Get George, Thomas and me back to Richmond? To the mansion? To get Mother off your backs?"

Abigail and Martha looked at each other but were silent.

Frederick replied, "Yes. At least you and Thomas. George can come along, too, if you want him."

Carrie spoke again. "So that's it. That's the offer. Come back, and all is forgiven." Carrie said. It wasn't a question, just a statement.

"Yes," Frederick replied. "But as I said, if George comes, I expect him to manage one of the tobacco plantations. For wages only, not as an owner. After all, Carrie, you've already received your inheritance. And one other thing Mother told me to tell you. None of the slaves can come back. They need to be sold. And not to anyone around Richmond. Sell them here, or sell them south."

Carrie looked at the three, her anger at them building higher within her.

"I will never sell Sarah or Emma to some slave trader," she said icily. "Never. They're my blood, my sisters, just like you two."

Martha replied, the anger in her voice matching Carrie's, "Carrie, that joke is not funny anymore. It never was. Those two are not our sisters. They're not anything to us. They are slaves. They are heathens, and we are Christians. You seem to think it's clever to make jokes about that, but it's not. You can't come back to Richmond and talk like that around Mother. It's disgusting even to say it."

Silence descended. Finally, Carrie gathered her thoughts, "Frederick, you're right; George is good at everything he does. You would be lucky to have him working for the family. But as for coming back—No. Not now." The room became quiet again.

Carrie said, "Please excuse me." She stood and walked out of the room. She went down the hall to the library, walked around the big desk, and opened the double glass doors to let in the night air. She looked out over the fields. Twilight was just fading into darkness, but she could still make out the top of the rocky knoll rising in the distance. As she stood there, the last rays of the sun disappeared, and the stars came out. She could no longer see the knoll, but she could feel it there in her heart.

She heard footsteps turning into the library. Without turning, she knew it was George. He walked up behind her, and in the dark, he put his arms around her waist. She reached down, grasped his right hand, and put it up against her cheek.

"He's not wrong, you know," George said softly. "He's not wrong about the land. This land here is nothing like what they have along the James. We'll never get rich off it. We can scratch out a living from it, but you'll never have the things Richmond could give you. Growing tobacco along the James means good money. I can never give that to you here, not even close."

Carrie turned, and in the dark, she wrapped her arms around George and held him close to her. She said, "George, you don't know what it would be like for us in Richmond. They won't ever take us back, not really. We would always be the sad little sister and her pathetic husband who tried to make it on their own but couldn't do it and needed to be rescued. To our faces, there would be smiles and sweet words. Behind our backs, they would laugh at us and make jokes about us. We would never be accepted back by them, never."

They stood there in each other's arms. Finally, George said, "Carrie, you say we will never be accepted. But Carrie, I've never been accepted, not once, by the people like that. Not before we were married, and not now. My whole life. First, I was a poor ragged preacher's kid. And then I wasn't even that, just a dirty orphan looking for hand-outs. You worry about being ridiculed? Despised? That's been my life, my whole life. But Carrie, I don't care about that. I care about you and Thomas. You're my home; the rest doesn't matter."

Carrie looked at George in the dim light. She had never told George the real reason she could not return to Richmond, about what happened when she was sixteen. About the man. She would not, could not tell him, ever.

She said, "George, wherever you are, that's my home, now and forever. But I will never, ever, ever, ever go back to Richmond. Never.

Don't ask me to do that." And she pushed the taste of bile and the panic and the anger back down, back into the crevices deep in her heart.

§

The next morning, Carrie watched and hoped, hoping now against delays, as the stagecoach turned off the road onto the cart path, pulling up to the front steps. George, Carrie, and Thomas gathered together with Abigail, Martha, and Frederick. As before, the slaves gathered around to see the three travelers off on their journey. Trunks, bags, and boxes were hauled up and packed. Hugs and kisses and good wishes were passed around. The travelers ascended the steps into the stagecoach, and the driver pulled away. George and Carrie watched until the coach was out of sight. Carrie walked over to where Sarah and Emma stood among the other Black people. With their light skin and blue eyes, they stood out from all the others. Carrie walked up to each of them and hugged them.

Sarah nodded towards the road where the stagecoach had now disappeared and said, "So, Missus Carrie, are we movin' back to Richmond?"

Carrie decided not to share with Sarah or Emma what her sisters told her about the little cottage in Richmond, the cottage where the two Black women were born, where the three of them grew up together, now burned to the ground. Or about their mothers, Mama and Auntie, and the children, their brothers and sisters and cousins, sold off and taken south by a Georgia trader. She might tell them someday, later. She looked over the fields toward the road and said, "This is home now, for George and Thomas and me. For all of us. Richmond will never be home again."

Chapter 6—1825—8 years on the land— Finances

C arrie awoke from a night of restless sleep. She twisted around and stretched her hand toward the other side of the bed. She was hoping to find George still there, sleeping in a little later than usual. She would touch him, turn toward him, snuggle against his warmth, and caress him with her lips.

It was empty. Not a trace of his body's warmth was retained by the sheets and blankets on that side of their bed. George, as usual, had arisen before light and departed silently, out early for his day's labor on the farm.

She listened out for Thomas, now eight years old, strained to hear his clomping footstep on the floor boards. She was hoping he might come bursting into her room and give her one of his sweet delicious hugs like he did when he was little. All was silent. Most mornings, he was up early, soon after George departed, headed down to the shanties to roust up Brock. She pictured the two boys down in the creek, red mud smeared over them, impervious to the chilly creek water.

With effort, Carrie rolled over and sat up on the edge of the bed. Morning was always the worst time for her.

A year and a few months previously, Carrie had begun to feel different. It came on stealthily at first, just fatigue. Of course, she was tired, she thought at the time, look at all of her obligations. She was a wife, mother, and mistress of a farm, plus there were all the slaves to look after. She tried to rest more, tried to take better care of herself.

The fatigue stayed, though, even with rest, a deep fatigue she never felt before. Then her fingers got stiff and crackly, like dried-out sticks. Soon after, the pain started, all over, all day long. Her fingers were puffed up and feverish. She felt dull, dragged down from head to toe.

George saw something had changed and, despite her protests, called the doctor out from town.

The doctor came, asked questions, looked, felt, and gave his diagnosis in one word. Rheumatism.

Carrie and George asked a few questions before the doctor left.

What caused it? No one knows. Maybe it was related to dampness, living near water.

Will it get better? It might, but mostly it gets worse.

What can she take for it? A bit of wine before bed to help her rest.

What else? Nothing, try to stay rested.

Carrie understood. She understood the message in the doctor's vague, imprecise words. With the rheumatism, she was on her own. Not completely, of course, she had George. She had Emma and Sarah. But there was no remedy, no cure. No secret elixir. It was hers alone to bear.

She tried to battle it, keeping herself extra busy. The farmhouse, like all houses, wanted to fall apart, so she commandeered a few of the field hands away from George and put them to work hammering down squeaky floorboards and replacing rotted wood, whitewashing and painting. She started having Toby drive her around in the wagon, stopping in at the small cottages and farmhouses along the road, getting to know those folk on their tiny patchwork farms.

She tried to get pregnant again, did all she could think of, hoping to see the house filled up someday with children and grandchildren.

Nothing worked. She needed to be distracted. She needed to do more, to be more. More than just a burden. She settled on a plan.

The day she married George, he became a rich man. All the money and land, all the slaves, all of her inheritance, was given over to him. In an instant, it was gone from her. That was the law. Carrie understood all of that. It was all his now, closed off to her.

But she knew she could help. If she could just work on the accounts, maybe balance the books, take some of the load off of poor George, that would be something.

A month previously, she approached George and asked his permission to look at the farm accounts. He put her off. No one else, he claimed, could make sense of his accounting system. It was too complex and confusing. But she kept after him, gently. In a week, of course, he relented and gave her his blessing. All of the farm's finances, all of the big ledgers stacked up in the library, were now open to her.

Today was the day she had resolved. Today she planned to plop herself down in the library and begin to familiarize herself with the ledgers.

She completed her morning stretches, kneading the muscles like dough and loosening the fibers and sinews. She slipped off her nightgown and pulled on her day clothes. She sat at her dressing table, gave her hair a couple of final pulls with her brush, gathered it, and secured it with a ribbon. She chanced one more peek in the mirror. She saw herself, the same and yet not the same as she looked a year before. There were new lines, new creases etched there from pain and worry. She looked away, sighing softly. Gathering herself, she pushed away from the dressing table and stood up, heading toward the door.

She descended the steps and entered the library. The room was warm, so she turned to the double glass doors behind the desk and opened them up. The doors were an expensive indulgence, specially crafted for the library from plates of glass brought by wagon from Richmond. The light they afforded made the library seem to glow, even in winter.

Standing in the open doors, she took time to look out across the scrubby farm fields toward the rocky knoll rising on the other side of the creek. Her mind reminisced, as always, to the first time she and George were there together, how they embraced, longing for each other, even as she held Thomas in her womb. The sweet remembrance of George's tenderness still stirred her.

She indulged in her reverie for a long moment. At length, she turned away reluctantly and sat down in the padded leather desk chair. She settled in to look at the ledgers and account book. She opened the first volume and began to study the columns and rows of numbers etched in ink by George's careful hand.

She decided to look first at the list of the farm's assets, including money in the bank and the dollar value of the lands and house. She was surprised to see how the cash part of her inheritance had dwindled from what she remembered. She looked back through the ledgers, trying to figure out when money came into their accounts, and when it was paid out, and how that was changing over the years of the farms' operation and growth.

She kept coming up with sums and balances that surprised, even shocked, her. The amount of money going out to pay bills and expenses exceeded, year after year, their earnings.

She knew in the first years it was going to be like that. After all, they started with a large tract of raw wilderness land, 1400 acres, and carved a farm out of it. It made sense that there would be high costs in the beginning. What didn't make sense to her was that eight years in, the draining away of their cash was getting worse. The numbers seemed to show that in the current year, they were earning less than last year. And last year, they earned less than the year before that. The cushion of money they possessed when they first arrived on the land was only a quarter of its original amount and dropping.

They were going broke. Their wealth, her inheritance, was flowing away, like apple cider flowing from a barrel with the stopper pulled out.

The cider still in the barrel was going down fast. They either needed to put the stopper back in the barrel; or they needed to find a way to make a lot more cider.

Carrie looked back at her list of the farm's property. She realized that there was one property class she was not accounting for—human property. She searched through the ledger, but it appeared that George never thought to write up a listing of their slaves. So she went back and made a list of all of the enslaved people on the farm, separate columns based on sex, and listed the name and age of each slave. She knew the ages of a few, like Sarah and Emma. For the rest, she put down a guess.

Carrie remembered that they departed from Richmond with 20 slaves. She could still recall the sound of their footfalls as they trudged along behind the wagon while she sat on the wagon seat next to George. Eight years since, she remembered that two of the twenty were dead, a couple of the older men. By her count, fourteen babies had been born among the ten slave women. Two of the fourteen babies died within a month of being born. To Carrie and George's good fortune, none of the Black mothers had died, neither from childbirth nor anything else. Totaling up the columns, Carrie was surprised, happily, to find that she and George now owned thirty people.

She knew what prices were being given for slaves from the newspapers. When she attached a cash value to each name on her list, she realized they were not going broke, not at all. They were as rich as when they first arrived on the land. The snag was that nearly all their wealth was tied up in the slaves. The value of their human property, even the young children who could not yet work, exceeded, by a lot, the value of all their other property combined.

Carrie thought about the other farmers in the county, the large landowners who owned lots of slaves. She wondered what they were doing differently to make money. She realized there was a big difference between these large landholders and her husband, George. All of the big landowners, those who counted their property in thousands of acres and scores of enslaved people, were lawyers, doctors, or ministers or ran businesses. They all did something else, something that paid, to make a living. For these men, Carrie realized, their farms and the slaves they owned were assets, treasures that they could pass on to their children. Their daily bread, however, was earned through their businesses or professions. George, Carrie knew, could never be one of those men. He would certainly never be a lawyer, even less a preacher. The thought of George in business, stuck inside some stuffy store, mades Carrie laugh out loud.

Carrie gazed again at the list of the slaves she had written out. It appeared to her that the farm had plenty of hands to do the fieldwork. And there were all those children born since the farm started, who would be big enough to work a hoe in the field soon. She knew slave speculators paid well for slaves, even young ones. She remembered seeing speculators in Richmond, bidding at a slave auction, buying up Black people, and forming them into caravans. She saw them on the roads when they left Richmond, marching along, chained together, heading south and west to the new cotton lands. If she and George sold a few slaves to one of these speculators, that might help put the stopper back in the barrel, at least for a while.

She kept studying the list. She made a new column in the ledger of the Black women, starting with the oldest and going down to the youngest. Next to each woman's name, she wrote the names of the babies born to them on the farm. There were four names with two or more baby names next to them. These, Carrie decided, were their prime breeders. If these women, these proven breeders, could be induced to keep having babies, even one child every two years, and if Carrie and George could convert a portion of that property stream into cash, the farm could survive. They would not go broke, not need to crawl back to Richmond begging for more money, more crumbs from Frederick.

Carrie's thoughts suddenly came up short. Two of the names written on her list of breeders were Sarah and Emma, her two sisters. Her best friends. In truth, her only friends in the world besides George.

Carrie's thoughts jumped, unbidden, to Richmond, to the little cottage, now burned to the ground. It was her world back then, her special world that she shared with Sarah and Emma. Back when they were all little girls, she didn't understand they were her half-sisters and that her father was also their father. They were her sisters, though, in her heart, and in their hearts, Carrie knew. Truthfully, they were more than sisters. They saved her that day, saved her life, she was sure. Even now, she could taste the fear.

And now she looked at their names, these sisters who served her faithfully for years, even risked their lives for her, scribbled down on a list on a piece of paper. Listed, along with other women, as breeders.

Carrie stared down at the list. She flipped the pages and looked back at the cash they held in the bank, how small and shrunken the balance had become. As she looked, her mouth became a hard line. She spoke to herself out loud. "Stop it. Just stop it. You're just being a stupid little girl. They're just slaves. Harden yourself up." She clenched her jaws together and forced back the tears filling her eyes.

She stayed seated at the desk, staring at the list of slave names. First, she looked at Sarah's name. She forced her mind to block out, wall off, every good and sweet memory, every kindness given and received, every feeling of love she held in her heart toward Sarah. She made her heart dead to Sarah. She did the same thing with Emma. Then she did it for each of the other women on her list of breeders, then the children. She finished with the men. She closed the ledgers and walked out of the library.

The next few days Carrie spent testing herself, checking her heart to see if the hardness was still there. She would reminisce, bringing up sweet memories from times past, playing with Sarah and Emma as children, or working together here on the farm. Whenever she felt a warming, a softening in her heart toward Sarah or Emma or one of her other slaves, she would push it down and cover it with a fresh layer of stone.

She decided she needed to present her ideas to George, get him committed to her plan, and do it quickly. Otherwise, if she waited, the hardness would crack. She would lose her nerve.

The next Saturday night, they sat together in the dining room following supper, Carrie sipping on her tea while George drank from his coffee cup. Carrie spoke softly, "George, dear, I thought perhaps that tomorrow afternoon we could sit and talk for a while about the ledgers. I had no idea how much time and effort and trouble you have been putting into taking care of our money. There were just a couple of things I didn't understand in the ledger, and I'm sure you could explain them to me easily. Would that be all right?"

George smiled, "Of course. That would be a fine time to go over the books."

Carrie smiled back and sipped her tea.

The next day, after church in town and Sunday dinner, Carrie and George walked down the hall to the library. George offered Carrie the padded desk chair. The day was warm, so he pushed open the double glass doors. A gentle breeze scented with the fragrance of cut hay wafted into the room. George pulled up a chair and sat beside Carrie.

Carrie pulled over the large farm ledger and opened it up. Instead of turning to the long columns written out in George's laborious hand, she turned to the back of the ledger, where she had made her notations and listings. She turned the ledger so George could see it clearly.

"George," Carrie began, "I didn't know where to start the other day, so I tried to make a listing of all of our property, so I could understand better the progress we've made the last several years." Gesturing to the different columns she had written out, she continued, "This first column is the money we have in the bank. In the middle column is a listing of the land, the house and our buildings, and how much those might be worth. Now this last column, I wrote down the names of all of our slaves and how much I thought each one might bring if we ever decided to sell any of them. I know you probably already have all of this in your head, but it helps me understand it better when I see it all written out like this."

She gave George some time to look at the different columns and the figures she had written down. She understood that some of this information must be new to George since there had not previously been any listing of the slaves or their value.

George studied the lists, his eyes moving intently down the columns. After a few minutes, Carrie said, "So, did I make many mistakes, George? A lot of the slaves, I'm not really sure how old they are or how strong they are. Wouldn't those things affect the price we could get for them?"

"No, Carrie, this looks wonderful. Honestly, I never really thought to write it all out this way."

"And, George, I just wondered, seeing all this, it seems like there's so many more slaves here now than when we first came. It crossed my mind that maybe we have more slaves now than we have work for them to do. Of course, you know more about that than I do."

George paused before replying, then he spoke more slowly. "Well, I suppose that's true to some extent. Some of the hands get their work done with plenty of time left in the day. But a few of the hands lag, and they slow things down for the others. 'Specially the older hands, they don't keep up with the others. Truthfully it's been getting worse that way."

The conversation lapsed as George continued to study Carrie's figures.

At length, Carrie spoke again, "George, there's nothing wrong with selling off a few of the slower hands. Everyone does that. It isn't fair to the other hands to have one or two slowing everyone else down. Maybe the faster hands might have to do more work because of the ones lagging. Maybe if we sell them, they can go work somewhere that's easier and where they don't have to keep up such a hard pace."

George remained silent for another long moment.

"Carrie, these people have been with you since you were little. They came here with us from Richmond. I always thought of them more as part of the family. I just don't know about selling them like that."

"George, family is the most important thing; we both agree about that. But George, this is different. Business is not family. Sometimes it can be unpleasant to run a business. We've been more than kind and fair to the hands over the years. We've worked right along beside them. But now, we might need to let some go. It would be for their own good, and it would be for the good of the rest of the hands here."

There was more silence. George still sat looking at the columns, his face puzzled. Carrie saw the puzzlement, the uncertainty and feared she was losing him. It was time to push through his reluctance. "So, George, you said that there were a couple of the hands that weren't keeping up, putting a bigger burden on the others. Which of the hands is slowing the others down?"

"There's only one that's worse than all the rest. Julius."

Involuntarily, Carrie flinched, then caught herself. Julius was Emma's husband and father to her two children. "Julius. Is he the only one?"

"He's the one who stands out. The other hands are all grumbling, saying Julius gets off easy, and they end up doing more work to make up for what he can't get done. I thought we might try moving him up to the house. Maybe, though, we should just sell him. Some of the older children are pretty near ready to take over for him."

Carrie was silent. Images of Julius came into her mind. Playing with her when she was a little girl back in Richmond. Julius and Emma standing together, the two of them arm in arm as Kee and little Samuel, their two children played nearby. As each image came to her, she pulled tighter on the cords of her heart, tightening it up, keeping it hard.

Toughen yourself up. They're just slaves.

At length, she spoke again. "George, if you feel Julius is the weakest, and we have the younger ones who can replace him soon, we should sell him."

George looked up from the ledger and spoke softly, "Truthfully, the worst part is going to be telling him and telling the others."

"It will be hard. But you can do it. I know you can; you are strong. You have to decide ahead of time what you are going to say. Then when you speak to him, put your mind somewhere else so that only your mouth is speaking. Just deaden yourself, say the words, and walk away. Don't look back. Then forget about it."

George was silent again. He finally spoke. "I'll do it this week."

A few days later, early in the morning before the first bell, George walked down to the shanty where Emma, Julius, and their children lived. He called out, "Julius, come here; I want you to go into town with me today."

Julius came out the shanty door, surprise on his face. "Yes, sir, Master, you wantin' me to go with you instead of out to the field?"

"Yes, that's right, Julius, come up to the barn. I want you to go into town with me. We'll go in the wagon."

"Master, I don't know how to drive the horse for that wagon. Toby always does the drivin'."

"I'll drive the wagon, Julius; you just get up to the barn, quick as you can."

Emma came out to the door and stood next to her husband, concern on her face. Their daughter Kee stood next to her, holding little Samuel's hand. Julius replied, "Yes sir, Master, I'm going up there now."

A few minutes later, the wagon was going down the cart path toward the road. George was holding the reins, and Julius sat beside him. That was the last time that Emma, Kee, Samuel, or anyone else from the farm, saw Julius.

Late in the afternoon, the wagon came back up the cart path from the road. George sat on the wagon seat alone. He stopped the wagon beside the barn, where Toby was standing. George got down and wordlessly handed the reins to Toby, and he walked back up towards the house. He stopped at the kitchen cabin to wash up and get some water. Emma and Sarah were in the kitchen, working on supper. George looked at Emma. He looked away, out toward the barn. He made himself dead inside. He turned toward Emma. He focused his eyes on a spot on the wall behind Emma's head.

George spoke the words he had practiced saying all the way home in the wagon. "Emma, I sold Julius to a trader. Julius just couldn't keep up in the field with the other hands. He was always falling behind. He just wasn't cut out for fieldwork. Emma, you can marry up with any of the other hands, you got my permission to choose anybody you want. You've got my word." Without further words, he turned and walked out the door and across the yard to the house.

Inside the house, he walked down to the library. Carrie was sitting there alone. Thomas was off, down at the creek, playing with Brock. Carrie looked up at her husband.

"So, how did it go?"

"There were no problems. The trader was there."

"Does Emma know?"

"Yes, I saw her in the kitchen. She and Sarah. I told them. I did like you told me, with the deadening. It helped."

"How much?"

"Four fifty."

"I thought we might get five hundred."

"Four fifty is all he would pay. So I took it."

"Fine, George, that's just fine. Four fifty is good." And Carrie pulled over the open ledger book. She picked up the pen and crossed out Julius's name from the list of the slave property. She entered $450 in the cash column and totaled up the balance.

"Thank you, George. For doing that. And for speaking to Emma and Sarah."

George nodded, his eyes down. In silence, he turned and walked out of the library.

In the kitchen cabin, Emma sat on the rough chair in front of the fireplace. The small wooden cross she wore around her neck on a piece of rawhide was clutched between her hands. She looked into the fire. Sarah could see her lips moving. As usual, she could not hear the words, not even a whisper. But she saw the tears filling her sister's eyes, streaming down her cheeks. She could find no words to say. She pulled up the other chair next to Emma's, sat down, and enfolded her arms around her sister. After a while, she did finally find some words. "Emma, honey, I'm sorry, I'm so so sorry. I'm just so so sorry."

Chapter 7—1830—13 years on the land— Pastor Parker

I believe that's enough for today, Thomas, you are dismissed," said Reverend Philip Parker to his young pupil. As soon as the words were spoken, the pupil, Thomas Jefferson Adams, age twelve, was up from his chair and heading for the door. Parker heard his footsteps racing down the hall, then up the stairs to his room.

Pastor Parker was still a young man. He still carried within himself a young man's vigor, and he moved with a young man's ease. He was ruddy in his face, with fading freckles across his cheeks. There was a collection of scars and creases on his hands, souvenirs from a childhood and youth spent working out of doors. Now, though, he spent far less time outdoors and too many of his hours inside, preparing for Sunday's preaching, spiritual food for his tiny flock. And even more hours were spent indoors preparing and delivering private lessons to Thomas and other children of the local folk for extra pay, since the church collections were pitiable, mostly nickels and pennies.

Left alone in the library, the half-smile on Pastor Parker's face faded back to worry, traced with resentment. It was all so unfair, so galling to go beggaring while others, his classmates from seminary, were moving along, moving up, gaining prestige and wealth. But not him.

He had followed God's calling, he thought, leading him out to this wilderness. Eight years, nearly nine, in this mountain valley. His own valley of dry bones, he mused morosely. He tried. God Himself could attest to how hard he tried, pouring himself out for God among these coarse people. But the bones were not rising, were not coming back to life. They lay on the sand, parched and dead, in a parched and dead land. And he was parched as well, in his spirit.

He didn't care so much for himself. But what of his poor suffering wife, Evangeline, her tummy swelling again with another child, and yet her face so gaunt, so drawn? What of his children, shoeless and dressed in rags and dependent on charity even for those?

He gathered up his texts and papers and packed them into his satchel. He stepped out into the hallway and looked up and down. No one was there, so he walked around, through the dining room to the slave pantry and out the back door. He headed toward the barn, where he had left his creaky secondhand buggy and his lean hollow-backed horse to be watched over by Toby.

As he approached the barn, he heard a voice coming from across the fields, calling out, "Pastor…hold up there, Pastor." He peered toward the voice, his hand shading his eyes from the sunny glare, and saw the voice was coming from Thomas' father, his employer, George Adams, who was hastening towards him. He sighed inwardly. The only reason he could imagine for Mr. Adams to speak to him would be to let him go, to tell him that his services as a teacher for Thomas were no longer required.

Adams approached closer to Parker. "Thank you, Pastor, can we speak a minute?"

"Fine, Mr. Adams, I have no other lessons to give today."

"Wonderful—how about we ride around a bit; let me show you the place. I recall, when we first met, you told me you grew up as a farm boy; I'm expectin' you can sit on a horse."

Parker was surprised but replied, "Fine, Mr. Adams, we can ride a bit." The two men entered the barn, where Toby had a pair of the farm's horses saddled and ready to be ridden. The two men mounted. Adams led the way out of the barn back towards the farm's fields and pastures. Parker followed behind. As he rode, he peered over the farm, sizing things up. He saw the hands, their Black faces sweating beneath their straw hats, down near the creek, hoeing along the rows of corn.

"So I can see now, Pastor, you sit on a horse just fine."

"Yes, Mr. Adams, I grew up on a farm, not much, we owned about 30 acres, over east, near Salisbury."

"And…brothers and sisters?"

"Oh yes, there were eight of us. I was fifth in line."

There was a pause.

"And…slaves?" Adams asked.

Parker paused before replying. He was not sure why Adams was asking about his childhood. "Yes, Mr. Adams, we owned slaves. Just a couple. Most of the work we did on our own."

"That sounds fine, very fine, Pastor."

They rode along for a bit in silence.

Parker spoke up. "Excuse me, Mr. Adams, why are you asking me about all of that? Aren't you firing me?"

"Firing you? What gave you that idea?"

"I don't know, Mr. Adams, I just assumed so."

"Well, hell no. No, Pastor, I don't want to fire you. In fact, I want to hire you. I need help here with the slaves and all. I want to hire you away from your church and put you on full-time here."

Parker was shocked. He blurted out, "Hire me? As what? As an overseer?"

"Well, yes, partly that, but more than that, Pastor, I want you to be a preacher for the slaves. Preach to 'em every Sunday. Oversee their souls, you might say."

Parker looked at Adams silently, his face puzzled by Adams' words.

"Now, Pastor, let me just tell you how I see it. We've been here, Mrs. Adams and me, twelve years now, and I've learned a bit about workin' the land with slaves. I'm sure you agree, Pastor, it's not much good usin' the cowhide on the slaves. With most of the slaves, the more you whip them, the worse they act. Slaves are funny like that; you think you got them figured out, and they surprise you."

"So Pastor, I hold back on usin' the cowhide as much as I can. What I've found is, you get the most from them by showing them kindness. I try to give the slaves nine parts kindness and only one-part cowhide."

Adams continued, "That's why I'm looking for somebody like you. They got to know about the cowhide, of course, but they also got to know, to really believe that we care about them. And they got to believe that God loves them too, and if they're good and work hard here on earth, they'll go to heaven when they die."

"So that's why I'm hoping to get a preacher to work with me. I'm not lookin' for the kind of man like most planters want. I don't want someone to just go out and beat the slaves down. What I'm looking for is someone to help them and love them, so the slaves are going to work hard just because they want to make the master happy. I guarantee, if you got slaves like that, and you go to sell them, word gets around, and pretty soon folks are wantin' to come to you, askin' to buy your slaves. And they pay extra for them."

"Now, Pastor, I know I'd be asking a lot from you if you do this, and I'll pay well. I think we could start you out at $300 a year. Plus, we've built a nice new cabin here on the property, you and your family can use, plus food from the house kitchen. That's a good offer, but you'll earn it."

Parker couldn't believe it. That was more than double what he earned from the church and his teaching put together. Plus, a cabin to live in and a whole farm of good food for his children. And, on top of all that, he would still be answering his call to preach, preaching to Africans, sharing with them the gospel. He knew a few classmates who had chosen mission work, sailing off to India or even to China, preaching to the heathen. Here he would do the same thing and not even give up the comforts of hearth and home. Parker felt elation rising within him.

Adams stuck out his hand, Parker grasped it, and the two shook.

The sun climbed up to its highest point. Adams yelled over to the hands in the field, "Alright, y'all, I'd say it's time for dinner. Come on over here and get in the shade. I'll send Brock down with the water."

The two White men turned their horses and headed toward the house. As they approached the slave shanties, Adams looked down towards the creek and spotted Thomas and Brock.

Adams called out, "Brock, it's dinner time; get those buckets of water out to the hands. Make a couple trips, they been working hard, and it's hot out today. And, Thomas, you head up to the house; it's about time for our dinner also."

Brock called out, "Yes sir, Master Adams," and immediately headed back up to the slave shanties to grab the buckets.

Thomas also called out, "Yes, sir, Father."

Adams turned to Parker, "Well, Pastor, you're welcome to stay for dinner if you like."

Parker replied, "Mr. Adams, thank you. I'm past due to get home, so I better go and check on Evangeline and the children. And let me thank you again for your generous offer. I will give you an answer on it tomorrow."

"Actually, Pastor, it was Carrie, my wife, who thought about hiring you. You'll find that she's the only one with any sense around here," Adams replied.

The two men headed back up towards the horse barn, where old Toby took the reins from them. Parker climbed up into the buggy, took his seat, and picked up the reins. He flicked the reins and the horse headed out of the barn and down the cart path toward the road.

As he turned onto the road, Parker's thoughts raced back to the offer from Adams. He thought about Evangeline, never complaining, but, he knew, struggling with the loneliness, the poverty. He thought of his children, their three faces turned up to him, trusting him, relying on him. The money would mean a lot for them and their future.

He began to think of verses and passages he could use for sermons to preach to the slaves, seeds he would plant in their hearts. Some might have never even heard preaching before, maybe never heard the gospel presented to them. He would plant the seed and tend it, and after a time, get to see the seed grow into a great harvest of salvation. He smiled, imagining the thrill on their faces and how word would get out that great things were happening for the Lord. The valley, this valley of dry bones, would indeed rise and come back to life.

Forty-five minutes later, Parker turned the buggy into the dirt yard at the front of his cabin. He looked over and saw Evangeline at the door holding Matthew. He saw her swelling, more pronounced every day as she came closer to her time. He could hear the voices of Nathaniel and Martha echoing from somewhere behind the cabin. A few chickens scratched around in the dust.

Evangeline's face was etched with worry. She walked out onto the dirt as Parker got down of the buggy and began to lead the hollow-backed horse towards the crooked one-stall shed. Evangeline followed him. "Goodness, Philip, I was starting to think something happened. You couldn't have been teaching Thomas Adams all this time, could you?"

Parker turned towards his wife, walked up to her and kissed her on the lips, took Matthew into his arms, and kissed him also. He turned to his wife and laughed at the shock on her face. He said, "Vangie, let me tell you, when I finished with Thomas, Mr. Adams called to me, and I thought he was going to fire me. But guess what, Vangie, he took me on a ride all over his farm, and when we were done with that, he offered me a job! He wants me to help manage his farm and his slaves, Vangie, and he offered to pay me well for it! My gosh, I can't believe it."

"What, Philip? Manage his farm and his slaves? You mean he wants you to be his overseer?"

"Well, in a way, yes, but in a way, no. Vangie, he wants me to work with the slaves, and manage them during the week, but then on Sunday, I would also preach to them. He says he wants to see the slaves getting saved, so I would be more of a minister to the slaves, not an overseer."

Evangeline looked at her husband, "A minister to the slaves. You said he was willing to pay you to do that?"

"Yes, Vangie, he said 300 a year to start, plus we could live there on the farm, and they would supply us with our food. The same food that

Mr. Adams and the family eat, we would get the same things."

Parker finished unhitching the horse and poured out a scanty measure of oats into the horse's bucket. They headed across the yard toward the cabin.

"So he wants to pay you the wage of an overseer, but you wouldn't be an overseer, you'd be a minister? Or a manager?"

"Well, see, Vangie, Mr. Adams needs help with the farm, and since he knew I grew up on a farm, he thought I would be a good person to help them out. And yes, I would help him to manage the slaves."

"Wait, wait, wait, Philip, tell me this again. So you won't be an overseer? Will you have a cowhide with you when you're out helping to manage the slaves?"

"Well, yes, I suppose I would need to, Vangie, the slaves need correction sometimes. But not mainly, Mr. Adams says he doesn't believe in that much."

"So you would carry a cowhide. What about a gun? Would you carry a gun?"

"Of course, for safety, but so what? Folks around here carry guns with them all of the time. I've seen some of the men in church with guns on their belts. It's the way they live around here."

Evangeline continued to look at her husband. "So all week, you're going to be going around the slaves carrying a cowhide and a gun, and when Sunday comes, they'll all gather around and listen to you preach to them?"

"Vangie, I thought you'd be excited about this. Why, the children would get milk to drink every day, eggs and butter, and meat. I think the Lord is opening a door for us here, Vangie, and I think we should try walking through it together in faith. God is wanting to bless us."

"Phil, what kind of a shepherd looks over his flock with a whip and a gun? It's not like you would have the whip or the gun to protect the flock. You'd be using them on the flock itself. So again, Philip, explain to me, what kind of shepherd does that to his sheep?"

"Evangeline, you're twisting things around, that's not at all what things would be like. All I want to do is take care of you and the children. Please, Vangie, you're not being fair."

Evangeline paused and looked at her husband for a moment. She walked over and took Matthew back into her arms. "Philip, you sound like you made a decision already. So what are you planning to do?"

"Well, I'd like to go back and tell Mr. Adams tomorrow that I'll take the job. And I'll tell the church on Sunday. Vangie, we can just give it a try for six months and see how things work out. If it's not going the way I think it will, I promise I'll look for another church."

Evangeline kept her gaze on her husband, her hands resting on her swollen tummy. Finally, she spoke. "I've got to go feed Matthew and the others. Come on in, I've got some cornbread and pork ready. We'll wait for you." And she turned and headed back towards the cabin, carrying Matthew tight against her chest.

Chapter 8—1833—16 years on the land— Fancy girls

Carrie stood at the glass doors, which were swung open to let in the warm October breezes. The sky was an uninterrupted azure expanse, extending across to the horizon, where it met the crimson and amber colors of the forest, their leaves changing colors as the land prepared for winter rest. The colors formed a frame around the rocky knoll, rising across the creek. The angular stone boulders thrust their way up out of the ground, providing a contrast to the palette of autumn colors.

The view from here, across the fields to the creek and then beyond to the rocky knoll, had always been Carrie's favorite. It was the reason she engaged an artisan skilled in glasswork to craft the double glass doors, why she had them built into the library. When they had first come to the land and begun to build the house, she would stand on this very spot, taking in its beauty and peace.

She stood in the doorway a few more moments looking out towards the knoll. Then she shifted her gaze, watching the hands across the fields doing their work. Dry stalks of corn were being pulled up, the un-shucked ears piled in the wagon, and the stalks gathered together. Farther on, she saw George and a group of the hands using a mule to plow across a field, cutting furrows through the weedy overgrowth, preparing it for sowing winter wheat and barley.

As she stood gazing across the fields, she heard children's voices. In a moment, she saw the children coming around the corner of the house from the kitchen cabin, being led and watched over by Kee, Emma's Kee. Kee was 12 years old now, nearly 13. Soon she would be big enough to work at hoeing the fields with the other hands. For now, though, she was a nursemaid and shepherd to these five beautiful light-skinned children, three girls and two boys. As Carrie watched them, playing and laughing, her heart surged with emotions. Conflicted feelings mixed and swirled together. She felt satisfaction, even pride, that her idea, her plan to breed these special beautiful children, had succeeded. Along with the sweetness of satisfaction, there came the bitterness of regret, the awareness of what these children had cost her.

She turned away from the doorway, took her seat at the desk, and pulled the farm ledger over to her. She opened its well-worn pages to the back, where she kept a listing of her slave property. She had separate columns for the women, the men, and the children, listing each slave, their age, and her estimate of their value in trade. Apart from the listing of children, there was a fourth column, headed simply "Fancy." Her eyes traveled to this column, which contained only three entries:

> *Angelique, b. 1829, Sarah*
> *Esther, b.1830, Emma*
> *Ruth, b. 1831, Emma*

Unlike the other slave names, Carrie had not written down any estimate of price or value next to these. So much depended on how they turned out when they got older. Would they be light? Would men, the rich men with the money to spend on them, look at them with desire? So she left the value off, but she hoped they would be beautiful when they were 12, 13, or 14. That would be the best age to take them to be sold in Richmond, where she could get the most money for them. Someday, Carrie knew that money might make the difference between staying on the farm, keeping her independence and her pride, or being forced to crawl back to Frederick, destitute and begging.

Carrie's mind traveled back through the years, to the year after she and George committed to keeping the farm afloat financially by selling slaves. An idea came into Carrie's mind back then. She pushed the idea away, pushed it out of her mind over and over, but it kept coming back to her. Finally, she let it stay.

Carrie had realized she owned a valuable property, sitting unused right there on the farm. She owned Sarah and Emma, her two mixed-race half-sisters. They were light-skinned and blue-eyed. They were beautiful, even now. They both had borne children, dark children from their slave marriages. Still, it proved that they were able to bear and were still young enough to have more. Carrie decided she would get them to have more children, but with a White man. Those children would be slaves, and, with luck, some would be girls, light and beautiful. Rich men would pay a lot of money for girls like that.

She realized that George needed to be the father at once. He was the only White man in the world that she trusted.

She remembered telling George and could recall the conversation word for word. As before, she waited for a Sunday afternoon and asked him if they could talk together in the library. They sat together at the desk, the ledger open in front of them.

"Alright, Carrie, what have you got in your mind?"

"George, first of all, I just want to express again my gratitude for all you do for us. We all depend on you so much to keep things going around here. It means a lot to me, George."

George smiled. "Carrie, I don't think you're giving enough credit to yourself. It's been your ideas, Carrie, that have helped us along the last few years. I couldn't do anything without you, sweetheart."

George leaned over and kissed Carrie on the cheek.

She turned back towards the ledger and said, "But, I do want us to look at the ledger for just a minute. I'm probably just worried over nothing, but it seems like most of the older hands are gone now. It concerns me, George, because now anyone we decide to send away will be one of our better hands, the ones who can work the hardest and the longest."

"Well, Carrie, it seems to me that's a good thing. We'll get better prices for those younger hands, so we won't have to sell as often. I don't see that that's any cause to worry."

"No, George, I'm not worried about things right now, but I was thinking more about down the road. If we start selling away some of the better hands, the better breeders, we won't have as many of the children coming along as we do now. And, you never know, George, prices could fall. Cotton prices are good now, but they could fall, and that could drag down the price for hands as well. That might be a problem for us."

"All right, Carrie, well, what should we do? Try to get the hands fired up, get them havin' more babies? Give out prizes for it?" George grinned.

"Actually, George, I thought we could do something like that. Not the prizes, exactly, but maybe we should give the hands a little bit more time off. Maybe give them Saturdays off, along with Sundays. And, I don't know, maybe a little bit more food. And, the women, when they are having children, give them a little less work to do, a little bit more time to rest. Maybe they would have it easier when their time came."

George looked doubtful. "We could try something like that, I suppose. Maybe a little more food, anyway. I'm mostly thinkin' that it wouldn't work, though. The women not having babies would get jealous of those that are, thinkin' the one having the babies are getting treated special."

"Oh, you're probably right, George; I just thought that maybe if we made it a little bit easier on the women to have babies, they might be more likely to try for it. But I can see how that sounds silly."

"Well, no, Carrie, I didn't say it sounded silly. I'm just not sure the hands are going to think like that. But we could try it maybe for a little while and see what happens."

"No, George, you're probably right; it probably wouldn't work. It sounds silly. I shouldn't have mentioned it."

"Well, like I said, Carrie, we could try and see. You never know how something is going to work out until you try."

In a softer voice, Carrie said, "I do have another idea."

"All right, Carrie, what is it?"

Carrie looked down. "Well, it's a little unseemly to talk about. But, you know, Sarah and Emma have both had children. So we know they're able." Carrie paused.

"Go on, Carrie," George said patiently.

"Well, of course, you know their children are all darker than they are, coming as they do from their slave husbands. But, of course, both of them are light. If they were to have more children with a White man, those children would be even lighter, maybe even light enough to pass for White. And those kinds of children can bring high prices up in Richmond."

Silence.

"So you want to breed Sarah and Emma with a White man, hoping to get light children? Light girls, I'm assumin'? To sell as fancy girls?"

"Yes."

"And just where is this White man going to come from?"

"Well...I thought it should be you."

"Me?"

"Yes. I think it should be you."

Silence.

"Carrie, that just...that just doesn't make good sense."

"Just think about it, George. It makes perfectly good sense. We know they both breed well. They don't have any diseases. You don't have any diseases. The children would be strong and healthy. It makes good sense."

Silence.

"Carrie, I'm not unhappy. Are you saying this because you think I'm...not being satisfied?"

"George, no, sweetheart, that's not it at all. It's just... business. I don't have any meaning beyond that. And, you know as well as I do, plenty of men do it. My father did it."

"But, Carrie, for me...for us...it just seems like it would be wrong."

"George, if you were going behind my back or lying to me about it, that would be wrong. But you aren't. You are not lying to anybody. You are not cheating anybody. You are simply using your property."

Carrie continued, "It's not immoral. The Bible approves of it. You would simply be taking care of your family and the farm. Remember, George, all the people here, including the hands, all depend on you. Without this farm, the hands might starve or get sent off somewhere much worse. It would help keep us all together in our home."

Silence.

George said, "I need to think about this." Without another word, he got up and left the library. A few minutes later, Carrie could see him through the glass doors, walking across the fields, slowly wandering.

Later that night, as they prepared for bed, George asked, "How would it work?"

"We could set aside one of the spare bedrooms here. You could do it when you come in for lunch. Sarah and Emma would both be here in the house then."

Silence.

"It would only take a few minutes, George."

"Have you told them?"

"Not yet. I wanted to have you agree to it first."

Silence.

"They'll hate you for it."

Silence.

"Eventually they will understand."

Silence.

"Alright."

They both lay down in bed.

"Good night, George."

"Good night."

The next morning, Carrie told Sarah and Emma. Of course, since

Carrie owned them, there was no discussion.

That was all five years past now. Once they started, things happened much more quickly and easily than Carrie had expected.

George fathered five children with Carrie's two half-sisters. There were the three girls listed in the ledger who were light, sweet, and precocious. Plus, there were two light boys, handsome even at their tender age, who would make superior house servants someday, Carrie hoped.

When the babies started coming, Carrie decided to move Sarah and Emma out of the slave shanties and up to the house. After all, there was more than enough room, they had built it with enough bedrooms for plenty of their own children, but only Thomas had come. Sarah and Emma could each have a room. They could do the housework and cooking and still watch over these special, beautiful, valuable children. The other children, the dark children that Sarah and Emma had borne from their slave marriages, stayed down in the shanties, being looked after by the other women.

Carrie hoped there would be more names on the list, but after Emma was pregnant with the fifth baby, George demurred. So Carrie pondered the names in her ledger over and over. She even began praying for them, for the three bright girls. She prayed that they would stay healthy, not get sick and die with a fever or get smallpox, which might leave them scarred and without value except as field slaves.

She sat at the desk, the brief list of names before her. She reflected again on what the three fancy girls cost her. She lost Sarah and Emma. Not as slaves, of course. They still cooked the food and cleaned the house, and still helped care for Thomas. But the last remaining spark of friendship, of sisterhood, was gone. Now they looked at Carrie with blank faces, their eyes revealing nothing. That was no surprise. Carrie expected that to happen from the very first time she considered breeding them with George. Even now, there was a tiny piece of her heart left that felt the stab of pain over that loss. Carrie knew, though, that the prize, if it came to pass, would be worth this cost.

Carrie lost something else, though, something she hadn't counted on. She lost George. She lost George's heart. The pain of that loss burned deeply into her own heart. She would undo it all, give back the fancy girls, were it possible. But it was too late.

George still loved her; she knew that. He would still kiss her in the morning and at night, rub her arms, shoulders, and feet to help relieve the pain of the rheumatism. He still counted on her ideas to run the farm. She didn't worry that he was sneaking down to the shanties at night. No other light-skinned blue-eyed babies were showing up among the slaves.

But his heart was gone. That eager spark, the intoxicating desire to fall into each other's arms, to spend hours in each other's embrace, kissing and touching, sometimes until dawn, was gone. Even after her rheumatism began, and she was not able to use her body the same way to lay on top of him and under him, they both still felt the yearning, the passion for the first kiss, the first caress. Now that was gone. Carrie had not expected it to die, but it did. Now it was too late.

They still made love, perhaps once per month. And it still was pleasurable, a release for both of them. But it was more like a shadow, a remnant of what they possessed before. Enough to bring out some of the good memories, but no more. The Fancy Girls carried with them a high price.

Carrie closed the ledger. She stretched her back and arms, trying to counteract the stiffness of the rheumatism. She turned the chair around and looked out the doorway across the fields. As she watched, low clouds moved in, and the rocky knoll became hidden, blocked from view. She saw the symbolism and felt sadness creep into her heart. She sat looking, hoping to catch a glimpse through the mist. Darkness fell. She sat in the dark until Emma knocked on the door and told her that supper was ready.

Chapter 9—1833—16 years on the land— Whipping

Thomas Adams awoke when he heard the slave bell ringing. The bell could be heard across the farm, echoing against the hills. It was rung every morning to rouse up the slaves, so they could be out of the shanties and ready to begin their labor at first light.

On most mornings, Thomas heard the bell and would fall back to sleep for a while before rousting himself and getting dressed. Today, though, he arose from his bed at the first sounding of the bell and slipped on his shirt and trousers. He didn't slip on his boots; he picked them up and carried them in stocking feet, hoping to keep his footfalls on the stairs silent. He slipped out of his room and crept by his parent's door. He peeked in and saw that his father was already gone, no doubt ranging around the farm. His mother, suffering as she did from her rheumatism, was still resting in bed. He moved slowly down the stairs, boots still held in his hands, and down the hall to the library. He entered and glanced at the farm's ledgers and books piled askew across the big desk. He crept over to his father's gun cabinet, locked up tight. The cabinet held the muskets and pistols used to keep control on the farm.

He pulled out the key from its hiding place, turned it in the heavy lock, and swung the cabinet open. And there in front of him were the trio of new guns, percussion cap muskets, transported to the farm from a Philadelphia gunsmith. He touched one, felt the wood stock and the cold metal of the barrel. He lifted it out of the case, testing its weight. He extended it out in front of him, aiming it through the double glass doors. He sighted out over the pasture and fields toward the wooded hills, searching for a target, somewhere to aim. The musket was weighty, heavier than he expected. He lowered the gun, resting the barrel on the desk, and took a look at the firing lock.

His Father had shown him the gun's lock when they picked them all up at the mercantile exchange in town. Thomas saw how the little brass cap was to be fitted onto the metal nipple, replacing the old flintlocks, making the gun much less apt to misfire when the hammer was triggered. Thomas let the gun rest on the desk and peered back into the gun cabinet, seeking to locate the paper cartridges and brass caps that would make the gun fire. He spotted them and dropped a few of each in his coat pocket. He picked up the gun with both hands, crept back to the door, and peeked down the hall. No one to be seen. He headed down the hall, turned into the dining room, crossed over to the slave pantry and out the back door. He peeked around again. Still nobody.

Assured that he was unseen, he crossed over to the kitchen cabin and walked around to the far side; so he was hidden from view. He realized he had not used the chamber pot before he left his room. He carefully laid the gun against the side of the cabin, leaned against the cabin, and pulled on his boots. He straightened up, loosened his trousers, and released a stream against the foundation stone at the base of the kitchen cabin.

Once relieved, he tightened his pants back up, took up the gun, and stealthily moved down the path toward the slave shanties. Full dawn was not yet come, and a light mist shrouded the shanties, rising from the creek.

He came down to the shanty where he knew Brock's family slept. He stood outside the door and called out to his friend. He knew he had only a few minutes before the slaves would be departing the shanties to head to the fields. As well, Parker, the overseer, might be lurking around on his horse and would put a stop to things.

In a second, Brock emerged from the shanty, dressed in his slave-cloth pants and shirt and shoeless, as he always was this time of year. "Master Thomas, what are you doin' out here, and what've you got that gun for?"

Thomas replied, "This is one of the new guns my father got. I want to go down to the creek and see if I can find something to shoot. Come on; you need to help me with it."

Brock said, "Master Thomas, I can't be missin' from the field, Master Parker will see that I'm not there, sure enough, and go huntin' for me, and when he find me, I'll get the cowhide for sure."

Thomas said, "Shut up, damn it, Brock, I'm your master, not that damn overseer preacher. I don't give a damn what he says. Get your black ass out here and help me with this gun."

Brock stared out over the field to see if he could spot Parker. Seeing no one, he turned back to Thomas and said, "Yes sir, Master Thomas, I'm coming. Let me grab my hoe. I been seein' copperheads down near the creek lately."

Brock picked up a hoe from several laying against the side of the cabin and followed Thomas. Thomas turned and handed the musket to Brock, "Here, Brock, carry this gun for me for a while. I carried it down from the house."

Brock took the gun that Thomas held out to him and carried it with both hands, along with the hoe.

As they were getting down into the bottomland along the creek, where the cover of trees was thicker, Brock said, "Master Thomas, can we stop for a minute? I didn't take a piss before we started."

Thomas laughed and said, "Yeah, sure, Brock, here, hand me that gun and hoe, and you take yourself a good long piss against that tree. Just don't do nothing else with that meat besides taking a piss."

Brock laughed and said, "No, sir, Master Thomas, ain't gonna waste any of this meat today. Gonna save it up for someone special." He finished and pulled up his pants. Thomas handed back the gun and hoe.

The two boys walked along, joking and cursing with one another.

They moved farther along the creek, and now Thomas said, "Brock, bring over that gun. I want to see what I can shoot with it."

Brock handed him the gun. Thomas took it and sat the stock on the ground, the muzzle aimed skyward. He pulled one of the paper cartridges from his jacket pocket, ripped it open, and let the powder trickle down through the muzzle. He pulled the ramrod out and pushed the ball and paper down the barrel on top of the powder until it seated and withdrew the rod. He picked up the gun and turned it horizontally, aiming down the top of the barrel across the creek. The barrel was too heavy for him to hold out straight, so he walked over to a small tree and laid the barrel across a limb. This allowed him to line up the gun sites while holding the stock up to his shoulder.

He pulled out a percussion cap from his pocket. He had never used one, but his father has shown him how to fit the brass cap onto the nipple. Pulling back on the hammer with his left thumb, he held the cap with his fingers and fit it onto the end of the nipple. But his thumb was not strong enough, and he was not able to cock the hammer. He struggled to pull it back, and the hammer slipped away from his thumb and flew forward. The hammer struck the cap and the powder charge detonated with a booming report, kicking the gun back against Thomas's chest and knocking him backward. The stock of the gun dropped into the mud, smoke still rising out of the muzzle. The ball flew off into the trees.

Thomas turned to Brock, his eyes bulging with surprise. "Oh shit, Brock, that was something. Oh, shit." He rubbed his chest where the gun stock had kicked against him.

Thomas looked down at the gun and said, "Brock, pick that gun up so I can load it. I want to see if I can hit something with it."

Brock said, "Master Thomas, I'm sure they'll be missin' me in the field. Master Parker will be lookin' to use the cowhide if he don't find me. Let me just grab my hoe and get up there."

Thomas said, "No, Brock, damn it, I need your help here with this gun; it's too damn big for me to shoot by myself." And Thomas stood the gun up again and pulled another cartridge out of his pocket.

As Thomas tore open the cartridge, they both heard horses coming from up the hill, the sound of the hoof beats reverberating. A second later, they heard the voice of Thomas' father calling out, "Tom, Brock, are you in there? Come out and show yourselves."

Thomas turned to Brock. "Keep your mouth shut," he hissed.

Brock called out, "We're down here, Master Adams. Master Tom and me."

Seconds later, George Adams appeared through the trees, followed by the overseer, Parker. Both men were on horseback, and both carried heavy cowhide whips curled against their thighs. Adams' face was flushed and contorted in rage. He looked at his son, who was holding the gun pointing upward, the stock resting in the mud of the creek bottom. Thomas was still holding the paper cartridge. Adams dismounted and came towards Tom, the coiled cowhide in hand. Parker remained mounted on his horse.

Adams grabbed Thomas by the shirt collar, twisted him to the ground, and began to beat him with the coiled-up cowhide. "Damn it, Tom, what the hell are you doing down here with my new musket? I never told you to take that gun. What in God's name are you trying to do down here? Well? Answer me, damn it!"

Thomas curled his arms around his face and head, seeking protection from the blows raining down on him. "I'm sorry, Father, I don't know. I thought it would be fine. I didn't think you would be upset," Thomas whimpered as he twisted himself in the mud, trying to make a smaller target for his father's anger.

Adams paused in his flailing at Thomas. He grabbed Thomas by his shirt collar again and pulled his son up to his feet. "What have you got to say?"

"Father, don't beat me. Brock was the one who wanted to come down here," Thomas said weakly to his father.

"Brock? You're lying right to my face," said Adams, sticking the handle of the cowhide into Thomas' chest. "How can you say that?"

"It's the truth. Brock told me that he saw a big buck down here by the creek. He wanted me to get your gun and bring it down here and try to kill it for the meat." Thomas looked down. "It's the God's truth, I swear. I wouldn't have done it except Brock kept after me."

"So, Tom," said his father, looking at him, "now you're going to blame it on your friend?"

"Father, it's true, I swear. Tell him, Brock. Tell them what you said to me." Thomas looked over at Brock, who was standing passively, his eyes cast downward, his face expressionless.

Adams kept looking at Tom and paused for a moment. "All right, Son, well then tell me, what should we do to Brock? I reckon he's deserving some punishment. What punishment for your friend here?"

Thomas thought for a few seconds, "Mr. Parker should flick him with the cowhide."

"Mr. Parker should flick him with the cowhide," Adams mimicked Thomas in a girlish voice, mocking his son. "No, Tom, that's not nearly enough. You told me that Brock tricked you and made you go against me. Any slave that does that kind of thing to a White man is going to get a hard beating and be thankful that he doesn't get worse." Adams grabbed his son's collar and pulled his face close. He looked straight into his son's eyes. "Tom, it's going to be you holding the cowhide, not Mr. Parker. Now wipe off your face. Brock, come over here right now."

Brock walked over to Adams. Brock set his face into stone and kept his eyes downcast. "Put out your wrists, Brock," ordered Adams. Brock complied, raising his arms and bringing together his wrists. "Mr. Parker, hand me that rope," and Parker handed down a length of rope he kept stowed on his saddle. Adams took the rope, twisted it several times tightly around Brock's outstretched wrists, and cinched it. He tossed the other end upward over a thick limb. As the rope fell, he grabbed it and pulled it up tight. Brock's arms were stretched up over his head so that he could just stand on his toes. Adams tied off the rope around the tree trunk and turned to Thomas, whose eyes were still fixed downward.

"Tom, look at me, damn it. I want you to take this cowhide and lay it on Brock's back."

Thomas reached out, took the cowhide from his father, and shuffled over to where Brock was dangling from the tree branch. Tom had never used cowhide on a person before. He raised the cowhide and slapped it down across Brock's shoulders, then he raised the cowhide again and slapped again. He glanced up toward his father.

"Damn it, boy; I told you this has to be a beating. No slave can get away with deceiving a White man, not in this county, and damn sure not on this farm. I want to hear that cowhide singing, and I want to see blood flying," Adams strode over to his son, grabbed Thomas' face in his hands, and roughly pulled it up, forcing Thomas to stare into his eyes. "Damn it, boy, if I don't see Brock's blood covering that cowhide when you're done, I'll string you up just like him, and it'll have your blood on it instead. Now get busy."

Thomas looked into his father's eyes, smoking and sizzling with fury. Thomas's face was etched with fear. He felt his throat tightening in panic, tasted the sour taste of terror rising onto his tongue. He looked over to Parker, seeking remedy or comfort. But Parker sat motionless astride his horse, his eyes focused at a point away across the creek.

Thomas turned back to Brock. Brock tensed as he knew the blows were going to fall. Tom raised the cowhide over his head and struck Brock's back with all of his strength. He lifted his arm back up and struck again, then again and again and again, his blows gaining a rhythm as they mounted up. Thomas' face turned red and twisted from panic into anger.

Brock could keep the pain in check for the first three or four blows, but after that, his resistance crumbled. He screamed as each blow of the cowhide whip struck his bare black skin, leaving a white crease that instantly turned red as it filled with blood.

Adams urged his son, "Keep it up, son, harder! You're not half finished."

Thomas, his eyes filled with tears of rage, could only see a red mass. He felt warm liquid over his face, like sweat. He reached up with his free hand, wiped his eyes, and saw a red glaze on his fingers and palm. He realized he was becoming coated with Brock's blood. Still, his father urged him on until Thomas could strike no more and his arm dropped to his side. Brock hung from the rope like a corpse.

Adams went over to the tree trunk and cut the rope with his knife. Brock slumped onto the ground in a heap. Adams said, "That's enough,

Tom. Pick up that musket, go back up the house, and put it away. Wait for me up there." He turned to the overseer, "Mr. Parker, please go and get a couple of the hands from out of the field and have them come down here. They can carry Brock back up to his shanty. Have one of the hands stay in the shanty this afternoon, so he can look after him. I'll be damned if I'm going to lose a hand over something as stupid as this."

Parker replied, "Yes, sir, Mr. Adams," and he turned his horse and rode off.

Adams turned to his son and said, "Well, what are you waiting for, do like I said, gather up that gun and get back up to the house and put it away and wait for me. And make sure that gun's clean when you put it up."

Thomas could not speak. He wiped his eyes, wiping away the blood and his furious tears. He looked down at the bloody mass at his feet but did not look towards his father. He walked over to the tree, where the musket still lay against the trunk. He picked it up and began to walk slowly up the footpath past the shanties and the barn and toward the house.

Adams swung his legs over his horse and watched his son walking back towards the house. He looked down at the torn red flesh covering all of Brock's back. He gazed up at the sky, then back down at Brock's bloody form on the ground, "What a stupid bloody mess." He spoke directly to Brock, "Brock, if you can hear me, I want you to know that I don't hold this against you. I know you were just doing what Tom told you to do. Tom was lying about all of that. We'll get you back up to the shanty, and you can rest there. I'm sorry this had to happen." He turned his horse and began riding back out of the creek bottom. He could see that Brock might die from the beating, which would mean one less hand for the coming season, one less hand he could sell to the speculators. But he also knew it needed to happen, somehow. It was time for Tom to learn the truth about how the farm ran. Tom was White, and the master. Brock was Black and was a slave. There was nothing else to be said.

The two hands that Parker sent from the field came and found Brock still laying in a heap, unmoving. They stared at his back. The blood was congealed, a mixture of dark red clots, shreds of black skin, and yellow fatty clumps. Flies were buzzing around and crawling across the wounds. He looked dead to the hands until they heard him give out a low moan.

"What did you do, Brock. What did you do?" they asked him. He could only whisper, "Nothin', I didn't do nothin'." One of the hands ran back up to the shanty and grabbed a blanket, and they were able to get the blanket underneath Brock. They dragged and carried him to his shanty and laid him out on the blanket. The hand took the water bucket back to the creek, brought it back up to the shanty, and poured it slowly over his back. They sat with him, waving away the flies, letting him suck drips of water from the end of a moistened rag as often as he could take it.

Adams rode out to the field, where he saw Parker overseeing the work of the hands.

"Any problems, Mr. Parker?" he called out to the overseer.

"No sir, Mr. Adams, everything's fine here," Parker replied, keeping his eyes fixed on the hands hoeing the rows of corn. Adams paused a few more moments, turned, and headed back to the house.

He stopped in the kitchen and washed his face and hands. He saw a wet towel with red and yellow smears laying by the water pitcher. Thomas's towel. Brock's flesh. He picked up another towel and wiped his hands and face, and realized that he, like Thomas, was coated by droplets of Brock's blood. He laid his blood-streaked towel down next to the one left by Thomas.

He walked into the house and down to the library. Thomas was there. His face was flushed red with emotion. He looked away when his father walked into the room. Carrie was also there, sitting in her side chair. She looked up at her husband, her eyes grim and her mouth a hard line. Obviously, she already had heard Thomas's version of the incident.

Adams sat down at the plantation desk. He turned the chair to look at his son. He forced the anger out of his voice, tried to make himself speak with a calm he didn't feel. "Thomas, son, what were you trying to do? What gave you the idea to take that musket out and try to shoot it?"

Thomas was looking away, his hair wet from his efforts to wash away Brock's blood. "Father, I swear to you this is the truth. Brock said he saw a big buck down by the creek. He wanted me to shoot it so they could have a meal off it, so I thought it would be…"

Adams interrupted, his anger rising again, "Tom, don't even bother with that damn lie, just don't even try it." Adams leaned forward towards his son, "Don't you know why I bought those guns? Don't you know why I have them locked up here? Haven't you heard about what happened up in Virginia?"

Thomas continued to stare downward. "I heard about some slaves killing some White folks, and then the White folks went and caught the slaves and hung them."

Adams said, "No, not just some White folk. Sixty White folks. Masters and children and women were butchered by slaves. The slaves were making knives and swords in secret and hiding them until they all rose up and attacked the Whites. They went all over the section up there, killing any White folks they could find."

Thomas said nothing. His face was still down, but his eyes were flashing with anger.

Adams paused, then said, "And Tom, you know why those slaves up there in Virginia did what they did?"

Thomas kept looking away but gave a sullen reply, "No sir."

"Well, it's simple," Adams said. "It's because the White folks let them do it. The slaves were roaming around at night, going to different plantations, and planning the attack, and the White folks didn't think anything of it. They just let the slaves roam around rather than put more patrols out on the road. A tool goes missing from the farm, and the overseer doesn't say anything, just goes and gets a new one. And meanwhile, the slaves are working at night, sharpening it, turning it into a knife or a spear, and keeping it hidden in their cabin until they went out on the rampage. The White masters and overseers turned a blind eye because they just never thought it could happen. And they let it happen."

Adams continued, "That's why I bought these guns. If any of the slaves around here try to start a rising like that or even think about it, we're going to put a stop to it. We won't be waiting 'til White folk start getting killed. I wanted to keep those guns secret from the slaves, but now, thanks to you, they know all about it."

There was silence in the room.

Adams went on, "Tom, it's time for you to grow up. You've got to start acting like a man, not a child. Things are different now, after Virginia. It's not enough to let Parker handle all the slaves. There's too many of them for him to handle. You're going to need to be out there, too, every day. We've got to show them that any White man on this farm has power of life and death over any Black man. Just like they were a pig or chicken. If any of them start to plot some bloody plot against us, we're going to find out fast and put it down fast. And then, by God, there will be plenty of blood. Their blood."

Thomas met his father's gaze. He said, "Yes sir," his voice filled with defiance and hate.

Carrie had stayed silent as George spoke. Now she said, "Tom, it's just a hard fact of life. When you get to a certain age, things have to change. That means you have to harden yourself up on the inside. It's easy to wish that the world was different, and we could be friends with our slaves. But we have to live in the world as it is. So, Tom, we have to put this day behind us and start over fresh."

Thomas looked over at his mother, his voice and eyes softened. "Yes, ma'am," he replied.

Adams said, "Tom, go change your clothes and put on your riding britches. I want you to saddle your horse, go out and find Parker. I want you to ride with him. We need to run these slaves, run them hard. Keep them busy enough that they don't have time to plot against us."

Thomas stood up and headed for the door. Adams called after him, "Tom, look at me." Thomas paused, then slowly turned to look into his father's eyes. Adams said, "Tom, we need our slaves, we can't work this place without them. We want to believe they'll always be loyal to us. But the truth is, the slaves don't think that way, they don't really understand about loyalty or honesty. If you let them, they'll steal, not do their work, or run off. That's just the way it is with them."

Thomas replied, "Yes sir, Father dear," acid filling his voice. He went down the hall and up the stairs into his room. He slipped off his clothes and put on his heavy riding britches, pulled on his boots, and put on a heavy shirt and coat. Then he headed out of the house toward the horse barn.

As he walked slowly past the kitchen towards the barn, he gave his mind free range to fill up with anger and rage. His father, what a damn, stupid, unfair, unjust son of a bitch. How could his father have taken the word of a damn slave over his own son? Didn't he see that, from now on, all of the slaves would look on him, Thomas, as weak? If it weren't for his mother, his precious suffering mother, he would shoot his son of a bitch father, shoot him in the heart, and head for Kentucky or maybe New Orleans. Anywhere to get away from his stupid father and this stupid little farm. His whole life was wasted, stuck on this stupid little farm, and no one cared. His face contorted in enmity and rage.

He got to the barn and saw old Toby. "Dammit, you dumb, stupid son of a bitch, get my horse ready. I gotta ride. Get off your stupid ass and get my horse saddled before I lay you open with a damn cowhide. Damn it, move!"

Toby, his eyes staring in shock, ran over and got the blanket and saddle for Thomas' horse. In a moment, the saddle and bridle were in place, and Thomas mounted. He turned the horse's head, kicked it, and went out the barn door, headed down to the slave shanties.

He raced down the hill, heading toward the door of the shanty where he knew Brock lay. He was planning to barge into the shanty and confront Brock to his face, but the sickeningly sweet odor of blood sent a wave of nausea surging up into his throat. He stood outside the door and yelled in, "Dammit, Brock, this is all your damn fault. Why did you let my father know where we were? You son of a bitch, next time I tell you to do something, you do it. All of this is just from you opening up your damn stupid mouth. Well, dammit, Brock, answer me. Answer me!"

The hand who was sitting next to Brock's prostrate form, trying to dribble water into his mouth from a wet rag, called out. "Master Thomas, he's in here. He just can't say much right now. But he heard you. Thank you, Master Thomas."

Thomas mounted back on his horse and began to ride toward the cart path. He had to get away from here, away from all these damned stupid slaves and his damned stupid father. Why did his mother want to stay here, on this stupid farm, in the middle of nowhere? Why did she want to stay with his stupid father? Why couldn't they, just Thomas and his mother, leave here and go back to Richmond? In Richmond, he knew his mother's family was rich. They owned hundreds of slaves to do the work for them. The White people didn't have to do anything. The slaves did all the work. Here on this stupid farm, he was forced to work hard every day, harder than the damn stupid slaves. And the slaves blamed him for everything. It was all so unjust.

He rode down the cart path and turned onto the main road toward town. He just needed to get away from this damn place for a while. He had a few coins in his pocket. There were plenty of people along the road who would sell him liquor, even at his age. He began to think about the corn liquor, the heat of it as he held it in his mouth before swallowing it. The pleasant buzz, how it would creep over him. His lips twitched involuntarily, and his anger started to lessen a little bit, replaced by the hunger and craving for the liquor.

§

As Pastor Parker rode over the rocky, uneven fields of the farm, he saw that the sun was ascending to its high point. He rode over and struck the heavy iron bell, sending the signal to the slaves that they could head for shade to take their noontime break. He began to scan around, hoping to spot Brock to tell him to go and get the water buckets filled. Then he remembered. Brock couldn't tote the water today. Brock, if he was not dead, was laying in the shanty, covered in blood. He called out to several of the other hands to take charge of the water buckets. Finished with that, he pointed his horse towards the overseer's cabin, where Evangeline would be preparing dinner for him and the children.

As he approached the cabin, he saw his children outside playing with the Black children. Usually, the sight of his children playing would lift his heart. Today, there was no joy. The nightmarish vision of Brock laying in the mud by the creek, his back stripped of skin, blood pooled on the ground, floated before his eyes. The smell of Brock's blood remained immovable in his nostrils.

The hopeful thought occurred that maybe he was just hungry and exhausted. He would not be so possessed by the horror of the whipping once he ate a bit and rested. He could smell bacon and coffee coming from the cabin, and that seemed to help block out the fetid scent of blood a little. He tied up his horse and went into the cabin, where Evangeline was at the fire, preparing his dinner. She turned and smiled at him, but her eyes widened in fear. "Oh, my goodness, Philip! Are you hurt? Did you cut yourself? What happened to you?"

"Nothing happened, Vangie; I'm fine. Why, what's wrong?"

"Philip, you've got blood all over your face and all over your shirt, and even on your hands. My word, Phil, what happened?"

Parker looked at the backs of his hands and down his shirt and saw a dried crust of blood. He mopped his forehead with his fingers and saw more blood. Brock's blood.

"Oh, that, Vangie. Mr. Adams told the slaves to slaughter a hog, and I must've gotten splashed with some of the blood. That's not my blood."

"Slaughter a hog? What on earth for? It's not hog season. Why would Mr. Adams have them slaughtering a hog now?"

"I don't know, Vangie," Parker replied, irritation hinted in his voice. "Maybe he was in the mood for some hog meat. But that's what he told them to do."

Parker hoisted the water bucket brought up from the creek earlier. He went outside and washed off his hands and face, wiping himself off with his shirt sleeve, itself already flecked with blood. He washed away as much of the stain of Brock's blood as he could, but he could yet see speckles of red around his fingernails. He gave up his efforts and re-entered the cabin.

Evangeline was setting out the plates with the sausage and cornbread and filling his coffee cup. She went over to the door and called out to the children, summoning them to the cabin for their dinner.

Parker's four children came boiling into the cabin, abounding with energy from their outdoor play.

Nathaniel jumped in first, "Ma, Ma, did you hear what happened? Thomas and Brock took a big gun down to the creek and fired it off, and then Mr. Adams came down, and he got mad at them, and he made Thomas whip Brock. He whipped him bad. There was blood everywhere!"

Evangeline scolded her son, "Now, Nathaniel, don't tell stories. Why would Thomas whip Brock? Thomas and Brock are best friends."

"Mr. Adams told him to do it, and he did it. Samuel told me. Samuel says he went down there to where it happened, and there's blood all around there. He said it looks like someone was slaughterin' hogs."

"Slaughterin' hogs," Evangeline repeated, shifting her gaze to her husband. "Nathaniel, are you sure about that?"

"Yes, Mother, that's what Samuel said. He said there was blood everywhere, just like someone killed a hog with an ax. But it was from the whipping."

"Killed a hog, imagine that," Evangeline said. She addressed her husband, "Isn't that something, Philip? So, tell me again about that blood that was all over your face? And on your hands and your arms? You still telling me that's hog blood?"

Parker kept his eyes on his food. He gave no reply. Without a word, he ate his sausage and cornbread and sipped on his coffee. After he finished, he stood up and headed for the door. "Gotta get back to work. Thanks for dinner," he called to his wife over his shoulder.

He walked out to his horse. He felt sick, felt a jittery jerking feeling inside. The food had not helped him one bit. The horrific image of Brock, with his back covered in blood, fat, and shredded skin, hung before him. He swung himself up in the saddle and headed back out towards the fields, his cowhide whip hanging from his belt and slapping against his thigh as he rode along.

Chapter 10—1837—20 years on the land—
Brock asks to marry

B rock carried a burden of hate. He knew it. He could feel it laying oppressively across his back, like a giant millstone trying to crush its way down into him and through him. Every day he was forced to endure the weight of the stone, carrying it about with him. Out to the fields in the morning, back to the shanties in the evening. As he ate, as he slept, the stone lay on his back, always present, always seeking to destroy him. He contended with the great millstone of hate every day, just to survive. He would try to imagine the stone was not there, or, on some days, he'd pretend it was just a little pebble, something he could bear without distress, without struggle. But the millstone, the hatred, was there.

Some days he thought he would surrender to the stone and let himself be crushed. It would be so easily done. Simply pick up the stone and cast it with all his might at one of the White people on the farm, at Missus Carrie, or Master Thomas or Master Adams. He could even hurl the stone at that mealy-mouthed counterfeit preacher who affected such concern for his soul. All that was required was to rise, to lift his hand once against any one of the White people, and his struggle and strife would be settled. He might meet death quickly from a pistol. Or his death might be prolonged, maybe dragged behind a wagon until his flesh was peeled off. Whichever way, the stone would be shattered.

Brock tried to shed the stone from his back, to shrug it off. But as hard as he tried to rid himself of it, even more, did the hateful stone cling to him, mocking him. Brock knew that made no sense, for how could a dead thing like a stone be mocking him? Yet it happened, day after day, year following year. All the years now passed since Master Thomas had been forced to whip Brock, to whip him to death. Except, for some unknown reason concealed in the mind of God, Brock didn't die. He lived and recovered and now bore the torment of the crushing stone.

Master Thomas, his Master's son, his lifelong companion, had not even bothered trying to make a plea to his father. Not a word was uttered to plead for Brock. Thomas just caved in, taking up the cowhide to scourge Brock's Black flesh, seeking absolution from his father by the blood of innocence. The blood of someone who committed no transgression, who was perfect in his obedience, exactly as that bloody overseer, Parker, preached to them again and again.

Brock recalled how, as he lay on the edge of death, suffering from the loss of blood, flies crawling over his flesh, Master Thomas had come down to the shanty. Brock lay stretched out on a filthy blanket, his tongue parched, his lips shriveled and crusted, and Thomas didn't even deign to come into the shanty. He stood at the threshold, raging and wrathful, screaming at Brock, showering him with curses. The thought, even now, filled Brock with fury.

But the greater part of Brock's burden of hate, the most crushing portion by far, was not for Master Thomas. It was for his master, Master Adams. Brock recollected little of what followed the whipping, but he could recall laying in a heap with his face in the mud. The cool mucky feel of the mud on his cheek must have revived him, bringing him to half-wakefulness. Brock remembered opening his eyes and seeing a horse's hooves next to him. He turned his head and recognized, through tears and blood, the form of Master Adams seated on his horse. The image would return to him every day, engraved in his memory, the awful sight of his master's face coated in crimson. The cowhide, dark with blood, lay curled against his thigh. And the master's words, darker than the whip, cast carelessly down at him as if that would even their accounts. Oh, don't feel bad, Brock. I don't hold this against you, Brock. I know Thomas was lying, Brock.

So his master confessed to Brock's very face that he was aware, all through the pounding and lashing, that Brock was blameless. Nonetheless, he chose to have Brock scourged, compelling his son to the task for two reasons. First, to rebuke Thomas for his disobedience and his lies. But the greater reason, far greater, was the second—to make it clear to every Black person on the farm that the single thing, the only thing, that mattered on the farm was Power. Not Truth. Just Power. And that the Power was real and would be used.

Every day since that day, after Brock didn't die and his body slowly recovered, leaving his black skin cross-hatched with pale scars, he had lived his life holding the oppressive stone on his back. Pretending it wasn't there, granting no one, White or Black, privilege to see the burden. That was the only way he could survive. He could not allow any of the millstone of hate to be found out, not even one tiny pebble, one tiny grain of sand. Were he to uncover it and let it be seen, he could be sold to a slave trader, chained in a coffle, and marched South for being insolent, a troublemaker, a difficult Negro, or such. He could be whipped again, this time to death, under the guise of "correction," the polite term that the slave owners invented, to gain the law's assent to a White man's murder of a Black one.

Now, he knew he must go to Master Adams and speak with him, bow and scrape to him, as hard as this might be. Because new feelings were alive within him. Not the giant millstone of hate. Not the love and loyalty and attachment his heart held for his mother and father and brothers and sisters. It was love, but different. And it was helping him to carry the stone. Or maybe the stone was becoming the tiniest bit less weighty.

He was in love with a woman and with children, yet unborn, that he foresaw coming from their love. And he knew that the woman Kee returned his love. Stealthily he would creep out of the shanty at night, while others slept, noiselessly moving over to her shanty. "Kee," he would call out softly, then wait for her.

She would steal out to him. They would make their way down to the creek, where soft sand collected in small drifts. They would stand together and embrace, his lips meeting hers. She would receive his kisses and return them to him, each seeking the other, hands moving over and around. They would slowly cast off their few clothes, rags really, and lay down on the sand, feeling the warmth of the sun still lingering there and adding to that warmth with the heat of their love. And the urgency would grow slowly and then quickly, each seeking the other, reaching its peak. Afterward, they would lay in each other's arms, listening to the sound of the water cascading over the rocks and boulders in the creek, each taking in the breath, the taste, the aroma of loving and being loved.

Too soon, they knew it would be time to separate, a last embrace laying together on the sand, slipping back into their rags, brushing their sandy bed smooth. Creeping silently back to the shanties to hope for some grant of sleep before the morning bell was ringing, calling them out to another day of labor. Labor is not given freely, not given for themselves or their future family, but taken from them for the wealth and comfort of their owners.

Later, as he moved down the rows, drenched with sweat in the shimmering flare of the southern sun, his eyes would search and catch her glance, and he would know that he was loved. And she would gaze at him across the rows, the ugly crisscrossing scars on his muscular back, and she would feel his desire and her own.

But they knew they must hide away what they held in their hearts. There were Black eyes and Black ears everywhere on the farm. A little extra tobacco, some side meat, or a little liquor at Christmas, and the White people would hear everything, all that could be told, about the goings-on in the shanties. There were some in the shanties who would see their love and seek to twist it, to use it against them.

Brock knew he had to confront his stone of hate. He could not have Kee as his wife without speaking to Master Adams and gaining his permission. Master Adams could withhold it. Some Masters would prefer their Black women to marry a man from a different farm, maybe even from a far-off town or county. Brock knew of that happening, Masters who would be aiming to breed in "new blood" among the Black children, the same as they would do breeding horses or cattle. They would be in hopes of stronger children, with more endurance or beauty, and, being thus, more valuable.

Brock knew he needed to face Master Adams, to speak to him as the obedient slave, and secure his master's consent to marry. He knew he would have to conceal the millstone, bury it beneath layers of servile smiles. One flicker of defiance in his eyes would be certain to trigger off misgivings or suspicions in the mind of Master.

Brock determined that he would approach Master Adams on a Sunday after the family returned to the farm following their church services. Brock observed that Sunday was the day when the White people would be in the best mood. There were fewer denunciations, fewer oaths, and curses showered down on the enslaved. Most often, on Sunday, the cowhide would stay coiled and laid aside.

Each Sunday morning, Master Adams, Missus Carrie, and Master Thomas would head to town in the wagon, Old Toby steering the team. And while the White owners were absent, the enslaved people would be gathered together to hear Parker preach about faithful servants and obedience and the rewards of heaven. As soon as Parker concluded and the echoes of the last hymn faded, the slaves were granted the rest of the afternoon time to repair torn clothes, grind corn, and collect wood.

So Brock considered his alternatives and settled on Sunday as his best choice to go to Master Adams, speak quickly, and, he hoped, take away the sought-after blessing. Now, as the moment approached, the taste of sick fear was rising into his mouth.

Brock spotted the wagon, Old Toby driving the team, turn onto the cart path from the main road and ponderously climb the gentle slope up towards the house. He paused himself, pushing down the anxiety he felt, his eagerness for action battling with his trepidation. He supposed it might take an hour for the White people to have time sufficient to settle in for the afternoon. He forced himself to look away from the house to keep his mind and hands busy.

He saw his mother sitting outside the shanty, pulling ears of dried corn out of a peck basket, knocking the kernels off the cob into a roughly carved oak bowl.

"Ma, you want a hand with the corn?" he asked his mother.

Sarah looked up from her work. She smiled. "Alright, Brock, come sit here and help me some."

Brock pushed a thick pine stump, cut off just above the roots, over next to his mother. He picked up an ear of corn and began knocking the hard kernels off, adding to the pile in the bowl.

Sarah stayed silent, but the soft smile stayed.

Brock worked steadily and silently for an hour. Without a word, he stood up. He walked over to the water bucket, picked up the calabash, and wet his mouth. He lay down the calabash, turned, and began his walk, stepping deliberately up the footpath towards the house, measuring his pace.

He walked up to the kitchen cabin, separate from the main house. He saw two slaughtered chickens destined to become Sunday supper for the White people. The birds' heads having been severed, the carcasses were hung up by their feet to drain out the blood. He spotted Vinie, the young Black women Missus Carrie brought up from the fields to learn housework. She was laboring to heat a big pot of water on the stove, feeding in sticks of wood, and getting the water hot so she could scald the chickens and remove their feathers.

"Hey, Vinie," Brock said softly.

"'Lo, Brock," she replied, looking him over, eyes smiling. "You here to talk to Master?"

"How do you know that?"

"Good Lord, Brock, everybody knows you been sneakin' down to the creek at night with Kee," Vinie said. "We've all been sayin' you better be talking to Master soon before that girl starts to swell."

Brock felt the warmth on his face. "Does everybody know?"

"What do you think, Brock? There's no secrets around here. We just all been waitin' for you to make your move. Now, go on, get in there and talk to Master before you lose your grit."

Brock turned and stepped up to the back door of the main house, which led into the slaves' pantry. He tried the door pull, which yielded easily, and he opened the door. He peered in and saw Lucy, the other young woman Missus Carrie was training for house service, wiping off the plates and cups. "Hello, Brock, you come to talk to Master about Kee? Stay here. Let me see if he can talk to you now."

Brock stood in the slave pantry while Lucy crossed through the dining room and disappeared down the hall. He heard her knock on a door. In a second, he heard it open. He felt his heart flying and pounding in his chest.

A minute later, she reappeared in the dining room. "He says to come on. I'll show you where."

Brock stepped gingerly through the dining room towards the hall, following his guide. He had never been in the house before, only in the slave pantry and front porch a few times. He trailed behind Lucy down the hall. She knocked on a door, and Brock heard the voice of Master Adams behind the door. She opened the door for him, and Brock walked softly, tentatively, into the library. Master Adams sat behind a large desk. A leather-bound volume was spread open before him. Light streamed in from behind him through the large glass doors. The two doors were swung open, and a warm sweet-scented breeze whispered its way into the room.

Master Adams lifted his eyes to Brock's and smiled benevolently. "So, Brock, they're all saying you want to tie the knot." Brock was unsure what Master Adams meant. "Sorry, Master, Sir, I don't know that."

"What I mean is, jump the broom, get married. Is that right?"

"Oh yes sir, Master Adams, that's what I want, and I want to ask you to say it's alright." Brock felt he was getting his words mixed up.

"And you want to marry Kee, is that right? That's what they're all saying."

"Yes sir, Master Adams, I'd like to marry Kee, and she has already said yes to me."

Adams leaned back in the padded leather desk chair. "Well, Brock, that would make me very happy to see you and Kee taking each other as man and wife. I've always felt it was important for the servants to have things to look forward to in life, and having a family and children is one of those things. So, Brock, you go and tell Kee and everybody that you got my permission, and I hope God blesses you soon with children."

Brock, despite himself, smiled broadly at his master. "Yes, sir, thank you, Master Adams, I sure do thank you for lettin' us get married. Yes, sir, I'll let everybody know. Thank you, sir."

Master Adams said, "I doubt you'll have to tell anybody. I have a suspicion everyone will know all about it by the time you get back down to the shanty. Well, go on, Brock, go tell your bride."

Brock turned and left, closed the door, and headed back down the hall to the dining room, crossed through it to the slave pantry, and out the back door. He bounded over to the kitchen cabin. Vinie and Lucy were there, plucking feathers out of the chicken carcasses. Brock still carried a smile on his face. Vinie looked up and saw the smile. "We best get the broom out and get you married up. We all gettin' tired of hearing you two gruntin' and groanin' in the middle the night when you're sneakin' out there to meet with each other. Get you moved into a shanty together, and you won't have to be goin' down to the creek and getting sand all over your skinny little backside," Vinie said, smiling. Lucy smiled, and her grin was as big as Vinie's. Brock smiled back at them, and the millstone, for an instant, seemed to lighten, and the hate burned a little less hot.

Brock headed back down the footpath towards the shanties. After he left, Vinie and Lucy got back to their work on the chickens. Vinie said, "I sure am glad to see Brock smilin' and bein' happy and bein' all in love with Kee. After that whippin' he got from Master Thomas, I never thought he was gonna smile again. I thought he was just goin' to get mean and mad and was going to stay that way. A slave who gets beat like that, 'specially a young one, they get mad, and then they get mean, and then they get hateful, and sometimes, they never come out of it. Sooner or later, that meanness comes out, and when it does, it just go on and on till some White man chops that slave to pieces."

"Yeah. Or hangs him up with a rope," said Lucy

"Yeah, or hangs him up with a rope," Vinie agreed.

Chapter 11—1838—21 years on the land— Letter from Pastor Parker

My Dearest Evangeline—

I plan on coming to see you and the children in several weeks, Evangeline. I am longing for the sweetness of your embrace and, just as sweet and dear to me, the sound of the children's voices gathered around us. It is my most fervent desire and prayer, even after the last year of separation, that we might regain a measure of the happiness we enjoyed for so many years together.

There is much for me to discuss with you, Evangeline; much has happened. So, please excuse the length of this letter, but I need you to be aware of these things before I come. It is only fair to let you know of these things and allow you an opportunity to consider your thoughts and your feelings before we meet.

So, my dearest love, let me just get started with the most shocking part of my news. My employer, George Adams, is dead. He was struck down by one of the slaves. I sadly was witness to the entire episode, and it is haunting me even now. At the risk of upsetting you, I need to let you know what happened and my role in it, for I need you to understand if I appear changed when I come to see you and the children in Salisbury.

A fortnight ago, Mr. Adams and I were riding out together to look over the work being done by the hands. All the work on the farm has been going well. The corn was planted on time and has been making good growth. We have been blessed with abundant rain and sun.

Mr. Adams was expressing to me his concerns about the changes he saw happening in the county. He increasingly had been agitated, even at times furious, because of the large number of foreigners, especially the Dutch, moving into the county. Most of the Dutch families are large, and they work only a small acreage and call on each other when help is needed. Thus, they mostly do not own slaves. Mr. Adams strongly disapproved of this. In fact, on that day, he seemed almost in a rage. He told me he was going to run for public office, and he said, "get rid of those thieving traitors in Raleigh." As I said, he was becoming more exercised and agitated as he spoke of it.

As we were riding across the fields, we saw a strange thing. One of the hands was using his hoe to chop down the corn plants. The stalks were up a good two feet and, as I said, were progressing well, and of course, the hands were in the field to chop out weeds and protect the stalks. And yet here was a hand who was going down the row chopping off the stalks close to the ground. It looked like he had already destroyed about 100 feet of the row, and each second was ruining more.

As I stated, Mr. Adams was already in a state of discomposure, and when he perceived this hand acting in such a destructive manner, he spurred his horse down through the field, yelling and screaming, leaving me behind. As he closed in, he pulled out his cowhide as if he was going to flog the hand. But the slave appeared to have been prepared for that, for as Mr. Adams approached, the slave twisted around and used the blade of his hoe to attack Mr. Adams, striking directly across his face. Taken off guard by such an action, Mr. Adams fell off his horse onto the ground, and immediately this devilish slave was on him with the hoe, beating him on his face and neck repeatedly. I was put into a state of shock, to say the least, by this attack on Mr. Adams, but quickly regained my senses and rode toward the offender.

I screamed at him to cease beating poor Mr. Adams, but he paid me no heed. I could hear the slave yelling over and over, like a voice from the pit of hell, "This is for Mary, this is for Mary, this is for Mary." As I came closer, the slave looked up from his bloody business and raised the hoe as if to strike me. I sadly had no choice but to pull out my pistol and fire. The Lord was looking out for me as the ball struck this devil square in the chest, and he fell back down dead. I quickly got off my horse to check on poor Mr. Adams, but I could see he was well past any aid that I could offer. In truth, I believe the first blow struck was, of itself, lethal to him.

It turns out that the slave who performed this horrid act, Robert, was the husband of Mary and father to her children. Days before, Mary and her children were sold to a slave speculator and sent off to Mississippi or Alabama. Robert, I knew him well, for he had always been one of the most loyal of the hands attending my Sunday preaching and teaching services. Somehow, the devil stole into his heart, leading him to perform such a despicable act.

I was shaken to the core, as you might imagine. I sent old Toby, whom I trust, into town to get the sheriff.

Sadly, it fell to me to tell Mrs. Adams and Thomas, who were up in the house in the library, of the sad events that had transpired. The three of us wept together.

The funeral was done quickly, and I gave the eulogy. Mr. Adams, as you know, greatly desired salvation for his slaves, but as for himself, he was no great lover of religion. I pray that God will have mercy on his soul on the Day of Judgment.

Thomas has now taken over as Master of the farm. He is young but, with God's grace, will do well. His mother is here with him and will give him much good guidance. He offered to keep me on with a raise in my yearly pay. But I have turned him down.

Truthfully, Evangeline, since all of this happened, I am tormented in my soul. I lay down to sleep but can only think of the image of poor Mr. Adams, the blade of the hoe penetrating through his neck and his head. As well, I think of the vile act, necessary but still vile, where I took the life of Robert. I truly believe that should I not have drawn my gun and fired, I would today be laying in a grave next to Mr. Adams, but I still feel flooded with guilt, having now taken the life of a man. And make no mistake, one thing I know after my years on this farm, a slave is a man. God does not see Black or White.

The truth is, Evangeline, I am sick of the stink of slavery. I am sick of the fear, sick of the blood, sick of the cowhide and the pistol. My soul is sick of this.

I cannot rest. I cannot bear to be around the slaves, even good and loyal slaves that I have known for years, ones with whom I have prayed. I cannot help, but every time I am near, I feel a great agitation. A great fear grips my spirit, and my heart pounds away in a fashion I've never before felt.

Evangeline, you spoke truth to me when you asked me once, could I approach my flock with Scripture on Sunday and with a cowhide and a gun *during the week. The answer is, for me at least, no, I cannot.*

Evangeline, I must get out of this country. I must move to a free state, a state where one man does not own another, where all men are united truly, and can fellowship together under our Lord Jesus. I'm going to write to churches in Ohio, Indiana, and Illinois. I hope to find a congregation that is willing to take a chance on me, damaged as I may be.

Evangeline, I am asking for you also to give me another chance. When I asked your father for his blessing, I asked him, and you, to take a chance on a poor preacher of the gospel. I am asking the same again, Evangeline. Please forgive me for my mistakes. Please let me recommit myself to being a poor preacher of the gospel, a husband to you, and a father to our precious children.

Evangeline, I know I have no right to ask for this. You told me so many times that this was not the way to serve the Lord, but I didn't listen. Evangeline, I listened to my own dark heart and not the words that God gave you to speak to me. But, if you can see your way to giving me another chance, I promise you today that I will live only for the Lord, and for you, and our dear and beloved children, all the days that the Lord sees fit to give us together on this earth.

With all sincerity, your loving husband,

Philip

Chapter 12—1839—22 years on the land— Thomas and Felicia marry

Thomas took a pull from the stub of his latest cigarette and blew out the smoke. He discarded the final scrap of the cigarette paper into the spittoon sitting next to his chair, intermixing with the others collecting there over the day and night. He lifted his glass and took another long swallow of the corn liquor, savoring the fiery burn of the liquor as it coursed down through his chest.

God in heaven, he thought, this couldn't be normal. How in hell could God allow him to suffer this way and not act in some way to end it? Thomas knew that giving birth was supposed to be arduous for women. But this, my God, Holy Jesus, something must be really bad wrong. No person could scream and cry out the way his wife Felicia was doing, had been doing for hours, unless something had gone wrong. He picked up his papers and pouch and began to roll another cigarette.

He noted the sound of another bout of screaming and pain starting in the next room, where Felicia lay, attended by his mother, Sarah and Emma, and the doctor from town. Every little bit, one of the Black women came out of the birthing room into this small side room, his prison cell. On each trip, they would speak to him, offer him something expected to comfort him, to deceive him.

"Missus Felicia is doing just fine in there, Master Thomas, just fine."

"You'll have a baby before long. She's just takin' her time."

"This is her first one and it can be like that."

He knew they were lying. He knew that Felicia's screams of agony, which were causing his whole being, body and mind, to go into spasms of torment, could not be ordinary.

A few hours earlier, when Felicia's screams had still been strong, not weak and muffled as they were now, he had slipped out of the room, down the stairs, and out the back door. He headed for the barn. If he could just ride some, ride into town, stop at the tavern, and have a drink to clear his mind. He would be back before anyone missed him.

He walked into the barn. Toby was there, but he was alone. All of the farm's stock, the horses and even the mules, were gone.

"Toby, get me a horse ready."

"Master, the horses are all out in the pasture."

"Well, go get one, you stupid son of a bitch."

"Master, Missus Carrie already told me not to do that. She called me in yesterday and told me to keep all the horses and mules out in the pasture. She said to do it even if you told me to go bring 'em back in."

"Damn it, do as I say. I'm your master, not her," Thomas screamed, grabbing the front of Toby's rough shirt and pulling him up so that their faces were only inches apart.

Toby averted his eyes. "I'm sorry, Master, but Missus Carrie told me to put the horses out in the pasture and leave 'em there."

Thomas pushed the older man back into the corner of the barn. Toby fell there in a heap.

"Damn you, you stupid Black bastard. Just wait 'til later. I'll make you sorry for this," Thomas screamed, his voice choking with rage. He turned and left the barn. As he walked back toward the house, the sky closed over him with dark clouds, and a thunderstorm poured down cold rain in a deluge. By the time he made it to the back door, he was soaked.

He climbed the stairs back to his cell and sat in his chair. He had no choice. He was a prisoner here. He sat and smoked his cigarettes and drank his corn liquor. And he waited for this long horrible nightmare to end, so he could be released from this prison of torture.

§

Carrie left the birthing room and wordlessly entered the small side room. She sat down in the chair next to her son. She looked at him, then looked away. Looking at him too long, she would inevitably begin comparing him to George. Then her anger would grow. She didn't need the burden of those feelings right now.

She had been hopeful that running the farm, or being married, or having a child, would have cultivated in Thomas a new level of maturity, brought out of him a capability for compassion. Sadly, at this very moment, when a grown-up, mature Thomas was most needed, she saw only the little boy, wholly consumed with his feelings, his own perceived suffering. She understood, though, that she had to put aside her disappointments and resentments. This angry child, hidden in a man's body, was all she had now, him and Felicia and the baby being born in the room next door.

§

Carrie was always mystified how someone like Thomas could be the son of a man like George. They were so different. George's mind was filled with visions for the future, and he possessed the drive to turn his dreams into reality. Thomas's mind never looked past the end of a day or maybe a week or a month. Even as a child, rather than looking to the future, birthdays or Christmas, he was captive to resentments from the past.

All of that was multiplied tenfold after the whipping, when Thomas was compelled to flay the skin, the very flesh, of his best friend. After the whipping, Thomas had slipped further and further away into his inner world. He shirked all responsibilities on the farm. He would disappear overnight and lie about where he was, where he had gone. He took up smoking, rolling cigarettes one after another. And Carrie knew he was buying liquor from neighbors all along the road to town. She smelled it on his breath and clothes. When George tried to speak to him, Thomas answered only with rage and curses.

Then George was killed, struck down by a slave, and Thomas became the master of the farm and its property. A few months of his slothfulness confirmed to Carrie what she feared and expected. Thomas simply did not have the interest, ambition, drive, or whatever one could call it to keep the farm going.

Carrie held out hope that Thomas could change. She had been witness to other men who, lacking drive on their own account, suddenly became imbued with it when a family came onto the scene. She could recall many examples among the slaves of a shiftless no account hand converting to hard work and virtue upon the arrival of a wife and children.

Carrie determined to get a wife for Thomas.

She wrote to her cousins in Richmond. A letter returned, acquainting her with the Fraziers, a Virginia family with a small plantation. Like George and Carrie, they started with wilderness land and carved a farm out of it. They lived on the land and worked it. They owned slaves, but not too many. Unlike Carrie and George, they were blessed with many children and had a surplus of daughters needing to wed. Letters of introduction were exchanged, and courtship visits were arranged.

With the machinery of society put into motion, Thomas soon proposed to Felicia, the middle of the Frazier's five daughters. A letter of acceptance was returned at once. The engagement was short. The wedding was stylish by local standards. Honeymoon travel to Charleston, and then the newlyweds arrived on the farm, as in love as only the young can be. For the first time in ages, Carrie saw Thomas happy, not morose or resentful. Carrie's play against long odds seemed to be paying off.

Two months into their life together, Felicia all at once began to feel ill and could barely arise from bed. Sarah and Emma nodded and smiled at each other. Thomas, consumed with fear, urgently summoned the doctor from town. Grinning at the dumbfounded Thomas, the doctor confirmed the obvious. Thomas was to be a father.

Felicia had an arduous time. The first few months, she could scarcely endure the sight or smell of food. Even as that passed, she unceasingly felt weak and lightheaded. She would barely struggle down the stairs, leaning on Sarah or Emma for support. Her legs, which she hid even from Thomas, were swollen, soft, like bread dough. And rather than gaining ground, week by week she got worse. Finally, she found it difficult to even sit in a chair. She would repeat over and over that she was thirsty and would ask plaintively for cup after cup of water, which never seemed to quench her dry throat. And yet she yearned to hold her baby, and to have a future filled with children and grandchildren.

Now her time had come, but the hopes for a rapid and uncomplicated labor were dashed. The doctor was summoned and had been in attendance for hours, remaining in the room along with Carrie, Sarah, and Emma.

§

Thomas heard Felicia's voice crying out again, but her voice was more and more faded. The screams were hoarse and throaty now. Thomas alternated sitting and pacing in the small room, smoking and sipping on the corn liquor, seeking to soothe his tormented spirit. Maybe he should go back to the barn again, force Toby to go out and bring in a horse, force him to put on a saddle, then ride towards town. But he didn't want to face his mother over it.

Finally, Thomas heard movement in the birthing room. He heard the doctor's voice, "Now, Felicia, it's time to push; it's time to deliver this baby." Emma's voice, "Now, Missus Felicia, you gotta push like the devil, push, push," and Felicia's voice, barely above a whisper, "I'm so tired, I'm so thirsty."

Thomas heard the doctor's voice, rising frantically, but Thomas couldn't understand the words. He strained to listen. He heard a tiny cry. At first, he thought it was the baby, but he realized it was Felicia's voice, weak like a kitten. Thomas smoked another cigarette and took another long drink from the cup. He tried to put himself somewhere else, anywhere but where he was, listening to the pathetic cries of his wife and no sound at all from his child.

The doctor came into the room, sat down, and faced him. "Thomas, you have a son, but Felicia went through a bad time. She tore badly. And she lost a lot of blood. She's small and the baby is big."

The doctor went on, "Tom, what is your son's name?"

"Thomas Jefferson Adams, Junior. That's what Felicia said to call him if it was a boy. She said to call him Jefferson."

"All right, Tom, so your mother said one of your slaves bore a baby a few weeks ago. We'll need to get her up here so she can suckle Jefferson and give Felicia a chance to get better, get stronger." Thomas was silent and puffed on his cigarette.

After a bit, the doctor asked, "Thomas, you want to see them? Felicia and Jefferson?"

Thomas sat and puffed on his cigarette. He took another long sip from the cup. "Doctor, I think I'll set here a while longer."

The doctor paused for a moment. He said, "Well, that's fine, Tom. Let me go back in there now. I'll talk to you more later."

§

Over the next few days, Felicia struggled urgently to get better. She asked Sarah and Emma to prop her up in the bed and cradled Jefferson closely against her. She tried to nurse him, but her breasts were empty, flat against her chest. Despite her desire to eat, to gain strength, she could not stomach more than spoonfuls of broth. She still craved water, asking for cup after cup. Her thoughts carried back to the pond on her family's farm. In winter, after a freeze, she would pick up ice from the pond's surface. She remembered how she would crunch the frozen shards between her teeth and let the sharp edges melt in her mouth before swallowing the cold meltwater. Now, except for holding her baby, she could envision nothing so pleasurable as a whole bowl of that ice. But there was none to give.

§

On the third day, Kee walked carefully up the rutted dirt path from her shanty, passed by the kitchen cabin, and knocked on the back door of the house, which entered into the slave pantry. Cuddled against her chest, she cradled her baby daughter, given the name Cat by Missus Carrie, now six weeks old. The door was swung open by her own mother, Emma, who smiled broadly as she took Cat from Kee's arms into her own. Extending out her hand, she helped her daughter up the two stone steps and into the house.

"Hey, kitten, you're such a sweet baby girl; yes, you are. You lookin' at me! What a good girl," Emma gushed over her granddaughter.

"Yeah, she's sweet, alright. But it don't feel so sweet when she grabs ahold of my nipples. I think she been born with a whole set of teeth," said Kee to her mother.

"You done the same thing to me, Kee. That shows how strong she's gonna be when she grows up." Emma snuggled and kissed her granddaughter.

Kee followed as her mother, still holding Cat close, walked across the dining room, out into the hall, and up the steps to Felicia's room. Emma knocked softly on the door, opened it up and went in. Kee entered the room behind her mother. Carrie sat on a chair, and Felicia lay in the bed, holding Jefferson.

Kee went to the bedside and said softly, "Missus Felicia, you want me to see if Master Jefferson might be a little bit hungry?" Felicia nodded, and Kee bent over to pick up Jefferson, where he lay nestled in Felicia's arm.

Until now, Jefferson was showing no enthusiasm for the breast, but as Kee laid her nipple against his cheek, he opened his eyes. He turned his mouth toward the nipple, latched on, and began to suckle.

Felicia had gained a little bit of color back. Her lips, which had been as pale as snow, now showed just a trace of pink, like a cherry blossom in the spring. Now, she looked on from the bed, watching every movement of her baby. When she saw him latch and begin to nurse, she said, "Oh," in a voice that was barely above a whisper.

Jefferson nursed hungrily on the right breast for about 10 minutes. Kee tried switching him to the left, but he would not latch on. As she lifted the baby boy, she saw that his left arm flopped over and that he was not moving it like the right side. She stood up, holding Jefferson with care, and said, "Now, Missus Felicia, I want you to hold that baby, he got a little bit a' good milk in his tummy now, and he should rest good. I'll be back up here toward suppertime to see if he wants to eat again." Felicia nodded and held out her arms. Kee gently laid Jefferson back in her arms, then received Cat back from Emma. She left the room, walked downstairs, and out to the kitchen cabin where she could feed Cat. Cat latched on and suckled hungrily.

As Kee and Cat were finishing their feeding in the kitchen cabin, Kee heard the faint clopping of a horse outside. She looked out across the field and recognized the doctor's buggy, headed along the cart path toward the house. Kee closed up her apron front and bundled up Cat. She walked around the house and called out to the doctor as he was stepping down from his buggy. "Master Doctor, sir, if you don't mind, I'd mention something to you 'bout Master Jefferson?"

The doctor turned, glanced over at the Black woman holding her baby, and replied, "Well, go on."

Kee continued, "Yes sir, so I was up there with Missus Felicia and Master Jefferson, lettin' him suckle off me since Missus Felicia ain't got no milk yet. And I picked him up, and I noticed that left arm is lookin' weak, like it got no strength to it. I've seen that before with some of the black babies, 'specially when a big baby came out of a tiny girl. I figured you already knew about it, but I thought I might say so. I didn't say nothin' to Missus Felicia about it."

The doctor frowned. "Well, that labor was one of the worst. We were lucky not to lose one of them or both. I'll check the baby's arm." The doctor motioned toward Cat, "I see you got your little bugaboo there. That a boy or girl?"

Kee looked down at Cat, bundled against her chest, and said proudly, "Yes sir, Master Doctor. This is my first little girl. I got my little boy down at the shanty."

The doctor nodded to Kee, crossed the porch to the front door, and knocked. Kee called out to him, "Master Doctor, there ain't nobody there to answer the door, Master Thomas been off at the barn, and Missus Carrie and the others all gonna be upstairs. You just go on in."

The doctor nodded again to her and grasped the door pull. The door swung open, and he entered into the dim light of the house.

Up in the room, the doctor knocked, then put his head into the room. Even in the dim light, he saw that Felicia's color looked a tiny bit better, her skin pinker and less pale against the sheets. Apologizing for his intrusiveness, he asked her to turn and spread her legs, pulled up her gown, and checked the lacerations. The oozing out of the wounds was lessened, and the wounds were scabbing up. He pulled the sheet and quilt back over Felicia.

The doctor shifted to studying Jefferson, sitting in his grandmother's lap. He noticed the left arm was hanging, limply, even as the right arm stretched out, grasping at the air. He bent over and took hold of both of Jefferson's hands and gently pulled both arms above Jefferson's head, then let them go at the same time. The right arm moved out to the side with the fingers spread. The left arm flopped weakly back to Jefferson's side.

The doctor turned to Felicia and spoke, "Mrs. Adams, I believe you're doing better today. You seem stronger, and your color's better. I do believe your wounds are healing. Just keep trying to eat. But stay in bed. You need to heal more fully before you try getting up."

He went on, "Jefferson has some weakness in his left arm. Now that's not to worry about. I've seen this before after a difficult birth. And it gets better, but sometimes it might take a few months. Right now, there's nothing to do for him, except we must just be careful not to let his arm get trapped in the bed clothing. So, please, Mrs. Adams, don't worry about that; worry about trying to eat and drink and get better."

Felicia's face betrayed alarm. "Is the arm problem dangerous? It won't still be with him when he grows up?"

The doctor smiled, "Mrs. Adams, I've seen this before; it is just a temporary condition. It always gets better as they get older. Your job right now is to rest and get stronger."

The doctor said his goodbyes and was coming down the steps off the porch when he saw Thomas near the kitchen cabin. The doctor called out to him, "Oh, Mr. Adams, I'm glad I ran into you. Can I talk to you for a minute?"

Thomas looked displeased with the doctor's words but came over. He tossed down his stub of cigarette paper and said, "Alright, Doctor, how are they doing?"

The doctor recited his words describing Jefferson's arm and his positive prediction for a full recovery. He gave his reassurances that Felicia looked stronger and seemed to be doing better.

The doctor climbed into the buggy, calling out that he planned to come back out to the farm the day after tomorrow. Thomas watched, a scowl twisted across his face as the buggy traveled down the cart path and turned onto the main road back toward town. When it was gone from sight, he went into the house and walked down to the library. He sat at the big desk and poured a glass from the jug sitting beside him, and took a long drink. He turned and looked through the glass doors, across the fields to the hills beyond the creek. He rolled a cigarette and smoked it, then rolled another.

After midnight, as Sarah dozed in the chair beside her, Felicia began to chill, shaking so hard that Sarah was roused not by Felicia's voice but by the sound of the bed rattling and banging against the wall. She touched her fingers to Felicia's forehead, feeling Felicia's body quivering through her hot, parched skin. Sarah got some cool water from the water bucket and bathed Felicia's forehead, face, and neck. Felicia roused up, and Sarah helped her sip some water, but after just a few sips, Felicia fell back against the sheets, continuing the violent tremble. "I feel so cold. Cover me up," was all she could say.

In the morning, Toby was sent to town to summon the doctor. When he arrived, Felicia was sinking further and faster, chilling one minute, sweating the next, and mumbling incoherent words to people who were not there. When the doctor pulled back the covers, the flood of drainage issuing from her wounds was changed, thick and yellow, clotted with blood. The noxious stench of it filled the room, permeating even the bed sheets. He laid back the cover over her.

The doctor left the room and went back down the stairs. He went out of the house and found Thomas near the barn. "Mr. Adams, I'm sorry, Felicia has taken a bad turn. She appears to have fever in the womb. There's little we can do. Some women are strong enough to pull through."

Thomas looked at the doctor, anger twisting his face, flushed crimson with rage. "Yesterday you said she was better; now today you're saying she is worse? Are you saying she'll die? Well, what is it? Do you even know?"

The doctor replied softly, "Yesterday, sir, she was doing better, but a childbed fever can come on even when things appear to be doing well. It's something we cannot predict and can do little to treat, save prayer and time."

Thomas glared at the doctor, hatred filling his face. "What good to us are your damn prayers, Doctor. Nothing you've done has helped her. And the boy is crippled, thanks to you. So now you want to pray for us? Do you think I don't see what you've done? Get your damn buggy off my land."

The doctor's face tightened. He said, "I'm sorry, Mr. Adams, I'll come out to check on her again tomorrow." He climbed up onto the seat of his buggy, flicked the reins, and guided his horse down the cart path and back towards town.

Thomas went into the house. As before, he did not go upstairs. He went into the library and sat again at the desk, looking across the fields. He rolled another cigarette and took another long drink of corn liquor. He sat in the library even after Emma knocked on the door to let him know that there was supper ready. By midnight the jug was empty.

In the morning, Toby was sent to town with a message to take to the doctor. It said not to bother coming out to the farm anymore. Felicia was dead.

Chapter 13—1844—27 years on the land— Financial troubles

Thomas stood impatiently on the stone steps of the brick church, staring down the muddy street, waiting to see Toby and the farm wagon come into view.

Every Sunday, it was the same damn thing, Thomas brooded. Get up early, ride the wagon into town, and sit in the damn church pew for two hours listening to some lazy son of a bitch preacher spouting off. Afterward, standing around, shaking hands and smiling at all the same lazy, stupid folks as they filed out of the church and got into their carriages and buggies and rode away. His mother was always wanting to wait around, be the last one to leave out of the church, so she could have her "talks," she called it, with folks, with other farm folks, and with the business folks of the town.

Thomas would just as soon tell them to go to hell, be done with the bastards, and forget about the church, but his mother said no. They both needed to come. He needed to be there, to pretend to care about the people and the preaching. So he did it every Sunday. Because she said he had to.

Thomas peered down the street and saw the farm wagon slowly coming toward the church, Old Toby guiding the team through the mud. As the wagon came to a stop in front of the church steps, Thomas scowled at it. What a piss-poor excuse for a wagon, a piss-poor team, and a piss-poor driver. Everyone else in town traveled by carriage, or at least a buggy, but his mother and he rode to town in this stupid dirty farm wagon. They had to nail down benches in the wagon bed just to have a place to sit. Back at the farm, they would pry out the nails, take down the benches, and use the very same dirty wagon to haul hay and corn from the fields and even to haul stinking loads of horse manure out to the fields. So here he was, riding to town, in front of everyone, in this stinking shit wagon. And all of it was because of one greedy, selfish bastard, his dead father.

Thomas watched as his mother shared a last dulcet word with the preacher, her voice coated in sweetness. She turned toward the street, and her lips tightened as she contemplated her necessary journey down the steps to the wagon. Thomas mounted back up the steps and cradled her right arm in both of his. As well, Toby bounded up the steps and took up her left arm. With expertise borne of years of practice, the two men guided Carrie's frail frame down the steps and up onto the bench anchored in the wagon bed. Toby pulled out a wool blanket from the seat-box and draped it over Carrie's lap, taking care to tuck it around her thin wasted legs. Then five-year-old Jefferson popped out of nowhere, mud coating his boots, and hopped into the wagon and took his seat. With Thomas settling in and Toby taking the reins, the wagon pulled away, the team pulling the wagon through the town's muddy streets, then back onto the road, rolling along toward the farm.

Thomas looked impassively at the small farms and cabins passing by. He felt in his jacket pocket and pulled out his tobacco and papers. As he rolled, he absently noticed another small farmhouse alone and abandoned, joining a string of others along the road. Weeks before, the owners, a family named Noonan, let it be known along the road that they were finished, they couldn't make it anymore. They jammed as much as they could in their wagon and sold their stock and the rest to whoever would pay cash for it. Then they struck out in their overloaded wagon, heading for Tennessee, praying for a fresh start. Thomas looked at the small farm falling rapidly into neglect. He looked down, striking a match to light up his tobacco.

§

Carrie also was watching the countryside passing by them, taking in the sights of the abandoned homes, the pastures empty of stock, wasted unplowed acres spreading away from the road. The fields were bare save for scattered patches of chickweed, mossy clumps laying atop the russet soil, racing to put out tiny flowers and drop seeds before being pushed aside, displaced by the sedges and bindweeds of summer.

The signs were all there, Carrie thought, for those willing to see them. But these were not hopeful signs, not like the warm air and the greening fields of spring, promising renewal of the earth. These were portents, signs of a calamity coming closer every day. A calamity that could strip Carrie and her family of their life and their land. Her land that she had broken and tamed, that she watered with her tears, that yet held poor George's precious blood and broken flesh.

The root of the present troubles, and the coming evil, the newspapers all agreed, lay with the greedy, vile bankers up North. Out of the blue, five or six years before, the big banks in places like New York and Baltimore broke their promises. They summarily announced, with infuriating arrogance, that their own banknotes, their own money, the very papers that carried the bank's own name, were no good, worthless. Only gold and silver were good now.

This treachery instigated by the Northerners had, for reasons no one could explain to Carrie's satisfaction, pushed down the price of cotton. Year after year, the money paid for a bale of cotton by the big buyers up North tumbled downward, falling farther and farther each season.

And even more calamitous than that, at least to Carrie's mind, the prices paid for slaves plunged with all the rest.

Now almost all the folks who owned land along the road, big and small alike, were hurting badly. Folks bought their land, their tools, stock, and their slaves on credit. Now they couldn't make payments, and the banks were forcing them out. All the work, all the years of toil, was being stolen away by the Northerners, the out-and-out criminals who ran the big banks. And it was all legal.

Carrie saw the signs for herself and Thomas and little Jefferson. The wolf was already at their door, looking to pounce. Taxes were due to be paid soon on their land and their house. And on their slaves.

There were avenues she could take to get money. When Felicia died, her parents set up an account for Jefferson. It was Felicia's portion, what would have been her inheritance if she had lived. But that money was held in a trust deposit at the bank in town, secure from greedy and grasping fingers. Jefferson was to receive it at age 21. Carrie was not naïve about the limits of the trust's security. If she asked them, the town's bankers and lawyers could use some legal trickery to get at least some of that money for her. So far, however, Carrie resisted the temptation to pirate away her grandson's inheritance.

As well, Carrie's family in Richmond was still rich. They still grew tobacco, still owned ships. But asking for help from her family would mean crawling back to Frederick. The thought of having to genuflect to Frederick and beg for his crumbs filled Carrie's mind with bilious rage and resentment. She swore to herself, even before George died, that she would sooner die on the farm, starve to death than plead for alms from her arrogant ass of a brother.

But they would have to make some move, and sooner would be better than later.

She glanced over at Thomas. He was unlike his father in nearly every way, but in one way, they were exactly the same. Like George, Thomas could shut his eyes to a looming catastrophe, even as it reared up before him. So, just as she had done with George, Carrie would have to compel Thomas to make the difficult decisions that would keep the farm secure.

"Thomas, after we get back to the farm, I'd like to talk to you a little bit about our bank accounts. Can we do that please?"

Thomas kept looking at the passing countryside. "Yes, Mother, happily." He puffed on his cigarette. He remained silent the rest of the trip.

The wagon approached the rutted turn-off leading away from the road. The team, knowing their way onto the cart path and that it led to the barn, to food and water, made the turn easily. Toby pulled the horses to a halt at the front steps, and Thomas, Jefferson, and Toby bounded out. Thomas and Toby repeated their actions from earlier, this time in reverse, aiding and supporting Carrie's thin limbs as she stepped down out of the wagon and over to the steps. With gentle, even delicate, support from the two men she bent and unbent her arthritic ankles, knees, and hips, climbing, one step at a time, onto the porch. Next, into the house and down the hall to the library, one halting step followed by the next. Finally, she took her place in the side chair next to the desk. Toby knew this task was completed, and now his job was to disappear. He moved noiselessly to the library door and was gone.

Emma came in, tapped on the door, and asked, "Hello, Missus Carrie, Master Thomas. Can I get you anything right now, Missus Carrie?" Emma's face carried a smile, but her eyes were hard and dark.

Carrie replied, "Emma, thank you so much; I'm fine. Thomas and I are just going to talk for a little bit. So I believe I will be alright."

Emma said, "That's fine, Missus Carrie. Sarah and I got that chicken ready for dinner in a little while. I'll be back and ask you if you need anything round about that time." And she left the room, closing the door softly.

Thomas stood behind the desk and looked out over the fields through the double glass doors. He puffed on his cigarette. He turned and sat down and looked toward his mother. "Well, Mother, are we going next, like the Noonans, dragging tail like some damn dog?"

Carrie looked straight at her son, "Thomas, we are not going to do that. Ever. This whole panic and depression was started by greedy bankers and crooked politicians. They just enjoy bleeding people like us."

Thomas gave an angry laugh, "Well, if they want to bleed us more, they better hurry. We been pretty well bled already."

Carrie said, "Thomas, we still have some cards to play, but we need to both decide together to do it. So look at me and listen closely."

Thomas looked over, curiosity in his eyes. "All right, Mother. Let's hear it."

"Thomas, your father and I were worried that something like this might happen someday, so we tried to plan for it."

Thomas' face darkened at the mention of his father, but he remained silent. Carrie watched the darkness cloud Thomas' face but continued.

"So, Thomas, I'm sure it's clear that Sarah and Emma are mixed. Both of them are lighter than the other servants. Their father was White."

Thomas looked disappointed. "Everyone here about uses yellow girls for their house slaves. Are you thinkin' those two would fetch us enough cash to get out of this mess?"

"Thomas, the truth is, Sarah and Emma are both my half-sisters. And they are half-sisters to each other. My father was also their father. That's why we grew up together in my parents' home, and that's why they came to me when I got married."

"Alright, Alright. That's interesting, I suppose. Granddaddy was a son of a bitch to your mother. I still don't figure how that's helpin' much. Half-White house servants aren't selling for much more than field hands, are they?"

Carrie paused, irritated that Thomas wasn't connecting to her words. "It's not Sarah and Emma where we can make the money. It's their girls."

Carrie paused again as she felt a lump building up in her throat. She steadied herself for a moment, pushing down her emotions, hardening herself as she had done so often before.

She continued, "Sarah's third child, Angelique, and Emma's fourth and fifth children, Esther and Ruth, are your half-sisters. Your father was the father of all three of them. Plus, Sarah's Johnny and Emma's Bobby."

As she spoke, Carrie absently fingered the ring hanging from a gold chain around her neck. She had given George that ring on the day they married. She placed it on the chain the day of George's funeral. She had worn it around her neck every day since.

Thomas saw his mother touching the ring and felt a surge of jealousy for his dead father rising and coursing through his heart. He could see that, even with the passage of so many years, it was his father, not himself, who was still first in his mother's heart. Hate boiled up inside of him.

Thomas spoke in an acid voice, "So, Daddy was knocking up the slaves. What a son of a bitch. He was cheating on you with your own damn sisters."

Carrie strained to control her rising anger. It would be pointless to scream at Thomas, to lose her temper. "Thomas, it was nothing like that. I knew what he was doing. I told him to do it, Thomas. He didn't want to, but I forced him. I knew that pretty Quadroon girls always sell for a good price. There's always a rich man, a planter, or some other big-shot man, who's willing to pay for it. So that's what we have to sell, now that we need the money. Sarah and Emma's children."

Thomas' face tightened. His father, his precious sainted father, his hated, scorned, loathed father, was coming back from the dead, offering him a gift, financial salvation. He would not refuse the gift. But Thomas was not going to release his hate. It was too delicious. He wanted to keep the taste of it, to savor it.

He looked back at his mother. "So what do we do?" he asked.

"I sent a letter to my brother's manager in Richmond, and he wrote me back, explained how these things are done. He knows people in the trading business in Richmond, people who get slaves just for the richest families. He says that we would need to take the girls to Richmond and let the traders look at them. If they are top quality, he could arrange private sales, which would fetch the best price. If he didn't feel that they were that kind of quality, he would auction them, which would bring less."

"How much?"

"He said that at a private sale, probably $3000 each. At auction, possibly around $2000 each."

"$6000, maybe even up to $9000. That would carry us a hell of a long way."

Carrie hardened herself again before speaking. "Actually, it would be more than that. If we sell the three girls, I also want to sell the two boys, Johnny and Bobby. And Sarah and Emma."

Thomas looked at his mother. The resentment and rage were set aside on his face, replaced by genuine surprise. "Sell Sarah and Emma? But they've been with you since you were a baby!"

"Yes, Thomas, that's why I want to sell them. Once we sell the children, I don't want to look in their mother's faces, not ever again. So, if we do this, you and Jefferson would have to take the slaves up to Richmond and carry through on it, and I would stay here."

"Why have I got to take Jefferson? Can't I go by myself and do it?"

"Jefferson needs to go and meet his Richmond family. And I don't want to tell the slaves about the sale, not until it's happening. You can tell the slaves that you and Jefferson are going to Richmond to visit the family there, and, being a man, you need all of them to go along to help take care of Jefferson. And I am staying home because of my rheumatism."

Thomas sat and was silent for a few moments. His face broke out in a hard smile. "Damn, Mother, I was fixin' to go out and rob a bank. And all along, we've got a pile of gold sittin' right here. All we've got to do is cash it in. What else have you got in that beautiful head of yours?"

Carrie looked at Thomas. Despite the hardening up, she was struggling to restrain the sadness and halt the tears. She missed George so badly. George would have understood. He would have understood that she was selling her sisters, her very own flesh and blood, for money. He would have understood her guilt and pain and loss and shared it with her, even as he understood the necessity of the sale. But Thomas was not George.

She finally said, "So, Thomas, you can think about this, but we have to decide soon. If we wait, we may lose out."

"No, Mother, I don't need to think about it. What's there to think about? Let old Uncle Frederick know we'll be coming soon as we can. Like you said, we need to strike hard now, so we don't miss our chance."

"Damn, I'm getting hungry," Thomas said. "I sure as hell hope Sarah and Emma got that chicken ready to eat soon." His fingers began to roll another cigarette.

Chapter 14—1844—27 years on the land— Shockoe Bottom, Richmond, Virginia

Shockoe Bottom, Richmond, Virginia. A long two-story wooden building, solidly built, with heavy doors and small windows. Iron bars are set into the framing around each window. A covered porch extends along the street down to the sidewalk. Behind the building, a courtyard surrounded by a stockade, like a jail, made of thick logs, driven down into the earth and extending 8 feet up, without windows or doors.

Signs face the street, advertising the goods for sale:

Slaves, Slaves, Slaves!
Cash for Negroes! Buy On Credit!
Best Prices, Guaranteed!
Every Negro Comes with a New Suit of Clothes and Pair of Shoes!
Our Negroes Don't Run! Guaranteed!!

All right, Joe, you get out there on the street. You talk them farmers up big, get 'em up on the porch, let 'em look all of 'em over. Dammit, Joe, keep them all lined up, tallest on one end and shortest on the other, keep them lined up good, that's good, Joe, you talk up the customers, get them up on the porch. Make them feel like they're takin' your time, make them feel like they owe you for something, let them poke around on the different slaves, just set them up and then send them indoors, and I'll finish the sale in here. I'll deal them, or I'll kill them, one way or another. Just don't send in no bums. I want to make deals.

Yes, sir, that's right, we got a big load of slaves from Colonel Highsmith. What, you've never heard of Colonel Highsmith? Why he practically won the war for Texas by hisself, had hisself three big plantations, right here outside of Richmond, and down near Charleston, but he died 'bout two months back. His children decided they couldn't keep all his slaves, brought the whole lot of 'em over to us. Now we got to get 'em sold, that's why we're givin' such good prices, 'cause, if we can't sell 'em, we gotta keep feedin' 'em.

Joe, that last fella you send in here was a joker, didn't want to buy nothin', just wastin' our time, don't send those dogs in here like that, that feller is just wastin' our time.

Damn, I wish I had 100 more of these, prices is low, but folks are buyin'. They must be figurin' that cotton will be high next year. Folks want to get in on the cheap prices now and get ready for next year.

Yes, ma'am, you like that yaller girl out there, the second one from the end. Yes, ma'am, we got her from a big plantation up in Maryland, right there on the Chesapeake Bay. That girl was brought up in the planters' house. Why I think she'd be fine to help you look after your babies, she's a real sweet girl, never given us any trouble here; matter of fact, we got her sister and her mama out there too, if you like to take all three, we'll give a good price. Oh, yep, I understand, I understand, yes, that would be quite a lot, you right about that. So you just want the one little gal? Why you could have her for 400, that's right, just count out the bills, and I'll write you up a bill of sale and get her loaded up for you.

Joe, get that little yaller girl, second one from the end, get her loaded up into this lady's buggy over there. I wouldn't worry, ma'am. They always scream and holler like that when they first start, why that just shows how much they love their mama. You get her to your house, and, quick as a bunny, why she'll be loving on your little girl, she's gonna be good as gold for you, I guarantee that. Don't you worry; she'll settle down and quit all that cryin' and screamin' before you even get to the edge of town. They all do that when they start, but they forget their mama real quick, the Blacks do, a few days, and she won't want to be anywhere else than with you. Thank you, Ma'am.

What's that, Joe, this man says he bought a slave from us last week, and now he's already run off? Well, holy lord, mister, we can't be responsible for that. Guarantee? Well, we guarantee that he's a slave. Anything after that is up to you. We can't guarantee that he ain't gonna turn rabbit and run off if you don't watch him close. You can go down to the newspaper and put in a runaway ad. Maybe someone will see him and lock him up so you can get him. Sorry, mister. Lord, Joe, get a load of that guy.

There is a fella out here wantin' to make a trade? What's he got to trade? Huh, he wants to trade those two broken-down old field hands?

For what? What, you want that likely buck? Is this a joke? That boy is only 15 years old, that's prime, he'll be a good hand for 30 years, he's worth 10 of what you're wantin' to trade, come on mister you're going to have to do a lot better, maybe give me 500 and throw in those two broken-down no-account hands, maybe we can make a deal. 300? Alright, sure, you got a deal, come on in, and we can draw it up. Joe, load up that buck.

Joe, I'm starving. Send your boy down to the saloon, get us some sausages and beer. I can't get away from here today. Damn, wish I had another 50 to sell. They must be planning to grow lots of cotton down there in Alabama this year.

Yes, sir, mister, come on in, get out of the sun. You say you like one of those pretty light-colored girls out there. That's fine, mister, but one like her is going to cost you some. I can send them down to New Orleans and get 2,000 for each one. I just put them out here to see if I could get a good price, save me the trouble. Plus, mister, don't you think your wife's gonna figure out something smells fishy if you come home with one of those gals? Well, tell you what most men do, they buy three or four other slaves along with the fancy girl all at once, so she don't stand out so much. So what you need to do is buy a couple of bucks and a couple of old wenches, plus the fancy girl, and when you get home, you tell your wife that prices was so good, you couldn't pass it up, and you make that young gal your wife's special girl. After a year or so, everyone forgets how she got there, and that's when you can start with her, and the Missus is none the wiser.

I can give you the girl, plus the older slaves for cover for, let's say, 3,500 altogether? I'm probably losing money; like I said, I could get a lot more down in New Orleans, but what the hell, maybe you'll do me a good turn someday. Yes, sir, 3,500. I think that seems fair. Let me write it up for you. Joe, get those four hands, the ones we traded for today, along with that pretty girl there, and get them loaded up for this man. Yes, sir, that wagon with the two fine-looking mules. Yes, sir, pleasure doing business. Yes, sir, you're right. Pleasure for both of us.

Hey, Joe, what's this going on with that one buck there in the middle of the row. He looks like he's got something wrong with the skin there. Damn, nobody wants to see that. They might think he's sick or got something bad wrong with him. Go get some of that boot polish and rub on those places. Maybe it won't show up so bad.

Yes, sir, all our old wenches out there, they know how to cook, raised up on some of the finest plantations in Maryland and Virginia. That one in the middle of the row, well yeah, now that you mention it, she does look part Indian matter-of-fact, now that I think about it, when we bought her, they said her father was an Indian chief, so I guess she's some kind of Indian princess, but I guarantee she'd be a good cook, good field hand, you get that Indian blood and Black blood mixed, you got yourself a fine slave, even better than pure African, they can work all day out in the sun, you can get them down and work them in a swamp, and they won't catch no fevers or nothin', why, a White man in that same situation would be dead in a month. Those Black Indians can do it year after year, no problem at all. Yes, sir, I guess we could let you have her for, I don't know, 850. 800? Alright, it's a deal. Let me write it up.

Hey, Joe, you done good with that last feller. Yeah, just tease them along with the low price, and I'll stick it to them when they get in here. Yeah, you earned yourself another fifty bucks on that deal. If we keep this up, we'll both be rich, go off somewhere and start our own damn plantation, just let the money roll in year after year. Alright, Joe, that looks like a buyer out there in the street. Drink up and see if you can pull him in. Yeah, I don't know, Joe, you can just tell sometimes when they want to buy or when they just want to look. Just something about the look in the eye. Yeah, just get them looking, get them to take up your time. That way, they feel like they owe you something. Then once they're hooked, shoot them in here to me, and I'll close it out with them, get them signed and sealed.

Damn, wish I had another hundred of these—when we're selling low, we gotta make it up on volume, we gotta make hay while the sun is shining, what I always say.

Yes, sir, mister, so you're wanting those two young brothers? Two of them together I could probably give you for 1,300. He told you what? A Thousand? No, dammit, Joe must be drinkin' again. I paid more than a thousand for them myself, let's see, maybe we could do the two of them for 1,200? I'll shoot myself later over this deal, but, alright, mister, 1,200, Joe, load up those two boys, yeah, the two brothers, while we finish the paperwork in here. Sorry about that, mister. Joe sometimes gets things a little mixed up, he works hard, but well, he just really ain't all that bright, especially when he's been drinking. He's my wife's brother, you know how that is, gotta look after your family. Yes sir, mister, good doing business, come back again.

Damn, wish I had another hundred and fifty hands. Hey Joe, let's wrap it up, get them all back in the pen, and get them locked up. I'd like to have another bunch of them sausages and beer, how about it? Yep, good day, we keep at this, and we might get rich someday. Hey, Joe, leave out that one gal, the one with the little boy, think I'll take 'em home tonight, try her out—Hey, I worked hard today, Joe, gotta have a little fun sometimes, too, right? You bet, Joe. See you tomorrow. Yep, you did real well today. Thanks, Joe.

Chapter 15—1844—27 years on the land—Traveling home

Thomas gazed out the window of the stagecoach, puffing on a cigarette and taking sips from his flask. The stagecoach was bouncing along, covering the last stretch of the journey home from Richmond. By tonight they should arrive in town, where Toby would be waiting with the wagon to carry them back to the farm. The same dirty little farm he left behind the month before. The closer he came, the more his mood turned sour.

When he first set out from Richmond, beginning the journey back to the farm, his mind had been soaring, still consumed with the thrills of the city. He remembered when he arrived in Richmond. At the first, his cousins, nephews, and uncles were standoffish. They didn't know him, couldn't get a read on him. Maybe he was one of those overly religious country types, sanctimonious or moralistic or the like. But with a few days to feel him out, they could see Thomas was one of them or wanted to be. After that, they took him under their wing, taking delight in showing him the pleasures of the city. They treated him to all manners of drink--whiskey, bourbon, rum. Fine spirits from all over the world, nothing like the nasty local rotgut corn liquor he drank on the farm. And Virginia tobacco, the best in the world, so smooth and sweet, it was like silk. And the women, damn, the women, so many, and all beautiful and all different. And all of it free for the taking. Well, Thomas admitted, smiling to himself, not exactly free. But his rich relatives, knowing about the farm's financial state, made sure he got to taste all of it, all of the pleasures that could be bought with money and not a penny pulled out of his pocket.

Even better, the sale of the slaves brought in plenty, even more than he dared to hope. Uncle Frederick's manager hooked Thomas up with one of the high-class slave traders he knew. The trader nearly wet himself when he saw the three light girls, the daughters of Sarah and Emma, brought in to be sold. They were the perfect ages and color, the trader said. Private sales were set up in just a few days, and each girl was sent off with her new master. On top of that, the two boys sold high. Even the two old hags, Sarah and Emma, fetched a bit of cash. Put it all together, even counting in the cost of travel, he was coming home with over $11,000 in his money belts. That would please his mother.

But as he traveled away from Richmond, dragging along his little turd of a son, he felt more and more that he was being cheated. There were so many pleasures to be had in a city like Richmond, and yet, out on that pissy little farm, he was cut off. He couldn't believe that his mother grew up there in Richmond, in that mansion, and left all of it behind, trading it for a poor desperate life on a dirty little farm. Just to be loyal to his dead father. His father stole that life from her. And Thomas now realized he stole it from Thomas as well. Here Thomas was, on this damn stagecoach, traveling away from Richmond. Back to that same little farm, where one day was the same as the next, year after year after year. And to top it all, dragging this little turd brat along with him.

While he was in Richmond, he bought a money belt, so he could carry the bank notes, the profits from the slave sales, safely back to the farm, out of sight under his clothes. The day before he left, he snuck away and bought a second belt, smaller than the first. Then he went to the bank and traded in $3,000 of the bank notes for gold coins. He wrapped the coins in flannel and put them into the second money belt. He secured this belt around his waist beneath the larger one. The coins were heavy, much heavier than the bank notes. Wearing the belt and feeling the weight of the money against his skin made him feel empowered like he was on par with his wealthy cousins.

The gold would be the wages due him for all the work he had done. Traveling to Richmond with the slaves and the brat, doing the sale, and dragging the little turd home again. His mother would never know. He would hide it somewhere on the farm, a hiding place only he would know about. If he ever needed to leave in a hurry the gold would be there, waiting for him. He looked over at the brat, and again he felt angry at the way he had been cheated. But his thoughts soon returned to the money and what it could buy. He smiled at that. He puffed and took another long sip.

§

Next to his father, Jefferson sat on the seat of the stagecoach, playing with the two tin soldiers his father bought for him before they left Richmond. But he was tired of playing with the soldiers. He was tired of traveling in the stupid stagecoach.

Jefferson remembered starting with his father on their trip to see his cousins in Richmond the month before. The trip was lots of fun because they were traveling with Sarah and Emma, who would always pick up Jefferson and hold him and love on him and kiss him and hug him, just like his grandma. And there was Johnny and Bobby, the two Black boys who would play with him and talk to him. And there were the three girls who would be nice to him and let him look at their needlework and let him try to do it. They would stop and eat. His father and he would go into the tavern and eat, and the others would have to stay outside, but still, it was fun, and there were always people to play with him, and there were new places to look at.

When they finally got to Raleigh, they got on the train, and Jefferson and his father sat on nice seats on the train, and it was not nearly as bouncy and rough on the train as it had been on the stagecoach. The others, Sarah and Emma and the Black children, all rode on a different part of the train, but still, when the train would stop, he could play with them, and Sarah and Emma would hold him and love on him the way his grandma would.

Then they got to Richmond, and he didn't get to play with Johnny and Bobby very much, or the girls, or Sarah and Emma. They all got put off far away. He wanted to have Sarah and Emma hold him and hug him like they did before. The adults told him to go play with his cousins, the ones who lived in Richmond, but his cousins were mean to him, laughed at the way he talked, and called him a rube and a hick. They made fun of how his arm was weak and how he couldn't move it the right way, so they wouldn't let him play games with them because he was bad at them.

One day a wagon came, and Sarah, Emma, Johnny and Bobby, and the girls got into the wagon and went away and never came back. All he was left with was his father and his stupid cousins.

Then it came time for them to go back home, and they got on the train, but it wasn't fun anymore. So his father bought him the two tin soldiers to play with. But that wasn't fun without Johnny and Bobby to play with, or the girls or Sarah and Emma to hold him and hug him and love on him. They went back to Raleigh on the train. After they left the train, they had to get back on this stupid bouncy stagecoach. His father said they were nearly back to the town, and old Toby would be there in town when they arrived. Toby would load everything into the wagon, and they would all go back to the farm.

Jefferson hoped that maybe when he got back to the farm, Johnny and Bobby, the girls, and Sarah and Emma would all be there. Maybe they came back to the farm on a different train and a different stagecoach, but they would all be there. He could play again with Johnny and Bobby and the tin soldiers, and his grandmother would be there to hug him, and when his grandmother was tired or had to rest, Sarah and Emma would be there to hold him and hug him and love on him. So he sat still, riding along in the stagecoach next to his father, waiting to get back to town and to the farm. And everything would be back to the way it was before.

Chapter 16—1853—36 years on the land— The runaway

Jefferson sat in the library, his thin frame dwarfed by the mahogany desk, the one transported by wagon, mile by mile, to the farm from Richmond years before. It once belonged to his great-grandfather, Grandmother Carrie's father. Carrie would describe how the old man would hunch over that very desk, keeping track of his vast wealth. And Grandmother Carrie, as a child, would play underneath it, playing with dolls as her father worked away.

It was rare, but his Grandmother Carrie would sometimes reminisce about her childhood in Richmond, about the huge mansions and the grand parties. She would recall the wonderful foods, cakes, and sweets, served by liveried slaves. And her father's plantations, vast slave farms, and thousands of acres along the James River where the tobacco, the source of all that wealth, was cultivated. How it would be dried and packed in barrels and sent off in ships, also owned by her father, to other countries or to the North. She would always conclude her stories by talking about how she met and fell in love with George and how they left Richmond behind. How they traveled here, starting a new life together in the wilderness.

Now, as Jefferson labored away studying Latin and Greek at the desk, Carrie sat next to him in her special side chair, padded with leather to try to protect her swollen, feverish hips. The rheumatism, year after year, continued to consume her, little by little, first taking away her youth, now taking away the rest of her. It was leaving her a cripple suffering as if she was burned, but a burn that never went away. She had a good day every so often, but then the weather would change, and the bad days came back worse than ever. She spent most days in the library, moving from there to the dining room. Her bedroom was downstairs now, in the parlor. But she still had her head, her sharp wit, her discernment. As well, she still had hard places in her heart, like the hardest stone. Those hard places were going to protect her family, Jefferson, Thomas, and herself, from those who would steal from them or, worse, try to tear the three of them apart.

Carrie realized years before that Jefferson was not like his grandfather, Carrie's beloved George, lost to her at such a young age. Jefferson did not have George's confidence, that strength that allowed George to push aside whatever lay in his path.

Nor, thank God, was Jefferson like his own father, Thomas, dark and resentful, quick to take offense and lash out.

Jefferson was like his mother, slight of build and fair-haired, and trusting. He was a quiet boy, not brooding like his father, just thoughtful. He loved to read, something Thomas never spent a minute doing. So when Jefferson was young, Carrie ordered books for him, stories of adventure and danger. Jefferson read them and read them again.

Jefferson would not live his life as a planter, of that Carrie was certain. Jefferson would need to go to University and read the law or go into banking or business. Of course, Jefferson could still own the farm and still live on the land, this land. But his life wouldn't be tied to the price of cotton or hogs. Or slaves.

At Carrie's behest, Thomas hired the young Presbyterian minister in town to teach Jefferson to prepare him for the rigors of University. Three times a week Jefferson traveled into town and received instruction from Reverend Clark. On the other days, Jefferson sat here in the library, working on those lessons, while Carrie read the newspapers or a book and kept watch. Watching to be sure Jefferson would get his chance and would be ready for University when the time came.

Of course, Jefferson didn't spend all his time indoors with books. Living on a farm in the country, Jefferson still enjoyed plenty of time out of doors, playing in the woods and exploring the creeks and hills. He grew up side by side with the Black children. Unlike his father, Jefferson shied away from the rough-and-tumble wrestling games the Black boys wanted to play. His special friend among the Black children was Cat, Kee's Cat. Carrie remembered how Kee suckled Jefferson and Cat, side-by-side sometimes, after Jefferson was born and after Felicia died days later. She wondered if that had fostered the closeness between the two of them, the Black slave girl and the White son of the master.

Jefferson finished up the work given to him by Reverend Clark. He held it up for his grandmother to review. Carrie looked it over carefully and finally nodded. That was the sign, the signal that Jefferson was released for the day. He jumped to his feet, bent over and gave his grandmother a hug and a kiss, and headed for the door. Carrie heard him racing down the hall, across the dining room, through the slave pantry, and out the door into the yard.

§

Once Jefferson was outside, he crossed back behind the kitchen and headed down the footpath towards the slave shanties. He could make out Cat's form in the rocky little yard, the space between shanties. That was where she and some of the other Black girls, too young yet to work a hoe, would be looking after the slave children while their mothers and fathers and older brothers and sisters labored out in the fields.

He ran towards her, but she spotted him coming down the footpath and waved him off, signaling for him to go back behind the shanty. She met him there.

"Can you keep a secret?" she asked him.

Jefferson thought he knew what she meant and smiled. As children, they would play this game, a guessing game, each trying to guess the other's secret. But as he smiled at Cat, he saw that her eyes were not playful, not childlike. Her eyes were hard and dead serious. His smile faded.

"What secret?" replied Jefferson.

She looked at him again, a look like flint. She said, "Can you swear?"

"Yes, of course, Cat, I always keep our secrets."

She looked at him again with hard eyes. "This is different. You have to swear to me you'll keep this secret."

"Fine, Cat, I swear. I promise to keep the secret."

"Wait here," she said. She dashed back around to the front of the shanty. Jefferson could hear her ordering the younger girls to stay there and look after the children while she was gone. She appeared again around the corner of the shanty. "Come on then."

She led the way down to the creek, and they waded into the chilly water. Cat hurriedly crossed over to the far side, Jefferson splashing along behind her. She began climbing the steep bank up into the woods. She moved ahead, grabbing tree branches and young saplings to help her up the hill. Jefferson struggled to keep up the pace, the weakness in his left arm still slowing his movement. "Slow down some, Cat. You're getting ahead of me." She turned around and reached out her hand. He grabbed it, and she pulled him upward. Finally, they came to the top of the bank and moved out onto more level ground.

Cat dashed forward, deeper into the woods. She pushed through the undergrowth of saplings and vines for about a half mile until she came to a tree that was leaning over. It had been partially uprooted years ago in a storm but survived, growing up crooked, forming an angled arch. In the dim filtered light of the forest, Jefferson could see that a multitude of branches and young limbs, with leaves still attached, were propped up against the angled part of the tree trunk, making a lean-to shelter. And in the shelter, under the limbs, lay a Black man.

The Black man's skin clung to his bones, his clothes were shredded to rags, and his hair was matted and wild. He wore an old pair of brogans, but the soles were coming apart, and his feet, calloused and stained, showed through.

The Black man spotted Jefferson and began to flail about, endeavoring to push himself back farther underneath the lean-to, hoping to make himself disappear among the leaves and branches. Cat called out to him, "Lem, this is the son of my master. I told you about him. He promised not to tell."

Jefferson stared wide-eyed at the man. "Cat, what is going on? Who is this?"

Cat said, "I came up here yesterday, looking for some blackberries for Ma, and I found him laying right there. I put up the branches for him. He told me he run away from down south, trying to get north."

Cat pulled out from underneath her shift an object wrapped in leaves. She unwrapped it and pulled out a corn cake that she gave to the black man. He picked it up and put it to his mouth. It was gone in a second, but even while devouring the corn cake, he kept his eyes on Jefferson. The image of fear remained on his face.

"Cat, why did you bring me here? He's a runaway. He needs to go back to his master. You know that. You know you can't help runaways. I'm going to have to report him to the sheriff."

Cat looked at Jefferson. "You can't tell. You swore." Jefferson was brought up short by Cat's hard stony eyes.

"You didn't tell me it was a runaway. How can you expect me to not tell?"

Stony eyes. "You swore."

Jefferson said, "Well, what do you want from me? Why did you bring me here?"

Cat gestured toward the man, "Look at his leg."

Jefferson took another step towards the black man, who tried to retreat further into his corner, but there was no further back he could go. Jefferson looked down and saw an iron shackle around the man's ankle and three links of chain hanging off the shackle. He saw that the skin underneath the shackle was red and swollen, and fiery streaks coursed up the man's leg to the knee. Jefferson said, "I'm just going to touch it," and reached down and pulled on the shackle, which was firmly secured. He touched the man's leg and, at once, pulled his hand away when he felt how hot the skin was. He touched it again, and the man winced in pain.

Jefferson said, "That leg is bad, Cat. He needs to see the doctor."

At this, the man cried out, "No, no, they'll send me back. I can't go back to my master. He wants to kill me."

Cat said, "Lem, tell Master Jefferson here what you told me. He's the only one that can help you." She turned to Jefferson. Her eyes were now pleading. "Please, Master Jefferson, just listen to him."

Jefferson looked down at the Black man. "All right, tell me."

Lem began, "My master been tryin' to kill me. He been tryin' to kill me ever since he got me. Every day, he's tellin' the overseer to whip me. Lem didn't work hard enough today. Go give him 20 with the cow hide. Lem didn't hoe his row today. Take away his corn. Lem needs to go down in the swamp and work grubbin' stumps. Every day it just gets worse and worse. He's buildin' up to killin' me, I know it. So I decided I might as well run. If I get killed on the run, that's no worse than gettin' starved or whipped to death."

Jefferson said, "What about the shackle there? That means you've tried to run off before."

Lem said, "No, sir, I've never tried to run before. That's the God's truth. Four weeks ago, my master told the overseer, he said go put a shackle on Lem, shackle him to a log, he's bein' too uppity. So the overseer puts on the shackle, with the chain goin' to a log, so all day I got to drag around that log everywhere I go and still do all the work my master says for me to do. Just to make it so I can't get my work done, so he can beat me."

Jefferson said, "What happened to the log? Did you break the chain?"

Lem replied, "No, sir, that chain was old and rusty. I'm draggin' it around, and the chain just busted. So I'm afraid my master will say I busted it on purpose, but I didn't. So I figured I should just run, and that's what I done. I run off about three weeks ago, and now I'm here. But that shackle is rubbin' away on my leg, so my leg got all hot and fevery, and now I can't walk on it."

Jefferson asked, "Where are you from? Where's your master?"

"Down there on the Congaree. He got a big old place right on the river. His daddy died a year ago and left it all to him. Plus, all the slaves."

Jefferson said, "Look, none of this makes any sense. Why would a master try to kill a slave when you can still work? Why would he want to kill you unless you were up to something? What did you do to make him treat you like this?"

Lem paused a moment before giving his answer, "It's not what I done, Master. It's what I saw."

Jefferson said, "Well, what did you see?"

Lem looked down. "Well, I saw my master," he paused and looked over at Cat, then looked down again, "well, I never told no one this, but I saw my master, well, he was humpin' on a sheep."

Jefferson said, "What did you say?"

Lem kept looking down, "It's like I said, I saw him humpin' on a sheep. I wish I hadn't."

Jefferson felt his face start to get hot, and he knew he was blushing. He heard Cat start to laugh, and as hard as he tried to suppress it, he started to laugh, also. Only Lem was left looking sad.

Jefferson finally said, "What in God's name are you talking about?"

Lem said, "I've never told nobody this before. So my master was young, maybe your age. 'Course, he wasn't my master then. His daddy was my master. So one day, I'm out in the field hoein' the cotton, and my hoe handle breaks. So I take it over to the overseer; he says run up to the barn and get another one, quick as you can. So I go runnin' up to the barn, I go in there to get a hoe, and there's my master's son, he got a sheep pinned up against the railing, and he standin' behind it with his pants down, humpin' on it. Well, as soon as I see that, I turn around, tryin' to pretend I didn't see nothin', but he musta seen me before I got out of there. I just go back down to the field and tell the overseer I couldn't find no other hoe, so he makes me pull weeds with my hands the rest of the day. But then, that night, I seen my master's son come around, and he looks right at me and gives me a ugly look like he knows that I seen what he was doin.'"

The smiles were gone away from Jefferson's and Cat's faces as Lem continued his story. "Well, then that son starts tellin' his daddy every day that Lem is no good, we ought to sell him, he's no account, he don't do no work. But his daddy, my master, knows I work hard and don't want to sell me. So this goes on and on, the boy is comin' around and givin' me ugly looks whenever he sees me, but he can't do nothin' because he ain't my master. But then, last year, my master dies. So now that boy is my master and, like I said, ever since then, he been starvin' me or whippin' me. I know he's just buildin' himself up to kill me. So, when the chain busted, and the log came off, I ran."

Jefferson said, "Why doesn't he just sell you himself now? Then you would be gone, and he would get the money."

Lem said, "Master, I don't know. I wish he would. I'd go anywhere. All I can think is he's afraid I would tell what I saw, and word would get around. But I never ever have told what I saw, not to anyone 'til today. If you send me back, I know he's going to kill me."

Jefferson looked at things for a minute. He turned to Cat. "I promised not to tell, and I won't. But I can't come back here. What do you want me to do?"

Cat said, "He needs food. I can't get enough food for him from what we get. And it's gotta be cooked, he can't build no fire up here, or he'll be found. And he needs a file to get that shackle off his leg. And he needs some medicine for his leg."

Jefferson said, "All right, I'll get some food; and I'll get a file. I'll put them in a basket and leave them behind the shanty. As far as medicine, all I could get is some of that bag salve they put on the milk cows. Maybe that'll help his leg. But I can't do anything more than that."

Jefferson looked at Cat, "And I can't be around you until he's long gone. If he's found out or caught, it'll all be on your head, Cat." Cat nodded that she understood. Jefferson continued, "I'll go back down to the creek by myself, and I'll try to get those things and put them behind the shanty by this evening." Jefferson began heading back towards the creek.

After he was out of earshot, Lem turned to Cat and asked, "You really trust him?"

Cat looked at Jefferson's back as he walked away. She did not answer.

Jefferson made his way back to the steep bank above the creek and worked his way down and across the creek. He walked back up the footpath and went into the kitchen cabin. He found an old peck basket, what the slaves used to get their weekly peck of corn, and looked around in the kitchen. He found some leftover corn mush and some bacon, and a leftover sweet potato from the night before. He put them all down in the basket. He also grabbed a calabash for water. He carried the basket down to the mule barn. The barn was empty, Old Toby was out somewhere. He hunted around and found an old file that Toby used to sharpen the hoe blades when they got dull. He went to the small keg of balm that was kept to rub on the milk cow's udders after they were milked. He found a piece of shingle on the ground, blown off the roof sometime in a storm, and used it to scoop out some of the salve and put it in the peck basket along with the other things. He carried his basket back down the footpath. The slave children were still playing in the yard between the shanties. He took his basket to the back of Cat's shanty and laid it up against the back wall. After that, he turned and walked away, back up toward the house, forcing himself to walk along at a slow pace.

The next day, following his lessons, he left the house as he had done the day before. But instead of heading straight down toward the shanties searching for Cat, he walked toward the kitchen cabin. No one was about, so he gathered up a supply of food. He remembered the image of the runaway, the starved look on his face, the skin hanging from his bones, so he hunted around and found some extra pieces of bacon and biscuits thrown in a bucket. He realized these were the remains of his own breakfast, scraps he pushed aside that very morning. They were collected from his plate by Kee, destined to be tossed to the chickens. Well, Jefferson thought, the chickens can wait today. He gathered together his gleanings, his leftovers plus some more ash cake and sweet potato and put them all together in another basket.

He walked down the footpath, feeling conspicuous with the basket held next to him. He went to the back of Cat's shanty and found yesterday's basket sitting there, empty. He picked up the old basket, replaced it with the new one, and walked back to the house. A few of the hands were about, and they called out to him. He gave a wave and kept walking. Finally, he reached the kitchen and put down the basket. He sat down on the kitchen stool. He felt drained and realized he was wet with sweat.

He repeated his hunt for the food scraps and his nonchalant walk down to the shanties and back every day. On the 10th day, he walked around to the back of the shanty, and the basket from the day before was still there, untouched, He turned it over, and the food fell out on the ground. Ants were crawling all over the ash cake. He switched the baskets anyway. The next day, he again found the basket undisturbed, the food untouched. He decided that the runaway must have recovered, his leg strong enough to go on, heading north. So he quit gathering the food and quit his daily walks down to the shanties. He waited a few days. Nothing happened.

He avoided Cat. If he saw her, he walked the other way, and he saw that she did the same with him. He wondered how long it would take before it would be safe. Maybe after another month passed. If nothing happened, he could stop walking away from her and start talking to her again. A month should be enough. Or maybe a month and a half. Maybe longer.

He walked into the library and looked up at the shelf of his books, bought for him by his grandmother over the years. He pulled down *Ivanhoe* and opened it up on the desk. He flipped to page 100 and circled the page number with ink. Then he flipped ahead to page 160 and marked it as well. Every day he would mark a page, starting tomorrow with page 101. When he reached page 160, that would be sixty days. Sixty days should be enough to be safe. In sixty days, he could talk to Cat again, go and see her down at her shanty, and have a friend again. Sixty days would be fine.

Chapter 17—1853—36 years on the land— The aftermath

Jefferson sat in the library, working on his lessons. He was working his way through a difficult passage of Latin, something that his teacher Reverend Clark insisted that he learn. He tipped his head back and stared at the ceiling to give his eyes and brain a rest. Carrie, sitting nearby, looked up from her newspaper for a moment as Jefferson shifted position, then turned her attention back to the paper.

Jefferson, still staring upwards, reached over with his right hand and massaged his left arm, and stretched and twisted his neck, seeking to work the stiffness out of the muscles. He finished the stretch but, seeking a bit more reprieve from the Latin, he turned the chair and glanced out through the double glass doors. A tiny movement, far off, caught his eye, and he focused his gaze on it. In a few moments, he could discern a rider coming up the cart path from the main road. As the rider approached, he recognized the man on the horse. It was the sheriff. An unpleasant sensation, like a thousand hot pinpricks, spread in a wave across Jefferson's scalp and arms. He felt his throat tighten for a second.

He had run into the sheriff in town before and met him a few times with his father, but Jefferson could not remember the sheriff ever coming out to the farm, not once. He watched the sheriff ride past the house on the cart path and around the side of the house, out of Jefferson's sight. He said to Carrie, "Grandmother, I think the sheriff just rode by. What would he want?"

Carrie looked up from her newspaper again and turned to Jefferson. "Well, I don't know, Jefferson. I would guess he's looking for your father."

It was now 31 days since Jefferson quit taking the baskets of food and medicine to leave behind Cat's shanty. Thirty-one pages of *Ivanhoe*, each page number circled in ink. He knew nothing more about the runaway. He had not uttered a word to Cat. He was still turning and walking away whenever he spotted her.

A few minutes passed by, Jefferson looked down at the Latin text, still open on the desk, but the letters were just floating, unrecognizable, on the pages. As he sat, he heard the front door open and footsteps coming down the hallway. Seconds later, his father, Thomas and the sheriff appeared in the library doorway. "Mother, Jefferson, the sheriff here wants to talk to us for a few minutes. Come on in, Sheriff, and have a seat." Thomas walked into the library, followed by the sheriff. Thomas pulled out one of the side chairs and gestured to the sheriff to sit. Thomas stayed standing next to the desk.

Thomas said, "Sheriff, why don't you just tell my mother and Jefferson what you told me."

The sheriff looked over at Carrie, "Well, Mrs. Adams, I'm really sorry to barge into your home like this, but I need to talk to you all about something. They caught a runaway up in Wilkesboro a few days ago. The slave patrol up that way stumbled over him by accident, camped out in the woods. Well, they took him to the jail and started asking him who he was. He said he belonged to a master down in Richland County, way down in South Carolina. Well, of course, Mrs. Adams, they get their share of runaways up in Wilkes, same as us, but usually, it's just one of the local hands, maybe sneakin' off to see his mama. We don't hardly ever get a runaway from that far off."

The sheriff continued, "Well, the sheriff and his boys up there was talkin' to him, tryin' to get more information. I guess they was leanin' on him pretty hard. He said he came up through this area and stayed 'round about here for a while. He told 'em he couldn't walk 'cause his leg was all lame. Told 'em a slave girl found him, and she got a White boy to give him some help, bring him food, and salve for the leg. Well, Mrs. Adams, Mr. Adams, I know you all wouldn't help no runaways, but you know how it is; we gotta check everything out. So, just so I can say I asked about it, you didn't have a runaway come through here in the last couple of months or so, have you?"

Carrie looked over at the sheriff and fixed him with her gaze, "Sheriff, you know as well as anyone that we make our living from our slaves, breeding and selling. How on earth could we ever help a runaway? Why we would never sell another slave again if word got out we were behind something like that. But, to answer your question, Sheriff, no, nothing like that has happened here. Thomas, you haven't heard anything about someone helping a runaway around here have you?"

Thomas said, "No, of course not. I already told the sheriff the exact same thing. We would be out of business if we did any damn stupid thing like that. Probably run out of the county, too."

Carrie turned to Jefferson, "And Jefferson, I know that you haven't been out helping any runaway slaves, have you?"

Jefferson's throat was dry, constricted, and he knew that he appeared pale. But he steadied his voice and answered, looking directly at his grandmother, "No, of course not. Nothing like that would've happened around here. It's like you said, Grandmother, nobody would want to deal with us if they thought we were helping runaways." And then he turned to the sheriff, "I promise you, Sheriff, I've not heard anything about this. He must've been lying to the sheriff up there."

The sheriff said, "Yes, ma'am, Mrs. Adams, I knew it was a waste of my time to come out here, but it's just part of doin' my job. I hope you don't hold it against me."

Jefferson asked the sheriff, "So, Sheriff, what will happen to that runaway, does he get sent back down to South Carolina?"

The sheriff said, "Well, most times his master would have to come up here and claim him and take him back. But, no, this time, that ain't gonna happen. See, like I said, they was leanin' on him pretty hard to get him to talk. But when they said they was gonna send them back to his master, they say he just went crazy, grabbin' and throwin' things and fightin' with 'em. So, what they say happened is one of the boys with the sheriff gets all excited too, pulls out his pistol, and shoots the damn runaway, shoots him dead right in the heart. So, no, I don't guess he'll be goin' back to South Carolina. I don't reckon anybody wants to pay to ship a dead slave down to Richland County. But you can understand, if he was getting help from somebody, we gotta find out. If some folks around here start helpin' runaways, why, there'd be hell to pay. That's why I gotta make sure nothing like that was goin' on around here."

The sheriff stood up. "Like I said, Mrs. Adams, Mr. Adams, Jefferson, I'm just doin' my job here. I appreciate your time. I can go along now. Believe me; this is no fun for me, any more than it is for you folks. I'll just see myself out." The sheriff walked to the door, and then they heard his footsteps down the hall and out the front door. In a minute, they saw him riding back down the cart path toward the main road. No one spoke until he was out of sight.

Thomas turned to Jefferson, his face burning red with anger. "Damn it, Jefferson, what in hell were you thinking? How in hell could you help a runaway? We could all end up in jail. We could lose everything, you damned fool."

Jefferson said, "Father, I didn't do anything. I don't know anything about a runaway. I swear, Father, it wasn't me."

Thomas walked over and stood over Jefferson, who was still sitting in the leather desk chair. Thomas' face grew more and more flushed, his voice rising in rage. "Damn it, you filthy worthless ungrateful baby, don't lie to me. You heard what the sheriff said. A slave girl and a white boy. How many white boys do you think go around with a slave girl like that? There's no one else it could be, you stupid bastard. You're just sitting there lying to me."

Jefferson said again, looking up at Thomas, "Father, I swear to you, it wasn't me. I haven't even seen Cat hardly at all in the last two months, she's been taking care of the slave children, and I've been busy with my lessons. I swear, Father."

Thomas' face went from red to purple. His face was twisted by anger and rage. His hands formed into fists. "Damn you, you stupid, stupid baby. You worthless, stupid, damned little baby. You sit there and lie to me." Thomas began punching Jefferson in the head with his fists and continued to scream out, "You stupid fucking damned stupid baby." Jefferson ducked his head down and covered his head with his hands, trying to get some protection from his father's fists, which continued to rain down blows on Jefferson's head wherever they could.

"Thomas, stop, stop this instant," Carrie commanded from her chair. Her voice was tremulous, but the steel in it stabbed through the air like a sword.

Thomas hesitated in his attack. He threw one more hard punch at Jefferson before stopping altogether and turning toward his mother. Sweat covered his face, and his breath came in heaving gasps. He looked his mother in the face. His features, defiant at first, melted, and he looked down. He stood in front of Carrie, trembling.

"Thomas, that is inexcusable. Go sit down and get control of yourself. Jefferson, please leave the room. Go out to the kitchen. Bring back some water for your father."

Jefferson heard his grandmother's voice but couldn't make out the words, as he had drawn his arms and hands up to protect his ears. He felt the blows from his father cease, and he lifted his head just enough to look around the room. He saw his father seated in the side chair, his face still flushed in a murderous rage.

Carrie repeated her order, "Jefferson, go out to the kitchen and wash yourself off. Give us a few minutes here alone. Bring back some water for your father." Jefferson arose woodenly. He was unsteady, his head spinning, his ears ringing. He grabbed the edge of the desk for balance and held himself there for a moment. Then he moved around the side of the desk, away from his father, and started for the library door.

He walked carefully to the slave pantry, stepped cautiously down the back-door steps, and across the yard to the kitchen. He found a towel, wet it in the water bucket, and wiped his face. He pulled it away, looked at it, and saw that it was smeared with blood. He dipped it again and wiped his face, then his neck and hair. He blew his nose onto the towel, wiping away clots of blood and mucus. He grabbed a cup and filled it with water and drank thirstily, refilled it, and drank again. He blotted his face dry on the towel and ran his fingers through his hair.

He poured a cup of water and headed back to the library. When he arrived, Thomas was sitting at the big desk. He was no longer gasping, but his brow and hair were drenched with sweat, his face remained flushed, and his mouth a hard line. His eyes gazed down at the desk.

Jefferson set down the cup of water, and Thomas picked it up and sipped it but did nothing more.

Jefferson sat down in one of the side chairs, opposite Carrie. No one said a word. The mantle clock ticked.

Finally, Carrie spoke. "Thomas, speak to your son."

Thomas spoke to Jefferson without looking up, his voice barely a whisper. "I'm sorry, Jefferson, I lost my temper. Please forgive me." Thomas finally looked up at his son, and Jefferson could see his father's eyes were still ugly with hate and rage. Thomas' apology was a lie, spoken only to appease his mother.

Carrie turned to her grandson. "Jefferson, I'm not going to ask you anything more about the runaway. You've already said you had nothing to do with it. If you're telling the truth, that's fine. And if you're lying, well then, you're stuck with it. You're going to tell this lie to everyone every day from this day forward. No one can know the truth. No slip-ups, no telling it to your friends, not even someday to your wife or your children. It ends here, today, forever."

Jefferson looked back at Carrie. "Yes, ma'am," he murmured, barely above a whisper.

Carrie went on, "Jefferson, you can't be friends with Cat. You have to be her master, and she has to be your slave. She is your property, and that is all. That's what our slaves are, that's how we use them, and if you feel anything else towards them, some sense of friendship or trust, it will hurt you. It won't do you any good, and it will be worse for your slave. Now go on, leave us alone. I'll stay here with your father until he's feeling better."

Jefferson said, "Yes, Grandmother." He stood up and walked out of the room. He felt emptied. Blood, air, feelings, everything was gone from him, drained away.

Two days later, he was in the barn. Old Toby had just finished putting the saddle on the mare so Jefferson could ride into town and have his lessons with Reverend Clark. Without a word, Toby slipped out of the barn, leaving Jefferson alone in the dim light. As he stood beside the mare, getting ready to swing himself up into the saddle, Cat ducked in through the open barn door and quickly moved into the shadows. He looked up at her and smiled. "Cat," he called out. Then he saw her face. The eyes were not stony now. They were like his father's eyes, burning and filled with hate.

Cat cast her rage-filled eyes on his. "You told."

Jefferson said, "What? Told what?"

Cat said, "You told them about Lem, and they caught him up north, and they shot him and killed him. You swore not to tell."

"Cat, I did not tell anyone about Lem. I just found out about it two days ago when the sheriff was here. And I didn't tell him anything. I swear to you I didn't tell anybody about Lem. And I didn't tell the sheriff about you."

"Well, how did they find out?"

"The sheriff said the patrol up in Wilkes County found him in the woods. They couldn't believe he made it that far unless someone was helping him. When they told him he was going back to his master, he went crazy, and someone shot him," said Jefferson.

Cat's eyes bored into his. "I think you're lyin' to me." Jefferson returned her gaze.

"Cat, I lied to the sheriff, I lied to my father, and I lied to my grandmother about it. But I'm not lying to you now. I didn't tell. But it doesn't matter. My grandmother told me we can't be friends anymore. I got to start being the master, she says. And masters don't have slaves for friends."

Cat looked at him for another long moment. Without another word, she darted out of the barn and ran back towards the shanties.

Jefferson moved to the open barn door and watched as Cat ran away. He wanted to run after her, plead with her, beg her to believe that he didn't tell anyone about Lem. That he wasn't to blame for Lem's death, his murder.

He couldn't. It wouldn't be safe. He couldn't talk to her anymore, not ever, not about Lem, not about anything. It was like his grandmother said, back in the library; the lie he told was the truth now. There was no runaway slave, no Lem. There never was. There was no going back.

He watched Cat as she ran down the footpath until she disappeared among the shanties. He mounted up onto the mare and headed for town to have his lesson.

Chapter 18—1856—39 years on the land— Kee remembers

Kee tapped on the door to the library and nudged it open. Missus Carrie was there, sitting in her padded chair, the same as she did day after day. Carrie looked up and gave Kee a slight nod, a tiny tip of her head, granting Kee permission to enter. Kee carried with her, arranged on a pewter tray, a small blue and white china teapot filled with hot water, a cup and saucer, and a tea ball. She set it down softly on the tray table next to Carrie.

Kee saw that Missus Carrie looked at her blankly now. Years before, when Kee was taken out of the fields and moved up to the house to cook and clean for the White people, Missus Carrie would have smiled at her. It would have been just a crooked half-smile, but at least it was something. Now, more times than not, there was nothing, not a flicker, certainly not a word.

Kee recited her words, the same words, or something close to them; she knew by heart from long use. "Missus Carrie, I'm going to go back to the kitchen and start getting dinner ready for Master Thomas and Master Jefferson, and you. Is there anything else I can get you right now, Missus Carrie?"

Carrie looked up from her newspaper, and this time, Kee was surprised to see a spark, a flicker of a smile cross past in Missus Carrie's eyes. "No, Kee, thank you so much. I think I'm fine for the time being." Missus Carrie looked down again.

Kee left the room and stepped softly down the hall and around to the back door, down the steps, and crossed the yard to the kitchen. As soon as she got to the kitchen, she pulled out the stool and sat down heavily. She sat, breathing hard, waiting for the smothery feeling to settle. She pulled up her long skirt and apron, both made of coarse-woven slave cloth, and looked down at her swollen feet, the skin tight like it was ready to split open. She saw, again, that it was getting worse. Before, a few months back, she would get up in the morning, and her ankles would be down, mostly. Now, even after a night's rest, her legs would still be puffed up. And she was always smothery. Just walking up from the shanties to the kitchen, she would have to stop to rest.

She knew something was wrong with her, badly wrong, but she would not tell Missus Carrie about it. If she told Missus Carrie about her ankles and her smothery breathing, she would have to sit and talk and answer her questions. And the fear, which Kee kept pushed down, might show. When Missus Carrie saw the fear, she would want to know why what was wrong. Then Kee would have to lie. How could she tell Missus Carrie that it was her, Missus Carrie herself, who filled her heart with a horrible dread.

She didn't remember how many years had passed, she lost track, but she remembered the day her life was smashed into pieces. She remembered Toby pulling the wagon up in front of the house, and her mother Emma and her Aunt Sarah and the children, her light-skinned sisters and brother and cousins, getting loaded onto it. She remembered Master Thomas and little Master Jefferson taking their seats in front, next to Toby, and the wagon pulling away.

That was the last time Kee ever saw her mother. The last time she got to embrace her mother, the last time her mother held her close to her, kissed and caressed her face. The last time she saw the others, the last time she laughed with them and shared her heart with them. They were all taken.

Missus Carrie and Master Thomas lied to all of them and tried to pretend the Black people were going on the trip to Richmond just to help with Master Jefferson, and they would all be coming back together. But Emma knew it was a lie. Sarah knew. They all knew the truth. Only Master Thomas and Master Jefferson were coming back. The slaves would be gone, sold off, or bartered away. It didn't matter. They were not coming back to the farm, not ever.

Emma, her mother, told her to guard her heart. Fill it up every day with faith, with Jesus, Emma told her over and over as she held Kee and the other children and grandchildren close to her. Guard your heart against fear because once fear entered it would never leave. It would stay and grow and bear seeds. But the seeds would not be good. They would be evil seeds. Seeds of despair. Seeds of hate.

Kee tried to do as her mother said, to guard herself. But from the start, the little grains, the little seeds, were there in her heart all the time. And after a few years, they began to grow, and she could not stop them. She could not chop them down or pull them out by the roots like she would a weed out in the garden. So the seeds grew, and they wanted to feed on Kee herself. They began by taking away her peace, making her nervous and jumpy. After a while, she saw herself getting more and more short-tempered and quick to anger with the children and even with Brock. Now they were taking her very strength, eating away at her flesh and consuming her. But she kept it hidden from Missus Carrie and Master Thomas.

Now, sitting in the kitchen, her feet up, she tried to gather her strength for the day ahead.

She heard the sound of horses down on the road. She looked down around the edge of the house, towards the road, and saw a wagon turning off the road onto the cart path. She recognized the wagon, and suddenly the fear, the deadly dread she kept pushed down and held back, burst its bonds, and reared up into her mind. She had seen this wagon, or a wagon like it, come to the house before. It meant only one thing. Missus Carrie and Master Thomas were going to be trading. Someone was going to be sold.

The wagon pulled up in the yard in front of the front steps, and the wagon's driver jumped down. He walked around and checked on the pair of horses pulling the wagon.

Kee heard the sound of more horses coming up from the other direction. She looked over and saw Master Thomas and Master Jefferson on horseback, walking their horses up the footpath from the fields. Walking in front of the two White men were three Black people. And she felt relief flow over her since she saw that none of the three were her children or cousins or nieces or nephews. The three hands were from different families. She knew all three of them, knew them since they were born. She worked with them, laughed with their parents, and grieved with their parents when someone passed. But they were not blood. So the fear retreated just a bit, and she felt a surge of hope that she might not lose one of her own, at least not that day.

As the little group came towards the house, Kee saw Jefferson turn his horse toward her and come walking up. As he came closer, he called out to her, "Kee, Father asks for you to bring the water bucket and some cups around the front of the house. We have a visitor, and he may be thirsty."

"Yes, sir, Master Jefferson, I'll do that quick," Kee answered back. Jefferson turned his horse and rode back to rejoin the group.

Kee grabbed the water bucket and the calabash. And she grabbed a bunch of cups and collected them all in one hand, picking up the water bucket with the other. She began slowly to walk around towards the front of the house. If she went slowly, she could do things without getting too smothery.

When she got around to the front of the house, Thomas and Jefferson were dismounted. Thomas was speaking to the wagon driver. Kee went ahead and scooped up water in the calabash and poured it into the cup, and walked over to the stranger, keeping her eyes averted, and offered the handle of the cup.

Thomas said, "Have a cup of water, Mr. Jones, you might be thirsty," and Mr. Jones took the cup of water offered and took a long drink. Thomas turned to Kee and said, "Kee, Jefferson and I would like a cup."

Kee turned wordlessly, and scooped up water into two more cups and handed them to Thomas and Jefferson. And she said, "Master Thomas, you mind if I give the hands some water, they been workin' hard, and it's warm today."

Thomas nodded absently, and said, "Yes, Kee, that's fine." She scooped up water in another cup and handed it to one of the hands, who drank and passed it on. And when it was empty, Kee filled the cup for them again.

Thomas said, "Kee, don't go back to the kitchen yet. We might need to have you go fetch something from the house."

Kee said, "Yes, sir, Master Thomas." She went over and stood next to the three field hands. She looked over at the slave trader. The trader was a White man but weather-beaten, and his skin was darkened from the sun. His clothes were raggedy and dirty, stained from long wear. A thick beard, stained brown with tobacco drippings, hung from his chin. His mouth was open, and Kee saw that his lips were reddened and chapped, and he was continually running his tongue along the scabbed-over spots.

Mr. Jones finished his cup of water, tossed the tin cup onto the ground, and looked over where the four Black people stood. "You wantin' to sell these four, Mr. Adams?"

Thomas replied, "No, just the three field hands. We want to keep our house girl."

Jones said, "Alright, just the three. Well, have them all slip off the shirts so I can look them over."

Thomas said to the three hands, "You heard him; go on. Slip off your shirts, and let Mr. Jones here look you over. Go on, hurry now."

The three hands did as they were told. Jones walked slowly over to the first, Elijah, who was 17 years old or maybe 18. Jones walked around him, checking on his skin. He felt around on the muscles of the neck and shoulders and arms, felt the hands and the wrists, and looked at the palms to see what kind of calluses were present. Kee could see Jones' intent dark eyes, taking in Elijah, assessing his value.

Finished with Elijah, he moved to the second hand, Lewis, a 19-year-old, and went through the same examination. He saw some healed scars on Lewis's back.

"This boy has been whipped. I can see that there on his back. What did he do, run away?" asked Jones.

Thomas said, "Oh, about four years ago, Lewis thought he was in love with a girl at a place a couple miles from here. He was slipping off at night to see her. But the slave patrol grabbed him one night, and one of those boys gave them a pretty good beating before they brought him back here. We've not had any trouble out of him since then. Ain't that right, Lewis?"

Lewis said, "Yes, sir, Master Thomas, I learned my lesson about that. I ain't gonna be runnin' off no more, no, sir. But Master Thomas, I sure would like to stay here with my Mama and Pa. Please, Master, can you not sell me. I sure would like to stay here with you and Master Jefferson."

Thomas replied, "No, Lewis, we've already decided about that. Now, Lewis, come on, promise Mr. Jones here that you ain't going to run. Say it."

Lewis looked down and said softly, "Yes, sir, Master Thomas. I promise." Kee could see there were tears in his eyes. But still, he wasn't her blood.

Jones turned his attention to the last hand, whose name was Annie, 18 years old. She stood there, shirtless, the sun shining on her brown skin. Jones walked around her, and his face broke out in a broad smile. The rough, scabbed areas along his bottom lip broke open, forced apart by his grin, and began to ooze blood. He walked behind her and did as he had done with the others, feeling the muscles in her neck and shoulders, checking out her skin. But unlike with the boys, he walked around in front of her and rubbed both of his hands across her bare breasts. He let his hands linger there as drops of blood trickled from his lip down into his beard.

After a moment, as Jones let his hands linger, Thomas became impatient and said, "Well, Mr. Jones, what do you say?"

Jones straightened himself up, dropping his hands down, and turned around to face Thomas.

"Well, Mr. Adams, they all look fine. You ain't never sold me a bad slave before. I imagine they would fetch a fair price. I reckon, for the three of them, I could give you two thousand."

Anger flashed across Thomas' face. "That sounds low, Mr. Jones. The newspapers are saying prime hands like these are getting sold down in Natchez for eleven hundred apiece. I think you can do better than two thousand for the three of them."

Jones smiled back at Thomas, a harder smile now. Behind the smile, his eyes were unyielding. "Yes, sir, Mr. Adams, that's for sure, but before they can get sold in Natchez, they gotta get there. We gotta hike 'em over the mountains. Some of these hands get away from home, even one that's always been good, and suddenly they turn rabbit and decide they gonna run. So I gotta take that into account. Now, for my part, I just take them over the mountains and down to Nashville. I sell what I got to one of the big boys trading there, and I buy me a big bunch of hogs. I drive my hogs back over the mountain and sell them in Spartanburg. That way, I make money on both ends. But, Mr. Adams, I got a good idea what they're going to pay me in Nashville for what I bring in, and it ain't going to be no eleven hundred per hand. So the best I can do today is two thousand for the three."

Thomas looked at Jones. Jones looked back with the same frozen smile and hard eyes. Thomas scowled in anger but said, "Oh, what the hell, that's fine, two thousand for the three. Get 'em loaded up in your wagon, and you can come in the house, and we'll settle up. I've gotta get something better to drink than this damn water."

Jones kept smiling and nodded, "That's fine, Mr. Adams, just fine. I always knew you was a sensible fellow."

Thomas spoke to the three hands, "Now, Mr. Jones is going to be your master. You be good and obey him just like you've done for us. I know you'll all end up with good masters down south. Just obey him and don't cause trouble for him."

Jones said, "All right, you three, get around to the back here. Get on in." The three hands moved around to the back of the wagon and climbed in. In the wagon were two benches built along the sides, facing each other. There were two iron rings secured to the floor of the wagon with heavy iron bolts. Jones opened a box, pulled out three sets of iron shackles, and put a set around the ankles of each one of the hands and secured them. He ran a chain through the rings and the shackles and secured the chain. When he was finished, all three hands were made fast in their seats in the back of the wagon.

Thomas said, "Mr. Jones, come on in the house. I want to settle this up. Kee, you can go on back to the kitchen now. Jefferson, you come with us." And the three White people started up the steps into the house.

Kee looked at the three figures in the back of the wagon. Their eyes were down, and despair covered their faces. She walked over to the wagon and said softly, "I'll let your folks know what happened to you. I sure am sorry." And she refilled the water cup for them, which they drank and passed and handed back so Kee could take it back to the kitchen.

Kee saw there was nothing more she could do for them, so she gathered up the cups, the calabash, and the bucket of water. She headed slowly back to the kitchen to cool off and get out of the sun, and begin to work on dinner. And she felt in her heart sorrow for the three hands, hatred for the three White men, and, alongside all that, a shadow of shame, of guilt. Guilt because she also felt relief, even a little touch of rejoicing, that none of hers were sold. Brock, her children, cousins, nieces and nephews were all safe for now.

Later in the day, the sun was beginning to sink, the wagon and the three Black people long departed. Kee labored on in the kitchen, cleaning up after dinner and starting to get things ready for supper. The sound of running footsteps came to her from outside, and she turned toward the door just as Cat appeared there. Kee saw the pain on her face, and there were tears in her eyes. She cried out as she ran into her mother's arms. "Ma, what happened? They sayin' that Elijah got sold away."

Kee spoke softly as she held Cat, caressing her. "Yes, baby girl, Elijah and Lewis, and Annie. That ugly trader Jones, he showed up before dinner, come with his wagon, and Master Thomas sold them, all three. I was standin' right there. I'm sorry, baby girl. I been seein' you an' Elijah havin' looks with each other, but all three of them is gone already."

Cat sobbed and shook and put her face on her mother's shoulder. Kee hugged her daughter close to her.

After a time, Cat said, "But Mama, how could Missus Carrie and Master Thomas sell them? Even their folks didn't know, none of 'em, they didn't even get to say goodbye."

Kee kept holding Cat against her chest, but she felt the seeds, the hate seeds, growing, pushing their way into her heart. "You know how, Baby girl. They just do it. They got the cow hide, the guns, and the chains. They got the patrollers and the sheriffs and the preachers. They got all that, and we got nothin'. And that means they can do to us whatever they want."

"But Mama, why? What did we ever do to make them hate us?"

Kee pushed her daughter away from her and looked her in the eyes. Cat's eyes were red from crying. Kee's eyes became hard. "No, Cat, they don't hate us. They don't even bother to hate us. They don't even think about us, at least not like that. We're just like a cow or a pig. Just somethin' they can trade. Even Master Jefferson. I suckled him right next to you. I can see it in his eyes. He's changin' over to being like that. I reckon they gotta feel that way, or else they couldn't be doin' this to us no more."

Cat, eyes red and lips still trembling, said nothing. Kee held her daughter to her again. She secretly rejoiced, again, that none of hers were sold. Cat, and the others, were still there, still with her. She could still embrace them, still hold them close to her heart.

Kee said finally, "I gotta go talk to Elijah's and Lewis's and Annie's folks about it. Let them know what happened. You want to come with me? If you don't, that's all right. I understand."

"Yes, mama, I'll go with you. You shouldn't have to do that by yourself."

"You're right, baby girl. I shouldn't have to. But I do."

Kee set aside her work in the kitchen, and the two began slowly walking down the footpath toward the shanties to let the families of the three sold Black people know what happened to their children.

In the library, Carrie scanned the figures, carefully written out in her hand, down the pages in the farm ledger book. She wrote in the two thousand dollars from the sale of the three hands and re-summed the balance. The bottom line was healthier now. Carrie's eyes smiled at the numbers. She was not religious, never had been, but she couldn't help feeling a sense of gratitude, of thankfulness, for what she saw. The price of cotton was up and rising, and that pulled up slave prices along with it. The bet they made all those years ago, she and George, to raise slaves, to breed them and sell them, appeared to be paying off. They would not need to beg her family for more money. Stuffy, arrogant brother Frederick, her stupid, shallow sisters, the whole damn lot of them up in Richmond, could all go to hell.

Chapter 19—1857—40 years on the land— Jefferson at Chapel Hill

J efferson hunched himself over the small cramped desk, squinting to see the page before him, illuminated by the dim light of a single candle. He listened to the icy rain and sleet beating against the small window of his room. Earlier in the week, the warm sun of autumn had been shining brightly. The maple and oak trees of the campus were putting on their display of brilliant reds, oranges, and yellows, the sun shining down through the leaves to create glowing walkways across the University. And now, only two days later, winter was bearing down.

He endeavored to focus all of his attention on the text that lay before him and ignore the pain, the tightening of the muscles in the left side of his neck. Jefferson lived with the tight pain in his neck all of his life. He remembered hearing the sorrowful story so many times about how he came into the world in a tumult of pain. His poor mother, her strength used up after days and nights of agony, could not finish her task. The doctor, everyone said, stepped in and, with hands bare, ripped Jefferson from his poor mother's womb, causing the crippling of his arm. How his poor mother, delirious and burning up with fever, died when he was only three days old. How the doctor said that everything would be fine when it wasn't, nothing was fine, and Jefferson was left with a weak crippled left arm. And without a mother.

All his life, his arm was weak, the elbow and hand floppy. If he strained too hard with it, or if he didn't get enough rest, the whole arm from his neck down to his fingers would knot up, the muscles painfully locking in upon themselves. When he was still at home, he would go find Kee and get her to rub on liniment. She would push her fingers down, deep down into the muscles, to unlock them, to work away the knots.

But on the farm, when he was out of doors every day, the painful locking might only occur every month or two. Now, three months into his first semester at Chapel Hill, he was contending with the pain nearly every day. The long hours of sitting and reading, hunched at his desk, staring at tiny text hour after hour, fed the fire of pain like never before. Two or three times a day, he would be forced to get up, stretching and bending and kneading the muscles, seeking some ease. About once a week the pain would get unbearable. He would have to go down to the kitchen, find the slave girl, Lily, and have her try to press her fingers down into the muscles to loosen the knots. But she could never hit the points of pain, down deep in the muscles. Not like Kee always could do, back on the farm, pressing deep with her strong hands.

The pain in his shoulder and arm was not the worst part of his three months at University. The worst part, far worse than the physical pain, was his longing for home. He was homesick. Every day.

He missed his grandmother, so fragile and so badly hobbled from the rheumatism but still able to speak to him with insight and wisdom, showing that the strength lost from her body still lived in her heart.

He missed his father, which he found shocking. His father, always so full of anger and profanity, was the one person whose presence Jefferson most wanted to escape. Yet Jefferson found himself missing even him, missing the rides across the farm fields, looking over the crops, assessing the work of the slaves.

He missed Kee, her years of labor up in the house and the kitchen, after Kee's mother was sent off to Richmond to be sold back when Jefferson was little. So many times, he heard how Kee nursed him when he was a baby, how he and Cat were suckled together, side by side, after his mother Felicia died.

He was missing Brock. Looking from a distance, he came to recognize that Brock was the one running the farm, not his father. Brock planned everything out, the plowing, the sowing, the gathering in. Jefferson recalled the crisscross of scars covering Brock's back, a maze of white and purple streaks, hard and cold to the touch. He missed how Brock's eyes, most often hard and dark, would soften and dance when he was with Kee and their children.

Most of all, he was missing Cat. He had been missing her for years, ever since Lem, since that last time when they spoke in the barn. But now, after three months gone by, he was missing her with a hard aching in his heart. He had no idea what Cat thought of him if she still believed he told the sheriff about Lem, breaking the oath he swore to her to keep. He wondered what work she was doing now—in the fields, the kitchen, or the house. He wondered if she was married, maybe even starting a family with one of the Black men on the farm.

He longed for the land, for the smell of the grass, the green of the fields, the sound of the creek, the fragrance in spring of leaves and wildflowers mixing together. And the beauty of the mountains, the ridges following ridges all the way up to the Blue Ridge, silhouetted against the sky. He knew other places in the South possessed all of the same sights and smells. The grass was just as green, and the dogwoods and the red buds bloomed in just as much glory everywhere. But he still longed to drink the water and breathe the air and hug the people, the ones on his land, his home.

His grandmother gave him advice before he began his first trip to Chapel Hill. "Jefferson, I know you'll excel in your studies. I'm not a bit worried about you failing there. But, Jefferson, make sure to make friends. Five or ten years from now, no one will know or care what your marks were. But 10 years or 20 years or 30 years from now, the friends that you make at University will still be with you and will still open doors for you."

She continued, "A lot of those boys will be from plantation families from Charleston or Savannah, families that own 10 times or 100 times more than we do. And some of them will want to show it off. They may even rub your face in it a little. Just give them a chance, Jefferson, don't judge them until you've given them a chance."

His father added, "And if one of those rich planter boys has got a little sister you could get ahold of, well, damn, Son, you could be set for life."

Yet here he was, three months into his first semester, spending Saturday night in his tiny cramped boarding house room, studying Latin. Feeling lonely and alone.

He heard footsteps outside his door, in the hallway, which surprised him, but just for a moment. The other boys taking rooms at the boardinghouse were indeed much wealthier than him and had a lot more money to spend. On most Saturday nights, they were roaming about, seeking liquor and love. Sometimes one of the group might run through his money too soon and come back to the house to refill his pockets before venturing back out.

But there was a knock on his door. Before Jefferson could answer, the door was shoved open, banging against its hinges. Jefferson looked up, startled, and saw Pinckney standing there, with Patrick and Teddy behind him in the hall. They barged into his room. Pinckney came up to Jefferson, who was still in his chair, and stood over him while Patrick plopped himself heavily on Jefferson's bed.

Pinckney spoke to the room, "Jeff, how about you put that damn book down and come out with us. We're gonna go to a place I know and take a few sips. I'm paying."

Jefferson felt himself tensing up inside. He realized he should go along, try to be sociable, and try to make friends like his grandmother urged him to do. But he didn't want to, not tonight. So he stared up at the hulking form of Pinkney looming over him and said, "Nah, I have to finish this little bit of work here, and then I'll probably go to bed soon. I really need to be up early tomorrow."

Pinckney reached down, slipped his hand under the cover of the Latin text, flipped it closed with a slam, grabbed the pen out of Jefferson's hand, and tossed it beside the text.

"Jeff, damn it, you gotta get out of this shitty room. You gotta quit all this damn studying all the time. Now come on, we're going to just have a drink or two, and you can come back and get all cozy in bed afterward. Like I said, I'm buying, so you got no reason to say no. Ain't that right, Teddy?"

"Damn right," said Teddy, his words coming out slurred. Jefferson saw Teddy's face was flushed, and he swayed as he sat on the bed.

Pinckney reached over and grabbed Jefferson by the arm, "Come on, Jeff, we got plans. We need you to come along with us. Don't worry; you can still go to church tomorrow, just one or two drinks." He pulled up on Jefferson's arm and said, "Come on, get your jacket and your hat. We're not taking any damn excuses." Pinckney grabbed Jefferson's coat and hat from the peg near the door, stuck the hat on his head, draped the coat over his shoulders, and yanked Jefferson to his feet, dragging him to the door. "Come on, Jeff, you gotta get your ass out of this damn room."

Jefferson opened his mouth and began to speak again, words of protest, but he could see the others were not listening, didn't care what he said, not one bit. He was going with them. The three other boys were bigger and stronger and were already mostly drunk. As Pinckney moved him out through the door into the hallway, Patrick stood up and glanced over at the Latin notes Jefferson had been taking. "Damn, what is all this?" he slurred as he turned toward the door.

The four left the boarding house and headed onto the street. Pinckney led the way. "Saturday night!" screamed Patrick, and Teddy screamed back, "Saturday night!"

Pinckney turned to the others, "Now boys, you'll scare poor old Jeff here. We're just going to have a couple of drinks. After that, he can come back and go to bed. Tomorrow he can go to church and pray for our poor damned lost souls."

They headed out into the street, Jefferson and the three bigger boys laughing and cursing, cutting a wide path down the street. The rain and sleet had stopped, but the wind was blowing hard and cold now.

They walked along into the wind, then turned down a side street, then down an alley then to a doorway where Pinckney stopped. Pinckney said, "What do ya' think, boys? Ya' getting thirsty?"

Jefferson looked through the narrow doorway into a dim interior. He could smell tobacco and liquor and sweat and urine. His three companions turned in, grabbing at his clothes to keep him in the middle of the pack. Inside there were three or four rough-hewn rickety tables with chairs scattered about. Pinckney sat down at one of the tables and called out to a man sitting in the corner, "Gus, bring us a bottle and four glasses, and keep it coming."

In a moment, Gus brought a glass flask and the four glasses. Pinckney sat a glass in front of each of them and grabbed the bottle, pulled out the stopper, and poured a generous measure into Jefferson's glass. "Now, Jeff, I know you're new to this, so don't try to keep up with us. But I want to see that liquor goin' down your damn throat. Come on, Jeff, let's see you kill that."

Jefferson picked up the glass and sipped. The burning liquor hit his throat, and he gagged and leaned forward and coughed and sputtered. The other three boys laughed. "Damn, Jeff," said Patrick, "that ain't the way to drink liquor. You got to drink liquor same way you hump a whore. Just close your eyes and let the liquor do all the work. Come on, brother, throw it back there."

Jefferson lifted the glass and took a larger drink, more prepared now for the burning of the liquor. He swallowed hard, forcing the mouthful of liquor down his throat, feeling the heat move down his chest into his stomach.

"That was better, Jeff, but; Son, you got a long way to go here tonight," said Pinckney. "Come on, Son, let it hit you again."

Jefferson took another drink and felt it again, the warmth, as it moved down into his chest. He didn't gag nearly as much. He started to notice a pleasant lightness swim around his head. Without any more encouragement, he took another drink, a little bit bigger this time. Again he felt the warmth and the pleasant spinning.

Patrick said, "Damn, boy, now you're getting ahead of us there. Maybe you'll find out that this stuff ain't so evil after all."

Jefferson smiled, and he was surprised that the tightness in his left shoulder and arm seem to dissipate a bit as he took a few more sips of the liquor. In fact, he found that he could move his neck around without pain.

Suddenly, Jefferson found himself laughing at Pinckney, Patrick, and Teddy and their funny jokes. He was laughing hard, laughing from his gut, laughing like he was never able to do before with these friends, these good fellows. He was so happy they brought him along. He laughed and listened to the other three tell story after story. Stories about the girls they had been with. Black girls, White girls. It was all funny. He noticed the lightness in his head was becoming a little less pleasant. In fact, the room seemed to be spinning, or maybe it was his head spinning. But the pain in his neck and shoulder was staying away.

Pinckney called out to Gus to bring over another bottle. Now Jefferson found he was feeling a little queasy, a little sick in his stomach. The room was spinning more and more. The feeling was not at all pleasant now, not like it was after the first couple of drinks. He decided to tell his new friends that it was time to stop. He needed to go home and lay in bed. When he tried to speak, though, he was shocked at how his words all slurred together, and he could not make them come out right. Pinckney looked at him, a leering smile on his face, and said, "Now, Jeff, we got you fucking drunk. We got to get you fucked all the way."

Jefferson looked at his new friend. He had no idea what Pinckney was saying. It was time to leave, to go back to the boarding house.

Pinckney said to the other two, "Come on, boys, let's take old Jeff here over to see Maude." The other boys let out yells of agreement, "Hell yeah, let's take him to see Maude."

Jefferson frowned in confusion and said, "Maude? Who's Maude, I gotta go back to the house, and I gotta take a piss."

Patrick said, "Don't you know who Maude is? Didn't your daddy ever tell you about Maude?"

Jefferson said, "My daddy never went to college. Who's Maude?"

Pinckney laughed. "Why, hell, Jeff, Maude was here when my daddy went to school here, and Patrick's daddy and Teddy's daddy too. You never heard of Maude?"

Jefferson said, "No, I told you, who's Maude, damn it?" Jefferson laughed at his own cursing. He had never heard his own voice cursing before, not out loud, and it seemed profoundly funny.

Pinckney said, "Well, Maude turns boys into men. So Jeff, tonight you're gonna become a man."

Jefferson began to register what his friends were talking about, and he wanted to protest, but his tongue refused to follow the commands coming from his brain. He could only utter a plaintive "NOOO" as the three boys stood up and grabbed Jefferson beneath his arms, lifted him, and dragged him towards the door.

Outside the door, Jefferson said, "Wait, I gotta take a piss," and laughed anew at the sound of the words he heard coming out of his mouth.

"Good idea," said Pinckney, and all four of them paused, grabbing at their crotches, loosening their pants as they turned towards the wall and let loose with streams of urine. Jefferson felt little drops of urine bombarding his pant legs, and that seemed funny too. He had to focus on his balance and not let himself sway too far to the right or left as he aimed his stream against the wall. He heard Pinckney say, "Damn it, Teddy, you're pissin' on my boots. Piss on your own damn boots." And that was the funniest thing yet.

One by one, the four boys finished and hitched up their pants. Pinckney said, "Come on, fellows, let's go see if Maude's busy tonight." The three bigger boys surrounded Jefferson, and they moved as a group, swaying and cursing, down the alley. They staggered along, turning left down a smaller alley. Jefferson was now feeling sicker and sicker, his stomach burning and turning over. The lightness in his head was gone now, replaced by a violent spinning that would not go away. Finally, they pulled up in front of a cellar door, and Pinckney banged on the door with his fists. "Maude, hey Maude, come on, we got a new customer here for you."

He continued to bang and call for Maude, the noise reverberating in Jefferson's ears until finally a scraping sound issued from behind the door, and the door swung open. A massive black woman, a head taller than Jefferson, stood in the door frame. She was wearing an old shift, cut of slave cloth. Her hair was streaked with grey. "I've done finished my entertainin' for tonight, Master Pinckney. I've already got in bed. I gotta get up early tomorrow to help my Missus before church," the woman said.

Pinckney stuck his foot against the doorframe, "Now, Maude, I already paid your master, and this will just take a few minutes. We got our friend Jefferson here. We promised him a good time tonight. Tell you what, Maude, you show Jefferson here a good time, and all three of us will each pay you a dollar; that's three dollars. Come on, Maude, let us in."

In the darkness of the alley, they couldn't see Maude's face, but she stepped aside and let the four boys come into her small room. Jefferson heard the sound of a heavy wooden plank falling over and Patrick saying, "Dammit, Maude, what's that board doing there? You got a candle, Maude. I got a match here; let me light that candle." Patrick struck a match and lit the small stump of a candle that Maude held out to him.

Maude motioned to the heavy plank laying on the floor. "I use that to keep my door shut up tight at night, Master Patrick." Patrick put his boot on the plank and shoved it into the corner.

In the dim candlelight, Jefferson saw that the room was bare, except only a low bed against the far wall, plus a small table with a washbasin. An old broken chair was set in the corner, heaped with dirty aprons.

"All right, Master Pinckney. You all here. What you want from old Maude tonight?"

The three bigger boys pushed Jefferson up to the front of the group, and Pinckney said, "This here's Jefferson. He comes from way out west, pretty near the end of the world. We told him you'd make sure he had a good time tonight."

Maude looked at Jefferson, "This boy don't look too good. What y'all been doin' to him tonight? What's wrong with your arm, Master?"

Jefferson looked down at his left arm. "It's from when I was born."

Maude looked around at the group, "Alright, Master Pinckney, I'll do him, but I can't do all four of you tonight. I already worked a full day and a full night. You boys help him get ready."

Pinckney replied, "All right, Maude, now you're talking. Come on, fellas, let's help our friend Jefferson here." All three of them began pulling off Jefferson's clothes and picked him up, and carried him over to Maude's bed. They dropped him down and pulled off his boots and pants. Jefferson lay on the bed naked. Meanwhile, Maude had slipped off her nightgown, throwing it over the rickety chair in the corner. She came up to the bed and stood over him. Jefferson looked up at the towering figure of the black woman, her two pendulous breasts hanging down over her chest. He saw, extending over the expanse of her belly, a crisscross pattern of stretch marks. At the same time, Maude looked down at him appraisingly.

"Huh, you don't look too excited yet, Master; you look kind of flat. That's alright, though. Old Maude'll get you up quick enough."

The three boys stretched Jefferson out supine on the bed, laughing and cursing, and Maude came over and mounted him. "Now, don't worry, Master, just let old Maude do all the work," she said, rocking back and forth rhythmically.

Jefferson cried out weakly, "No, no," but he was being compressed by Maude's weight, her stomach pressing on his and making it difficult for him to breathe. With each of her rocking motions back and forth, her breasts inched their way up toward his neck and began pressing on his throat. He began to feel panicky. But, as Maude kept rocking, he felt himself start to become aroused. His left arm was entrapped up against his side, and now as the numbing effect of the liquor abated, the pain was returning. He was helpless, as he could not stretch out his arm, he could only lay there absorbing the worsening pain and gasping to catch shallow breaths.

His perception of time was suspended. He vaguely heard his three friends laughing, yelling out in the background, but the words were unintelligible, more akin to animals squealing at him. His vision began to dim.

Despite all the pain, the climax came quickly. Maude gave a couple more thrusts and said, "I think he's done, Master Pinckney." Quickly she rolled off of him, stood up and grabbed a rag from the rickety chair and wiped between her legs, and began putting her nightgown back on.

Jefferson's vision began to clear as he gasped, desperately sucking air into his lungs. He felt his panic begin to wane. Pinckney and Patrick came over, looming over him and grabbing Jefferson's arms and shoulders, pulling him up into a sitting position on the bed. Jefferson screamed out as Patrick pulled on his left arm, the pain burning and throbbing as bad as ever. Patrick said, "Oh, sorry, Jeff, forgot about your arm, but, damn boy, that was something to watch. You're one of us now."

Jefferson sat on the edge of the bed, still naked. His throat began to constrict, and he realized he was going to vomit. He leaned over the edge of the bed and puked on the floor. He gagged repeatedly, but only a small pool of yellow-stained vomit spilled out onto the floor. Maude said, "Oh, Master Pinckney, look at that mess you leavin' for poor old Maude." And she took the rag she had just used to wipe herself and threw it on top of the puddle of vomit.

Pinckney said, "Sorry, Maude, sorry. Come on, Jefferson, get your clothes on. We gotta get back to the house before it gets locked up." And the three boys grabbed Jefferson's clothes and got him dressed again as quickly and roughly as they had stripped him before. They picked Jefferson up and started propelling towards the door and out into the alley.

Maude called after them, "Master Pinckney, what about my three dollars? You told me three dollars."

Pinckney replied, "Yeah, Maude, I'll bring it back to you tomorrow. Thanks, Maude, you were great as always. Nobody takes care of us boys like you do, Maude." And the four boys headed down the alley.

They heard the door close behind them, and Maude put the heavy plank against the door as a barricade. And as they headed away, they heard Maude utter, expressively, "Shit! Shit, shit, shit! Shit!" Laughing and cursing, they headed back towards the boardinghouse.

They got back to the house and found that the door was not yet locked, so they entered, dragging and carrying Jefferson up the stairs to his room, and tossed him heavily on his bed, still dressed in his clothes. Pinckney said, "Jefferson, you just sleep this off. You have sweet dreams. Come on, boys, let's leave him be. He'll be fine. Damn, that was something. I ain't never seen anyone who can hump like Maude."

Jefferson lay crumpled on his bed, awash in misery. The bed was spinning, his head pulsating in pain. His mouth was parched, and the pain in his arm was scorching. He managed to sit up and grasp the pitcher of water off the table next to his bed and pour a glass. Carefully he set down the pitcher. He picked up the glass with both hands and drank it down quickly. He repeated the process, drinking quickly. Finally, he fell back on the bed, drifting into a fitful twilight between sleep and wakefulness.

He aroused slowly into wakefulness in the morning. The restless sleep had not purged away his pain. In fact, he felt even worse than the night before. His throat felt withered, his tongue glued to his palate. His head was throbbing and pounding, his neck and arm searing, and his bladder bursting. He fumbled around, searching on the floor, finally finding the chamber pot, and, with difficulty, was able to open his pants and aim the stream of urine into the pot. He touched the crusted, dried semen on his pubic hair, and a wave of shame and revulsion came over him. Then the awful, disgusting smell of his urine, wafting up from the chamber pot, hit his face. He quickly finished and put the chamber pot in the corner of his room and covered it with a spare blanket. He gulped down another 2 cups of water and lay back down on the bed, letting pain, shame, and disgust roll over him. He dozed back off.

He was awakened again by a knock on the door. The door swung open, and Pinckney stuck his head in just like the night before. This time, though, it was Pinckney alone.

"Hey, Jeff, I just wanted to check on you, make sure you were alright. Damn, that was a hell of a bash last night."

Jefferson sat up on the edge of the bed, looked down, and said nothing. But he could feel a seething anger building.

Pinckney waited for Jefferson to reply, but when Jefferson remained silent, he continued, "Anyway, Jeff, I just wanted to be sure you were alright. You looked a little rough last night when we got back here, but looks like you're doing fine this morning."

Jefferson looked up and said, "You damned son of a bitch."

"Hey now, Jeff, that's not called for. We didn't do nothing wrong. That was all just some fun. You're not gonna go to hell for one night of fun."

"You damned son of a bitch."

"Jeff, I didn't know you'd never drank or messed around like that before. Hell, I figured, growing up on a farm with all them slaves, you messed with bunches of the Black girls. I mess with the Black girls in our plantation, my brothers all mess with them, and my daddy messes with them. Hell, I bet your daddy messes with them too. Ain't you got any light slaves running around on your farm? Where the hell you think they came from?"

Jefferson said nothing and just sat there looking at Pinckney's feet, his face contorted with anger.

Pinckney continued, "Alright, Jeff, I'll just leave you alone, but if you ask me, we did you a big favor last night. Looked to me like you was enjoying yourself plenty. So just get off your big horse. You ain't any holier than any of the rest of us."

"You damned son of a bitch, get out of my room."

Pinckney turned and stomped out, slamming the door closed behind him

Jefferson sat there a few minutes more. He reached his hand down into the water pitcher. There was still a little bit of water left in the bottom. He pulled out his hand and wiped his face with the water.

He was very hungry. He went downstairs and out to the kitchen and found Lily. She gave him two biscuits and some bacon, which he ate hungrily. He drank and drank cups of water.

He turned back to Lily, "Lily, I really need to have a bath today. Could you help me with that? I'll pay you a dollar to help me."

At the mention of the dollar, Lily lifted her head, turned to him, and smiled, "Why, sure, Master Jefferson, I'll help you get a bath this afternoon. I just gotta help get dinner ready for the folks comin' back after church. After that's done, I'll help you. I can get out the big tub and heat some water on the stove, and you can scrub yourself all you want. And I can scrub your back and the parts you can't reach because of your arm. That sounds real good, Master Jefferson."

Jefferson said, "Oh, thank you, Lily, that sounds wonderful. I'll come and find you after dinner." He finished the last bites of the biscuits and the bacon and drained the last cup of water. He got up, went out into the hall, and up the stairs to his room.

He sat on the chair at the desk and closed his eyes. The fiery burn in his stomach from the liquor was lessened, and the throbbing and pounding in his head was easing. Inside, though, in his heart, all he felt was loneliness, emptiness, and longing. He wished he was at home. He wished he was 12 or 14 again, back on the farm, roaming out in the woods, not in some stuffy boarding house. More than that, more than anything else he could think of, he wished to be, yearned to be with Cat. He sat there, his eyes closed, as the loneliness rolled over him.

Chapter 20—1861—44 years on the land— Death of Carrie

Jefferson looked again at the envelope he held and felt a tremble of unease go through him. The handwriting on the envelope was not right, not what he expected.

The letter arrived earlier in the day while Jefferson was at recitation. After that, he was required to attend the evening chapel service, so he was late getting back to the boardinghouse. Mrs. Landry, his landlady, handed him the envelope as soon as he came in. He assumed it was from his grandmother, one of the monthly letters she had been sending to him ever since he started at Chapel Hill. But when he turned over the envelope, he did not see his grandmother's thin, shaky script. The envelope was addressed with the pointed and disordered lettering of his father. And he knew something had gone wrong. His father had never written him a letter, not once, the whole time he was attending University.

He pulled a penknife from his pocket, slit open the envelope, and pulled out the letter. Unfolding it, he began to read.

Dear Jefferson,

Son, I'm sorry to tell you, but your grandmother passed away last night. She didn't get up this morning, so Kee knocked on the door. When there was no answer, she went in to check on her, then straightaway called for me to come. Mother was laying there on her bed as always. She was cold to the touch. She died in her sleep. I think her heart just gave out.

You know, Jefferson, how much she suffered. Lately, she just was having one bad day after another. Some days she was having to stay in bed all day, she couldn't even make it to the library. She couldn't even hold the newspaper to read it.

I miss her already, and I know you will too when you read this. But I can't be sad that her suffering has now come to an end. I am glad that she died peacefully, without the pain that she experienced throughout so much of her life.

Jefferson, we are planning to bury her today, up on the Knoll, next to Father and your mother. We are planning to have her memorial service in about three weeks, so you can be there. I am also writing to her family up in Richmond. Some of them may come, but I don't know how many if any.

I know that you are in the middle of your final semester, Son, but I do want you to try to come home as soon as possible. I do believe we need to talk about the future.

With love,

Father

Jefferson read the letter through several times, each time finding it unbelievable.

He was not shocked, not even a little bit surprised, that his grandmother had died. When he was home at Christmas, he saw that she was fading. And he felt loss. Even now, he felt the heavy loss in his heart. He could not feel sad, however, that her suffering, the terrible suffering she experienced all through Jefferson's whole life, was now at an end.

What did shock Jefferson was the seeming tenderness of feelings expressed by his father. Jefferson had never, in his whole life, known his father to say anything that wasn't wholly focused on himself. Now, suddenly, here were expressions of deep feelings, even love. The handwriting was his father's, but the thoughts were not. Jefferson wondered if his father paid someone to compose the letter for him and copied it over.

His father must want something from him badly, to expend time and trouble on this letter. Jefferson wondered what it might be.

He went back downstairs to find Mrs. Landry to inform her that he would need to go back home. She would help him make the arrangements. She would no doubt have Lily help him to get packed. One of her other slaves would drive him in the buggy to the train depot.

He also would have to go and inform his professors. He was certain they would give him leave, but Commencement was only a few months away. They would no doubt want his promise to come back to receive his diploma. He wondered if his father would come for that.

He daydreamed a bit, thought about the farm, the people, what it would be like there without his grandmother. He realized with relief that, on the farm, he would at least get respite from the one topic that was inescapable around the University. The drumbeat of war was omnipresent on the campus, the subject of every conversation. Not whether war would come, but how soon, how long it would last before Lincoln was whipped. Jefferson was sick of it, sick of secession talk, sick of hearing his loud-mouth classmates bragging about their imagined bravery and their righteous cause. He hoped when he returned to University in a few weeks, all of the incessant inflammatory war talk would be fading away.

§

The sun was starting to sink behind the trees in the west as Old Toby drove the wagon up the cart path from the road toward the house. With expertise gained through long decades of enslavement, he guided the team, stopping the wagon next to the front steps. Thomas and Jefferson both stood up and stepped down over the sides of the wagon. They walked up the two steps onto the porch, the warped wooden planks creaking under their weight. Old Toby shook the reins, and the wagon headed towards the barn.

The memorial service for Carrie filled up the Presbyterian Church in town earlier that day. The pastor delivered an effusive eulogy. Carrie's wasted, thin body had already been buried weeks before, next to George on the rocky knoll, so there was no graveside service.

Thomas and Jefferson and the few relatives who came down from Richmond stood in line and accepted condolences from all the local businessmen, professional people, planters, wives, and children. When all the local people finished sharing condolences and the church was emptying, the Richmond relatives announced that they would stay in town rather than make the trip out to the farm. Their journey back home to Virginia would begin the next morning, early.

Jefferson and Thomas rode back to the farm in silence, listening to the sounds of the horse's hooves on the road and the squeaking of the wagon wheels as they sat side by side.

Now they were back home. It was finished.

As they stepped onto the porch, Thomas turned to Jefferson and spoke, "Son, now that that is all over and done with, I need to sit down with you and go over things. With Mother gone, it's time to look at our future." And he headed down the hall towards the library. Jefferson followed behind.

His father turned into the library and took the chair behind the big desk. Jefferson saw the farm's business ledgers spread out across the desk. There was also a jug and a glass. Thomas poured out a measure of liquor into the glass. He sat, took a sip from the glass, pulled out his pouch, and began to roll a cigarette.

Jefferson pulled up the side chair, the chair where his grandmother would sit for hours at a time, and turned it so he could look at his father.

Thomas started, "Jefferson, you don't know this since you never wanted to involve yourself with the farm business. But the truth is, we're about to go bust here. That's nothing new. From what I can tell, this place has been on the edge of goin' bust since it started. But in the last few years, things are just gettin' worse. The truth is, our land is no good now; it's been farmed out. And our slaves, they ain't much damn good either. I've been havin' to sell off most of the younger hands to make ends meet. That means the ones we still got ain't workin' much, and, plus, they ain't havin' babies. The jig is just about over here."

Jefferson was surprised. The farm appeared the same to him. "I thought that's why Grandmother wanted me to go to University, so I could be in business or law. That way, I would have a way to make a living without depending on the farm."

"Well, that's fine for you, Jefferson, but what does that leave for me? Hell, I'm only 43 years old. I don't really care for the idea of spendin' the next 40 years stuck on this damn little patch of dirt, just so I can be buried here, next to Mother and Felicia. We been puttin' our blood and sweat into this damn farm for over forty years, and it ain't givin' anything back to us."

Jefferson was taken aback by the way his father spoke about the farm. He always assumed his father loved the farm with just as much love as his grandmother loved it. Just as much as he loved it.

His father went on, "Look, it's time to move on. We've done all we can do here, and I don't want to keep throwin' good money after bad. There's plenty more out there better than this. So I've been talkin' to a land agent, and I've got a bid made to buy some land in Mississippi. They got new land out there openin' up, cotton land. That's where the smart money is goin', Jefferson, not back here where you break your damn back and got nothin' to show for it. We need to move on this, Jefferson."

"But, Father, we could do other things here. We could raise more pigs. We've got the land for it. Plenty of folks are making money raising pigs in the mountains. We don't have to just raise crops."

Jefferson noticed his father's face turned red at the mention of raising pigs. "Damn it, Jefferson, I am never goin' to be a damned Tennessee pig shit farmer. Just the idea makes me want to puke. That's damned stupid, Jefferson."

Jefferson paused. He said, "Alright, fine. But what about the house? What about our things here on the farm? What are we going to do with them?"

"Well, whatever we can sell, we sell, the stock and tools, the whole lot of it. The damn house ain't even worth tryin' to sell. There're 10 houses in the County just like this one for sale, and no damn buyers. We just leave it. Eventually, the county will take it for taxes. Same thing with the land. It's just worthless. Nobody wants it."

Thomas continued, "And the slaves, we sell all of them. There ain't only a few left, Toby and Kee and them. We sell 'em here local or let a speculator take 'em."

Jefferson thought of the years he spent at University, homesick for this land. His grandmother loved this land and this farm. She fought so hard, gave up so much, to keep it. Suddenly he was learning that, to his father, the land was worthless. Worse than worthless, it was a burden, just something to cast off, to give away for taxes.

Jefferson spoke, "But, Father, that land in Mississippi, if it's so rich and valuable, and this land here is worthless, how can we possibly buy it? Not only the land but new tools, new barns, and a new house. Plus, traveling there. All that will cost money. If the farm is broke, where's the money coming from?"

Thomas looked past Jefferson at the wall behind him. "Well, like I said, we sell our stock. That'll give us a little bit of money. And I sold slaves last fall. I still got a little of that money. And we'll need to use the money you have in the bank. That would help us get started."

"My money in the bank? You mean the money from Grandfather Frazier? That's my inheritance money. That's what I got when Mother died. That's my money."

"Yes, Jefferson, I know it's your money, and as soon as we get settled there and get our first few crops brought in and sold, you'll get it back. But, dammit, son, that money is just sittin' there. It doesn't make sense to not use it. It'll give us money to get started. After the first crop gets sold, you get it back."

"Wait, Father, wait, you keep talking about the money. So just tell me, just how much money does this new land cost?"

"We need some for the land, and we got to get moved, and we need some to get started, for tools and to put up a house for us and shanties for the slaves. So we need about $8000 in cash. And I checked with the bank, you got plenty in that account, you got that much and more. And now that you're 21, you can get to it."

"So this would take my entire inheritance? What happens if it doesn't pay off like you think? What happens if cotton prices fall again? Have you thought of that?"

"Don't get pissy with me, Jefferson. Look at all I've given up for you. You've hardly ever lifted a finger around here. You had slaves to do all your work and cook your food. Who the hell do you think paid for all that? I did; your grandmother and I did. And we never asked before for a damn penny from your damn precious inheritance. We've even paid for you to go to that damn school. Now when I ask for a little of that back, you turn stingy." His father's face was starting to turn red again.

Jefferson could feel the muscles in his neck and arm start to tighten up and become more painful. He felt twinges of guilt from his father's words.

"I'm sorry, Father. I don't want to be stingy. I'm just trying to understand what you're telling me. First Grandmother is gone. Now, you hit me over the head with all of this. And the money. I never thought I would have to use up all that money so quickly, just as soon as I turned 21."

"Damn it, Jefferson, I already said I'll pay that money back to you just as quick as we get a crop from the new land. And the land is so rich the landowners don't even have to live there. They got enough money to go live any damn place they want to."

Jefferson paused for a moment, then asked, "So you sold some of the slaves? What for? Won't we need them down in Mississippi?"

His father said, "Son, I sold Brock because he was just getting more and more ugly like he didn't know his place anymore. And when Jones came to get Brock, he was paying good prices. So I went ahead and sold Cat and Jim to him and a few more. And I got good money for them, and that will help us get set up in Mississippi."

Jefferson felt stung again. "You sold Cat? And Brock and Jim?"

Thomas replied, "Yes, Jefferson, they needed to go. You and Cat, that ain't no good. It just needed to be done. Son, I did it for you."

Jefferson looked over at his father. Now he knew for sure it was all a lie. His father never did anything for anyone but himself.

"It sounds like you've got it planned out. How soon?"

"This land agent is saying that the land is being snapped up, so we need to get our money down fast. We need to get that money of yours put down this week. And we gotta get down there quick, maybe two weeks, three, make sure no one tries to go squattin' on it, tryin' to steal it from us."

His father's voice changed, less angry now, more imploring, "Jeff, I am asking for your help. Please, son, I can't do this without you."

"So you're saying I have to drop out of University, my last semester, and not get my diploma after four years of work? That's what you want?"

Thomas' voice turned angry again. "Dammit, Jefferson, I've already said it to you five times. Everything will work out as soon as that first crop gets sold. Once we get that cotton money comin' in, you can go back. Get as many damn diplomas as you want. But who needs some damn diploma when you're rich?"

Thomas continued, "I could order you to do this, Jefferson. You're still my son. Rightfully, that money is as much mine as it is yours. And Jefferson, your grandmother would tell you to obey me."

Jefferson said nothing. He looked over his father's shoulder out the big double windows. In the distance, he could see the barn and the slave shanties. Behind them, the wooded hills rose. The dogwoods were in bloom, giving the hills a frosty appearance. Standing above the hills was the rocky knoll. After a moment, he turned his eyes back to his father.

"Yes, Father, I can see that everything you said makes sense. Plenty of the boys down at Chapel Hill have told me how their families are doing the same thing, buying up new lands down in Mississippi and Louisiana and starting up new plantations to take the place of the old ones."

He said, "Father, I'm going to go out and take a walk around. I think I'll go up to Grandmother's and Mother's graves. I want to start saying my goodbyes now. I think it will be easier when we leave in a few weeks."

Thomas' face showed satisfaction and relief. "That's fine, Jefferson, just fine. Take all the time you need. We can talk later about some of the details. We'll need to go into town this week, get the money out of the bank."

Jefferson left the library. He was still wearing the mourning clothes he wore to his grandmother's funeral, so he went upstairs, changed into his farm clothes, and put on his boots. He headed out the door, past the kitchen and the barn, and down past the slave shanties. He noticed most of the shanties looked empty now, weeds overgrowing the spaces between them.

He splashed across the creek and clambered up the side of the hill, up to the family plots perched on the rocky knoll. He stood in silence, looking at the gravestones. He walked to the edge of the knoll and peered out at the distant ridges. He left the knoll and walked farther back into the woods.

He found the spot where Cat led him to see Lem, the runaway slave. He remembered how he helped Cat feed the runaway and supplied her the medicine and a file so Lem could make his try for freedom. He remembered how he lied about it to his father and grandmother, and the sheriff. But Lem was caught and killed. And now Cat was gone, sold away to Jones, the slave trader, along with her father Brock and her brother Jim, and most of the others.

After a while, he turned and headed back through the woods toward the house, kicking at the fallen leaves as he walked along

As he came back down from the woods, crossed the creek, and walked back up towards the house, he noted the beginnings of an idea. It was not really a plan, just a grain, a seed of an idea. Tomorrow, he would have to decide. He could trust his father, give him the money, and have his same old life in a different place. Or he could do what his grandmother did at his age, casting the old aside to make a bet and take a chance on something new.

Chapter 21—1861—44 years on the land — Jefferson begins his journey

The next morning, as Jefferson awoke, for a moment he felt disoriented, finding himself laying in his childhood bed, looking over at the shelf of books his Grandmother bought for him years ago. Then remembrance came back to him in a flood. His grandmother was gone. His father wanted to steal from him, to take away his inheritance.

He looked out from his bedroom window over the farm, the fields, and the pastures. He realized that, in some mysterious fashion, overnight his mind had reached its decision. Even if his father was telling the truth about the Mississippi land and the money, Jefferson didn't want it. He didn't want to live his same old life in a new place. He wanted something new, a new kind of life, but he wanted it here, on this land. The land he loved.

He went out looking for his father and found him at the barn, getting set to mount on one of the horses. Jefferson made his voice soft and pleasant, purging from his words any edges of deceit.

"Father, good morning. So what is to be done today?"

Thomas turned at the sound of Jefferson's voice, squinting at Jefferson, a cutting smile on his face. "Well, Jefferson, up early, I see," his voice mocking, "I imagine away at school you stay in bed til noon or so."

Jefferson smiled wanly back at his father. "Well, not every day, Father, some days we are up out of bed by nine o'clock. I suppose that will all change when we get to Mississippi."

Thomas looked over at Jefferson, his eyes searching his son, "Look, Jefferson, I know this has come on fast. But it's something we can't wait on. Just a year, Jefferson, and I swear you can get your money back. Just trust me. I swear it will all work out."

Jefferson considered his words. "Father, I—I'm sorry that I spoke the way I did yesterday. It wasn't right of me to question you, and I ask you to forgive me." He was surprised by how easily the lies slipped from his lips.

Jefferson continued, "Father, I know we have a lot to do, but I was hoping to go into town today, see Reverend Clark for a while, maybe eat supper with him this evening? Would that be acceptable to you?"

Thomas paused, his face hardened again. "Jeff, that's fine, but you gotta keep quiet about the Mississippi land. I haven't told anyone about us leaving. I don't want any of them damn town folk knowing our business, not until we're packed up and riding away. So don't say anything to Clark. And don't talk about the money, not to anyone."

Jefferson smiled at his father. "That's good sense Father. I get it. If it's all right, I won't have Toby take me in the buggy. I'd like to ride the mare. I've got to get used to sitting on a horse again. I need to be able to help out down in Mississippi."

"Fine, Jeff, fine. And tomorrow, we can go into the bank and see about pullin' out the money."

Thomas turned his horse and, without a wave, rode off toward the overseer's cabin.

Jefferson watched until his father's figure receded in the distance. As his father passed out of sight, Jefferson asked Old Toby to saddle the mare. The mare was smaller than the other horses, and Jefferson could handle her better than the others. Plus, she was tough. Jefferson had seen her go for days on just grass and water.

Jefferson's plan depended on traveling to town quickly, getting what he needed, and heading out on the road just as quickly. So he grabbed the bundle of clothes and food he gathered up earlier and packed them into the saddlebag. He climbed onto the mare and flicked the reins. The mare moved out of the barn and headed down the cart path towards the road. Old Toby yelled after him, "Sure good to see you again, Master Jefferson," and Jefferson raised his hand in acknowledgment without looking back.

As the mare walked along, Jefferson looked around, enjoying the familiar fences and fields, the undulations of the road as it passed over hills and streams. The trees were still in the flush of springtime. The sun was warm. A soft breeze caressed his face. Jefferson felt a surge of hope as he traveled the miles along the road toward town.

Jefferson came into town and rode straight to the bank, where an old Black man, stationed next to the bank to look out for the bank's customers, came out into the street. He held the mare's reins while Jefferson got down out of the saddle. Jefferson gave the man a nod of thanks and headed into the bank.

He knew he would have to speak forcefully and assert himself, so the banker would listen to him like people always had listened to his grandmother. He spoke to the cashier, "Good morning. Is Mr. Johnson in today?" Mr. Johnson had been the head of the bank for years, as long as Jefferson could remember. The cashier got up and went to Mr. Johnson's office, knocked, and in a moment, Mr. Johnson appeared, smiling and approaching Jefferson and extending his hand.

"Hello, Jefferson. Let me say again how sorry I am about your grandmother. She was a wonderful woman. This whole town owes her a lot, her and poor old Mr. Adams."

"Thank you, Mr. Johnson. I thought I would come by to talk about my accounts. Can we go into your office?"

"Of course, yes, by all means. Come around the corner here. Here you go, have a seat there, Jefferson." Jefferson sat in a chair in front of Mr. Johnson's desk. Mr. Johnson walked around and took his seat.

Jefferson spoke first, intending to move the conversation along. "So, Mr. Johnson, you know, I've turned 21. And I have that trust account that was set up for me by Grandfather Frazier after my mother died for my inheritance. So now that I'm 21, I'd like to set it up in a new account in my name."

"Let me go get the ledger of that account, Jefferson. I'll be right back." Johnson left the office. In a moment, he was back, looking at the account ledger.

"You are right, Jefferson. According to the trust, you are to inherit the money on your 21st birthday. That would mean that, as of now, you are entitled to the money. We need to set up a new account in your name and transfer the funds. So, it looks like, with interest accumulated, you would have, let's see, over $8,000. Goodness, Jefferson, that's quite a nice birthday present. Congratulations."

"So when can we transfer the money to the new account?"

"Well, Jefferson, that type of transfer ordinarily will take a few days, possibly a week."

"Mr. Johnson, I really want to do the transfer today. Since you have the documents, and since you know me, you've known me since I was born, could we not do that all today? It's like you said, it is my money now since I turned 21."

"Well, yes, that's true, Jefferson. Since I know you and can attest that you are who you say you are, I guess that could be done today. But usually, we don't do things like that."

"Yes, Mr. Johnson, I'd like to do that, and I also would like to make a withdrawal today, please."

"A withdrawal today? In what amount?"

"All of it," said Jefferson, trying to keep his voice steady.

"All of it?" Johnson repeated, his voice rising with alarm. "Jefferson, I don't know if we can do that. What do you need that amount of money for? It's not safe for you to carry that amount of money. I don't believe we could let you withdraw all of it like that."

"But Mr. Johnson, you just said it is my money now," Jefferson replied.

"Well, yes, Jefferson, of course, it is your money, but I'm just worried for your safety, carrying that much money with you. Does your father know about this?"

"Mr. Johnson, the money is mine; it came to me from my mother's father. My father is not involved. I would like to make a withdrawal. How much can I withdraw today?"

"Well…Perhaps half of it, although even that would be really quite unusual. If you wanted to use the money away from here, we could arrange a transfer to another bank. Then you wouldn't have to carry the money and risk losing it."

"No, that is not going to work for me. I would like to withdraw all of it today. And I'd like to get it done quickly."

"Quickly? How quickly do you mean?"

"Well, Mr. Johnson, when I came in, there was no one else in the bank beside you and me and the cashier. I'd like you to get it done and let me take the notes in an hour. Is that possible?"

"But Jefferson, I still would ask you…"

Jefferson cut the banker off. "That's wonderful, Mr. Johnson, an hour. I'll wait right here."

Johnson looked back at Jefferson. He closed his mouth, puckered his face in a disapproving look, picked up the ledger, and walked out to talk to the cashier.

An hour and 15 minutes later, the bank cashier handed Jefferson a large envelope filled with bank notes. Jefferson peeled off fifty dollars in smaller notes and put them in his pocket. He put the rest inside of his jacket, out of sight. He went out and found the Black man, who had watered and tended the mare. Jefferson asked him to hold her for a while longer and held out a quarter to him.

"Yes, sir, thank you, Master Adams, sir," the man said.

Jefferson walked down the street to the Mercantile Exchange and entered the building. He saw Mr. Greene, the store owner, and listened to the same recitation, the same words of condolence, and effusive praise for his grandmother.

"Mr. Greene, I'd like to buy a money belt. Do you have one?"

Greene pulled a money belt off a high shelf and showed it to Jefferson, showed him the different pockets and how he could cinch it around his waist, underneath his clothing out of sight. Jefferson tried it on.

Jefferson said, "That looks fine. I'll take this one. Also, Mr. Greene, I'd like to get a revolver."

Greene showed a look of surprise. Jefferson said quickly, "Father has several, but they all feel too big for my hand. I thought I might get one of the pocket revolvers, so I thought I would see what you might have."

Greene went into the back storeroom and returned carrying a small wooden box. He set the box down on the counter and folded back the lid, so Jefferson could peer into it. Nestled inside was a pocket Colt, brand new and covered with grease from the factory. Jefferson picked it up and tested the heft of the pistol in his hand. He asked Greene to show him how to load the gun. Greene pulled out a box of paper cartridges and showed Jefferson how to pack the loads, how to set the percussion caps, and how to pull back the hammer.

"Jefferson, you need to practice loading and firing that gun if you really think you'll need to use it. The sound and the kick that comes when you fire it the first time is pretty shocking. It's a lot more than you expect. So let me give you extra cartridges and caps. You take that out somewhere on the farm and practice with it."

Jefferson took the money belt and revolver along with the caps and the cartridges, and he pulled out the small notes from his pocket.

"That's all right, Jefferson. I can just put that on your father's account. You don't have to pay me now."

Jefferson lay down the notes. "No, Mr. Greene, this needs to go on my account, not on my father's. In fact, if he comes by, I would appreciate if you didn't say anything about seeing me today."

Greene shrugged and picked up the bank notes. "Fine, Jefferson. It's good to see you, even under the circumstances, with your grandmother and all. You college boys don't always come back here much after you finish your schooling. I hope you stay around. Well, so long."

Jefferson took his purchases and headed up the street, where his horse was still being looked after by the bank's Black man. When he got there, the man helped Jefferson get up into the saddle. Jefferson handed the man another coin and turned his horse to the east.

Jefferson actually wanted to head southwest. He remembered how Jones, the slave buyer, once talked to him and his father at the farm. Jones was bragging about how he made his money, how he was making money on both ends of his trips to Tennessee. He would drive slaves west to sell in Nashville. After selling the slaves, he would pick up a herd of hogs and drive the hogs east, selling them to traders and butchers in South Carolina.

That meant that Jones would have been traveling on the Drovers Road, the set of good roads and turnpikes built specially to bring Tennessee hogs through the mountains into North Carolina. Once they were through the mountains, they were driven south to the lowlands of South Carolina and Georgia. Each year, tens of thousands of hogs would be driven east, food for the great plantations of the Cotton Country, where cotton was grown on every available acre. If Jones was driving hogs from Tennessee, he must have used the Drovers Road. There was no other way.

Jefferson decided he would get on the Drover's Road and head west, talk to people, and try to see if anyone along the Road knew Jones. Maybe Jefferson could find Jones, and Jones could tell him where he sold Brock and Cat and Jim.

Jefferson knew the closest town that touched on the Drover's Road was Rutherfordton, and it lay southwest.

But there was a problem, Jefferson thought, with leaving town and traveling directly southwest. Someone might see him, and word could get back to his father, who might try to come after him, try to stop him, or try to steal his money again. He decided to leave town heading east for a few miles before turning the mare southwest. He could travel on back-country roads, eventually bending his path toward Rutherfordton. This would add at least a day to his travels, but his trail would be harder to follow, he hoped. He headed east.

After a few miles, he came upon a buggy trail that looked to be heading southwest, and he headed the mare onto it. He soon found the trail crisscrossed by other trails. It was well past noon now, so when he came to a fork or a path crossing his, he would choose which trail to take, trying to keep the sun in front of him. The trails, really not more than dirt strips through the countryside, were empty.

He walked along, letting the mare set her own pace. He looked across the farm fields lining both sides of the trail. There were verdant fields of wheat and barley, come back to life from winter dormancy, alternating with bare brown fields, destined to be sown with corn or planted with sweet potato.

As he studied the fields, a thought struck him. He pulled the mare to a halt, his eyes widening, pondering. Back at home, on the farm, the fields were bare, all of them. No fields plowed, no seed sown. There were no greening fields of wheat, not a patch. In usual times wheat would be sown in September and October for a harvest in June. The grain would provide sustenance for the stock and the people on the farm until corn could ripen later in summer. Jefferson's father evidently never bothered, way back in the fall, to plant any of the fields with wheat.

Jefferson realized his father never cared anything about the routines and rhythms of working on the land. Years before, Brock had taken it all over, directing the other slaves on the farm and managed the plowing, the sowing, and the harvest. But Brock was sold away last fall by his father, and the wheat crop had not been planted. It could be his father had been greedy for the money offered by Jones and too lazy to get the planting done himself. Maybe, though, there was something else, something deeper, behind the bare fields. Maybe his father didn't bother to plant any wheat because he was already planning, in September or even before that, to leave. Might his father have been plotting all of this, scheming to steal Jefferson's inheritance money, all this time, six or more months in the past?

But what about Grandmother Carrie? Jefferson's father couldn't have known back in September that Grandmother Carrie would pass away in her sleep months later. Would Thomas have abandoned his own mother? Or...

A new, much darker thought occurred to Jefferson, a thought that sent a wave of sickness through him. Grandmother Carrie was so feeble, so weak. It would have been simple for his father to do something to her, alone with her in the house. A pillow or a blanket pressed over her face for a few minutes would have done her in without a trace. Suddenly, Jefferson felt like he couldn't breathe. A shiver moved through his chest. That was going too far. It was too terrible to contemplate.

Jefferson forced his mind away from this new line of thought, forced it back onto the road, back to the here and now. He moved the mare forward again.

As the shadows lengthened, he came to a small creek lined with trees, crossing the road. He slipped down off the mare and led her off the road. He found a nice sandy spot with a grassy area. He took the bridle and bit from the mare's mouth so she could graze on the grass and drink and slipped off the saddle. He made do for himself with some scraps of ham and bread from the saddle bag. Pulling his jacket tighter around him, he didn't bother with fire, and just dozed off, curled up in the big exposed roots of a tree.

He woke before sunrise stiff and cold. He filled his canteens, ate the last scraps of bacon and biscuit, and quickly got the mare ready. Flailing a bit, he finally got up in the saddle and got back out on the little path. He kept heading, as well as he could reckon, to the southwest, hoping to come to a more likely, well-traveled road,

In the afternoon, he saw ahead of him a small figure walking in the same direction. As he came up to the figure, he saw it was a Black boy, about six years old, ambling along slowly, carrying a big basket with both hands. Jefferson called out to him, "Hello there, where you headed?"

"Back home," said the boy.

"And where is home?"

"At my Missus' house."

"And what town does your missus live in?"

The boy frowned for a second before his eyes brightened and he smiled. He said, "Ruffton, I think."

Jefferson said, "Rutherfordton?"

The boy nodded.

"What have you got in the basket?"

"Eggs. My Missus sent me to get eggs." And the boy lifted the lid of the basket, showing about two dozen eggs.

Jefferson looked down at the boy. "You want a ride?"

The boy nodded. Jefferson said, "Hand me the basket, then I'll lift you."

The boy handed the basket up to Jefferson. "Don't bust them eggs. If they get busted, I get a whippin.'"

Jefferson took the basket of eggs and held them in his left hand, then reached his right hand down. The boy grabbed his arm, and Jefferson hauled him up and sat him in front on the saddle. He picked up the reins and flicked them, and they moved on. Jefferson handed the boy the basket of eggs, which he held in front of him.

"How far is it to Rutherfordton?" Jefferson asked.

"I don't know. A long way."

In about an hour, the boy pointed towards a log building surrounded by stout wooden pens and outbuildings. "That's my missus' house."

Jefferson rode into the yard. He slung down the boy and handed down the basket of eggs. When the boy and the eggs were safe on the ground, Jefferson dismounted. He looked around and decided this was a hog stand, a way station on the Drovers turnpike. The pens were there to hold, overnight, several hundred hogs while the drovers ate and slept indoors. But hog season did not start until October, so the pens were empty.

Jefferson said to the boy, "How are your eggs?"

The boy lifted the lid on the basket. "They are all good."

"Can you take me to your missus?"

The little boy took off around the side of the building, and Jefferson followed after him. They arrived at a kitchen cabin where a Black woman and a White woman were working. The little boy went in and handed the basket of eggs to the Black woman. "Here, mama," he said.

The White woman looked up at Jefferson, surprise on her face, and Jefferson said, "I found this young fella on the road and gave him a ride. He was kind enough to show me the way here. I assume I'm in Rutherfordton?"

The White woman answered, "That's right, this is Rutherfordton. Where are you headed?"

"Up towards Asheville. Maybe you can help me. I'm trying to find a trader who might've come through here a few months back, around September or thereabout. He would have been driving a coffle, maybe 30 slaves, heading over towards Tennessee. His name is Jones."

The White woman's face turned angry. "Jones? Yeah, I know that son of a bitch. He came through here and stayed the night. Said he'd be back through with hogs in December. He told me we would settle up then. But he never came back. That bastard owes me $10. Are you a friend of his?"

Jefferson spoke back to the woman quickly, "Friend? No, he just bought a couple slaves from my father, and I wanted to see if I could find out where they went. Nope, I've only met him once in my life. He's no friend of mine."

The White woman still looked angry, "Yeah, I wouldn't figure he would be."

The White woman was silent. Jefferson finally said, "Well, thanks. So are you taking boarders? I need to spend the night, and my horse needs to be brushed and watered and fed."

The White woman's expression changed. "Sure, Mister, we sure are taking boarders. It ain't hog season, so you got the place to yourself. You can get yourself a bed, and we'll take fine care of your horse."

The White woman looked at the little boy, then back at Jefferson. She moved in closer to Jefferson. She lowered her voice. "Are you the law?"

Jefferson was surprised. "No."

"Are you some kind a preacher?"

Jefferson had no idea why the woman was asking about that. "No," he said again.

The woman approached until she was just inches away from Jefferson. She spoke in a low voice, "I can let you have the boy if you want. A dollar for an hour or five dollars for the whole night. Ain't no one here to know."

Jefferson was bewildered for a second until understanding dawned on him. He could feel his face flushing. "No, that won't be necessary." His throat constricted; he barely could get the words out. "I better go check on my horse."

Jefferson left the kitchen and walked back around to where his horse still stood, saddled. He considered getting back on the horse and heading further west, looking for someplace else, a different stand, to spend the night. But he was tired and hungry, and the mare needed good food and brushing. So he grasped the reins and walked the mare back around to where the two women were still working. The little boy was in the yard playing with the dog.

Jefferson stretched out his hand to the White woman. She reached out her palm, and he laid two dollars in it. "That's to get my horse fed and cared for, my supper, and the bed. Breakfast in the morning. That's all." He slipped off the saddle bag, turned, and headed back to the front of the stand. The White woman scowled at his back as he walked away. As she turned back to her work, she stuck the money into her apron pocket.

Chapter 22—1861—44 years on the land— Jefferson meets peddlers

The next day, Jefferson followed the road west from Rutherfordton. The road was wide now and made for easy going. The mare moved along smoothly, barely burdened by Jefferson's slight frame.

Every five or ten miles, he would pass another hog stand. They were simple to distinguish along the road, rough log buildings surrounded by pens and corn cribs.

The road was mostly empty now, and the stands were mostly empty, just a few travelers like himself. As he came to each stand, he would stop, search out someone, and seek to determine if he was following the path of the slave trader Jones. And, as often as not, the same story. "Jones? Yeah, I know Jones, that son of a bitch. He came through here in the fall with a coffle, said he was coming back with hogs. Said he would settle up his bill then, but he never showed. He's a damn liar."

Jefferson became exasperated by these people at the stands, always asking if Jones was his friend as if they expected Jefferson to pay off Jones' debts. So he concocted a story to tell that Jones has bought some slaves from his father but did not pay for them, and Jefferson was searching him out, aiming to settle up accounts. After listening to that story, the people at the stands would offer Jefferson their good wishes and try to help him. But the trail was cold, and Jefferson uncovered no new clue about Jones and his coffle.

The road changed, going uphill, steeper and steeper, following a rocky fast-moving river through a narrow gorge. Twisting and turning, the road led him up through the mountain gap, jumping along from one ridge to the next. At last, he stood atop the highest ridge, the rugged eroded Blue Ridge. He remembered looking out from the farm nearly every day growing up, seeing the Blue Ridge silhouetted against the sky.

In winter, the Ridge would be covered with a frosting of ice and snow. In summer, as the last light of the day faded, the mountains would change to cobalt as the sun sank below the summits.

He looked east. Spreading out far below was a wavy carpet of green forest stretching out to the horizon.

He turned and looked to the west and saw he was entering a narrow valley with steep ridges rising on his right and left. From here, he knew, all streams flowed westward toward the Mississippi. He would move westward as well, tracking Jones, hoping that would lead him to the three Black people, to Brock and Cat and Jim. And if he found them, what next? He didn't know.

He came to a small stream and climbed down off the mare, letting her rest and drink and graze for a bit. The he mounted back into the saddle and continued on the road west towards Asheville.

As he rode along, the sun sinking in the sky before him, he spotted ahead in the road two men, both of them straining, pushing in front of them a two-wheeled open cart. When he approached closer, he saw one was a Black man dressed in coarse slave clothing. Beside him was a White man, long whiskers falling across his chest. The White man was dressed in black, and wore a wide-brimmed black hat. The cart was piled high with pots, pans, ropes, belts, and buckles. Jefferson knew the White man was a peddler, traveling along through the country and stopping at small farms and cabins, making a few pennies selling to folks on the back roads. He called out to the peddler, "Hello, friend, can you tell me how far it is to Asheville?"

The peddler turned and answered, his words carrying a heavy accent, "Asheville, dat still is about 10 miles. You won't make it by dark."

Jefferson asked, "Is there a stand up ahead where I can stay the night?"

The peddler replied, "Ya, a stand about 5 miles. We gonna stop for the night at the campsite we got about a mile ahead. Stay with us if you want. You be welcome."

Jefferson hesitated. It was common knowledge, everyone said, that peddlers were thieves or worse. But maybe he would have information about Jones. Jones had disappeared. He told everyone along the road he would be coming back through, driving hogs, but he never did. Maybe the peddler would have some information since he was out and about, traveling the roads, talking to all kinds of people. And, Jefferson supposed, he could be robbed and murdered at one of the stands, just as much as out on the road.

Jefferson called back, "Thank you, sir. I would be thankful for that. Lead the way, and I will follow."

After a while, they came to a clear grassy area near a stream. The two men pushed their cart off the road, and the peddler called out to Jefferson, "Dis is it."

Jefferson followed the two men off the road and swung himself off the mare. He took off the saddle and bridle and let the mare drink from the stream and graze.

The peddler offered his hand to Jefferson. "My name is Avram." Jefferson grasped his hand and shook it. "I'm Jefferson or just Jeff," he responded.

Avram said, "And this is Vincent," gesturing to the Black man. Vincent came over and stretched out his hand to Jefferson. Jefferson froze for a second. He had never shaken hands with a Black man before. He recovered from his surprise, reached out, and shook Vincent's hand.

Vincent let his eyes meet Jefferson's as he said, "Pleased to meet you." The voice was flat, guarded. Jefferson nodded to him, returning his gaze. Like his voice, Vincent's eyes were hard, unrevealing.

The men busied themselves, setting up a small camp. In a little while, Vincent had a campfire going.

Avram said, "Sorry to say, all we got is some corn cakes and coffee, but we can share."

Jefferson said, "Well, I can add molasses and salt," and he got those from his saddlebag. Concealing himself from the others, he also pulled the pocket revolver from the saddlebag and put it in his jacket pocket. Just in case.

Jefferson found a spot next to the fire and sat. The three men ate their supper and sipped on the coffee.

After a bit, Jefferson looked toward Avram, "So, I take it you're not from around here."

Avram grinned, "Oh, a smart fellow. No, I'm not from around here. You people here would say I'm Dutch. But where I come from, Bavaria, they don't claim me. I am not one of them. To them, I'm just a Jew. Yes, I'm a long way from my wife and son. They still back in Bavaria."

Jefferson was taken aback. How could a man, any man, leave his family behind like that? "What are you doing here? Why would you leave them behind?" he asked.

Avram's eyes turned dark as he replied, "Jeff, I'll tell you about Bavaria. If you are a Jew in Bavaria, you can't own land. You can't live in a town or city. The Christians there won't allow it. You can go to the town to work if they let you, but you only get the work the Christians don't want. You can't even get married unless they say it is allowed. What does that sound like to you, Jeff?"

Jefferson paused. "Sounds a lot like being a slave."

Avram laughed and looked over at Vincent. "No, not as bad as being a slave. The Jews get treated bad there but not that bad. Here in America, if a slave tries to leave, runs away, they are hunted down and brought back to the master. In Bavaria, they want us to leave. They are happy when we leave. Unless they are fighting a war, then the Army come into the village to take us away to fight."

Jefferson said, "But what about your wife? And your son? You left them behind?"

"We get money, so I can come to America. I work here, work to make money, so I can pay for my wife and son to come. I hope they can come in two or three years."

Jefferson was silent. After a pause, he said, "How did you end up way out here? Why not in the city? You have to work so much harder here, pushing your cart all along the roads."

Avram said, "So, I get my money to come to America. I take my money, and I go to buy a ticket. Everyone says, 'don't go to New York, too many Jews there already.' So I just buy the cheapest ticket they told me was going somewhere else. When the ship comes to America, I find out I'm somewhere called North Carolina. Wilmington, they say. I get off the ship. I think, here I am, free to do what I want. But then I see Black men working, unloading the ship, and a White man is beating the Black men and cursing them. Then I walk farther, and I see lots of Black men, and Black women, and Black children, and they are all sitting in the sun, and White men are all around them. The White men are calling out, buying the Black men and the women and the children. I hear screams, children crying out for their mothers, and men for their wives. I think, God, if they do that to Black people, what will they do to the Jews like me."

Jefferson said nothing. Vincent looked into the fire.

Avram continued, "Finally, I see another Jewish man and ask him where to find the Jews. He takes me to the shul. And they tell me there's already too many Jews here. They don't like us much. They all say, go west, be a peddler. They like Jewish peddlers good enough out west."

"So I came west and found a place where they don't have too many

Jews. I buy a few things, carry them on my back, go out in the country. Sometimes people shoot guns at me, sometimes, dogs chase me, but I sell a few things. Buy more things, sell more. I get enough money to buy a cart, so I can carry more things and sell more things. Soon I'm gonna set up my own store, get enough money to send for my wife and son."

Jefferson said, "Well, you must be making good money. You got yourself a slave to help push the cart."

Vincent's eyes flashed anger in the firelight, and Avram quickly spoke, "No, no, Jefferson, Vincent is my business partner. Well, ya, he is my slave according to law, but between us, he is my partner. We both push the cart."

"So you're free?" Jefferson asked.

"Not exactly," said Vincent softly.

"Go ahead and tell him your story, Vincent. After all, if he wanted to kill us, he could've already done it with that little gun in his pocket," said Avram.

Jefferson looked down and saw that the outline of the revolver was visible through his jacket pocket.

Vincent looked at Jefferson. The eyes were still hard. "You swear to keep this secret?"

Jefferson felt a hard lump come up in his throat. He remembered when Cat asked him the same thing before she would tell him about Lem. "Yes," he said.

"Well, all right then. I was a slave down east, outside of Wilmington. My master owned land out in the piney woods, and he kept a whole mess of slaves in those swamps, workin' at collectin' turpentine from the pine. Ain't no work harder than turpentine. He was master to my wife too, and our little ones. My wife worked out there collectin' just like any man, even when she was expectin'. He always gave us Saturday and Sunday off, said we needed the rest because the work was so hard."

Vincent paused for a moment. He sipped from his cup before continuing. "Most of the Black folk would just lay around on those days or earn a little and drink it all up. But Janie, that's my wife, and me, we decided we wanted to be free. So Saturday and Sunday, we would do anything we could to make money. Cut up strips of pine wood and make baskets. We go out and pick blackberries and blueberries, sell 'em to the White folks livin' nearby. Took in laundry, cut firewood, whatever we could do. My master knew what we was doin'. He said if we could get together a thousand dollars, we could buy freedom for us and our boys.

So we worked and worked and saved every dime."

"But then our master died, and our new master was his brother. So finally, we got a thousand saved up, and we went to the new master with the money, but he said it wasn't enough. He said he could sell us, me an' Janie an' the young'uns, in Wilmington and get double that. Then, he said, he would take the thousand for me, so I could be free and work full time to earn money so I could buy Janie and the young'uns. So I say fine, we gave him the money, and he goes to court, gets the papers draw'd up."

"The day after he give me my papers, he comes and tells me to get off his land, I'm trespassin'. He don't want no free Black folk around, givin' the slaves ideas about being free. He's got the sheriff with him, and the sheriff says I gotta get out of the state. 'Cause the law says if a slave gets freed, he's got 90 days to leave, and if you don't leave in 90 days, they'll catch you and sell you back to bein' a slave. Well, I go down to Wilmington, tryin' to figure out what to do to get the money, so we can all be free together and go north, go to a free state. But no White man's gonna let a Black man borrow that kind of money."

"Well, I'm walkin' around Wilmington, tryin' to figure out what to do, and I run into Avram here. He looks about as low as I feel. I can't understand a word of his jibber jabber, but he's got one of his Jew friends there who helps us talk to each other. So Avram tells his story, and I tell mine. And he tells me he can be my master, just on paper, so I don't have to leave the state, and we can be partners, split all the money right down the middle. Course, it all has to be in his name since no slave can't own nothin'. But once I get the money saved up, I'll go back down to Wilmington, to my old master, and I can buy Janie and the young'uns. Avram says one of his Jew friends down there is a lawyer now and will help us and not cheat us. After that, me and my wife and our young'uns, they ain't young no more, we'll head north, so they don't take us and sell us back to bein' slaves."

Jefferson pondered it. Finally, all he could say was, "Holy Jesus."

Avram laughed and said, "Jefferson, Jesus was a Jew, and I promise you, speaking as a Jew, Jesus got nothing to do with Vincent's story."

Jefferson thought about the bank notes in his money belt, wound around his waist out of sight. That money would be a Godsend to the two peddlers, save them years of toil. Avram could send for his wife and son from Bavaria. And Vincent could buy his wife and children from slavery and go north. But if he did that, he wouldn't have the money he needed to buy back Brock, Cat, and Jim.

Jefferson stood up. He walked over to his saddle and picked up his blanket roll. "I think I'll turn in. Does it matter where I put my blanket?"

Vincent continued to look into the fire. "It's a free country."

Jefferson stretched out his blanket and used his saddle for a pillow. He slipped the pocket revolver out of his jacket pocket and tucked it underneath the saddle, out of sight but within easy reach. The other two men sat a while longer. After a while, they both spread out their blanket rolls. The fire died.

The next morning, Jefferson awoke as the two peddlers were moving around, breaking camp, and getting the cart ready to go back on the road. Jefferson sat up, worked on stretching out the muscles in his left shoulder, which became tight and painful overnight.

"Say, Avram, I have been looking for a trader that I think came this way a few months back. A man named Jones. Have you and Vincent come across him?"

Avram said, "A peddler named Jones? I haven't heard of such a man. Have you, Vincent?"

"I don't think he means a peddler, Avram. I think he means a different kind of trader, ain't that right?" replied Vincent, looking over at Jefferson.

Jefferson looked away from Vincent's gaze. "Yes, I mean a slave trader. He would probably have about 30 slaves with him, heading west over towards Tennessee."

"Oh," said Avram. "No, Jefferson, I know nothing of such a man. Do you, Vincent?" Vincent shook his head no.

Jefferson rolled up his blanket roll and saddled the mare. He put the revolver back into the saddlebag. He mounted the horse and headed her west on the road toward Asheville. After about 100 yards, he looked back and saw the two men, the Jewish peddler and the slave who bought freedom for himself yet was still a slave, pushing together on the handles of the big cart.

Chapter 23—1861—44 years on the land—Jefferson finds Brock and Cat

Jefferson finished his last bit of breakfast, spearing the corner of a flapjack with his fork and pushing it through the streaks of molasses still clinging to the plate before lifting the bite to his mouth. He drained the last of the coffee from his cup and pushed back from the table, leaving his napkin on the chair. He went to the front of the hotel and settled up his bill. Then he went back through the dining room and went outside, crossed the alley to the kitchen, where he found the kitchen boss, a Black woman in a stained apron.

"How about fixing me up a sack of that bacon and some of those delicious flapjacks to take with me on the road?" he said to her. He held out his hand with two dimes. She looked at his hand, took the two dimes, and slipped them into a pocket under her apron. Wordlessly she grabbed an old flour sack and piled a couple of handfuls of bacon and four or five of the flapjacks into the bag, wrapped it up, and handed it to Jefferson. He nodded, headed out the door, and crossed the alley to the stable. He found the stable boy and gave him a dime to get the mare saddled up and ready for him to go. The stable boy helped him up into the saddle, and Jefferson headed out into the street.

Jefferson arrived in Asheville the day before. As he traveled along the streets of the city, he saw the sign for the hotel. Sundown was still a few hours off, and he could have pressed on, gained a few more miles trailing after Jones. He passed the hotel by and made it another block, but he pulled the mare to a stop and looked back. Well, the mare could use a good rest and a good feeding and brushing. He sat still in the road for a moment, pondering, before turning the mare and heading back.

Now, after a supper served at a table with a tablecloth and a night spent on clean, crisp sheets, Jefferson was back out in the streets, carrying a hint of guilt in his heart over the time lost.

Jefferson turned the mare's head west toward the valley of the French Broad River, and soon he was traveling on the Buncombe Turnpike, cut out of the hillsides and ridges beside the river. Even more than the roads east of Asheville, the Turnpike was kept in good repair, held in readiness for its annual surge of travelers.

Every fall, a porcine invasion would surge into North Carolina via the Turnpike. The invasion would begin each spring quietly. In the forested hills of eastern Tennessee, tens of thousands of sows would give birth to hundreds of thousands of piglets. The piglets would fatten and grow over the summer, turning into hogs. As fall approached, the hogs would be rounded up, gathered into herds, and driven onto the Turnpike. They would become a raging torrent of swine, numbering a hundred thousand or more, moving west to east. The great hog drives would last from fall into winter. Corn and oats, grown on bottomlands all along the Turnpike, would fuel the herds on their journey. The river of swine would follow the Turnpike road to Asheville, then break up into smaller streams, heading south or southeast. Regardless of their path, all would finish their journey at the inevitable destinations, butchers and smokehouses scattered across South Carolina and Georgia.

As the mare paced along, Jefferson could see that in some places the river valley was broad, and the Turnpike cut across fields, avoiding bends in the river. In other areas, the river cut straight through a mountain ridge. There would be a rocky bluff 100 feet or more high, right down to the water's edge, with no place for even a footpath, much less a road. In these places, the Turnpike ran right into the river. Jefferson would have to walk the mare into the shallow water, sometimes as far as 50 yards, until the road picked up again on dry land.

The sights and sounds of springtime were just emerging now from winter. He remembered back on the farm; spring had arrived. The maple and oak trees were putting on their leaves, the dogwoods and the red buds giving their show of color. But up here, in what these folks called High Country, spring was just starting. Where the road passed through shady places in the shadow of a steep ridge, the air carried a sharp chill.

§

For the next several days, Jefferson pushed along the Turnpike. As often as he came to them, he stopped at the stands, asking always for information about Jones. Sometimes he would get only blank looks. In other places, Jones' name elicited sour looks and curses. But no one could tell Jefferson where Jones might be found.

He arrived outside the village of Warm Springs. He recognized the name of the place; it was a favorite topic of conversation among his college classmates, the boys who grew up on the big plantations in Charleston and Savannah. He heard over and over how their whole families would travel here by stagecoach for the summer, escaping the heat and diseases of the Low Country, taking suites of rooms in great country inns. How they would spend summer days and nights playing cards, drinking liquor, and smoking cigars.

Jefferson saw immediately that Warm Springs, with its hotels and tea-houses, was not in the same world as men like Jones, driving along their coffle of slaves in chains. It would be a waste of time to stop there. He kept the mare moving, and soon the town lay behind them. The road now ran close to the river. In a few more miles, he saw a sign for Garnett's Stand, and he turned the mare into a dirt yard fronting the same old rough log buildings. He slipped off the mare and led her around the side of the big building to the barn, hoping to find someone who could get the mare watered and fed. No one was about. The yard by the barn was empty.

He walked through the open door into the barn. In the dim light, he saw a Black man brushing and rubbing down one of the horses. Despite the cool air, the man was bare-chested. Jefferson was going to call to the man, but before he spoke, he saw the man's back, and stopped. There were scars, hard white stripes, all over the man, from his shoulders to his waist. A web of crisscrossing scars that Jefferson had seen, day after day, since he was little, on the back of a man he knew. He couldn't believe it.

"Brock," he called out to the man.

Brock's movements froze for a second when he heard his name called out. Then he turned.

"Master Jefferson! Oh my God and Jesus, what are you doin' here?"

"Looking for you! I've been traveling the road looking for you. You and Jim and Cat. But I thought that Jones was going to take you down to Nashville."

"Lookin' for us? Master Thomas sold us. We ain't run away. Why would you be lookin' for us?"

Jefferson suddenly felt flustered, felt the color rising in his face. He wanted to answer Brock, explain why he was looking for them, why he lied to his father, pulled his money from the bank, and bought a gun. He wanted to answer Brock because he wanted to know the answer himself. But he couldn't, not really. Instead, he just spoke, letting a string of nonsense words roll out from his mouth.

"Well, Brock, you see, my father wants to sell the farm and move to Mississippi and sell all the slaves away. I thought about that. I just couldn't go along with leaving the farm; it's all I've ever known. And when he told me he sold you and Cat and Jim to the trader and was planning to sell Kee and Joe and Tim and Belle, I don't know. I just felt I needed to do something. It just didn't seem right to split you up like that. So I came looking."

Brock said nothing for a moment. His eyes were hooded. "You found us, Master. Me and Cat."

"Well, what about Jim? Is Jones here? Is Jones still your master?"

Brock looked down. "We lost Jim. And Jones is gone too. Master Garnett is our master now. Cat, she's workin' in the kitchen. Though he'll probably try to sell us soon."

"Well, what happened, Brock? Everywhere I went, along the road, they said Jones owed money. He was going to come back, but he never did. Did he sell you?"

Brock looked at Jefferson, looked down, then back again at Jefferson. "It's a story, Master Jefferson. You want to hear it?"

Jefferson nodded.

"Well, after Master Thomas sold us to Master Jones, he put us together with his other Black folks. There was about 30 of us, I reckon, about 15 men and about 10 or 15 women, plus a few young ones. I was the old man of the bunch. So he chains all the men up together, side by side. The women and the kids, he just let them walk along without any chains. I guess he's figurin' they wouldn't run off. It was just Jones and two boys who was his sister's boys. Just two young skinny White boys, they call him Uncle Pete, and he calls them Billy and Bobby. They ain't no older than my Joe, back at the farm. Maybe they wasn't even that old. Those two boys don't know nothin' about nothin'. They each got a cowhide, but Jones won't give em' a gun. So it's Master Jones on a horse, and Billy and Bobby walkin' along, and us 30 slaves."

"So we move along, and every day Jones is yellin' at us, hurry up, move faster, we gotta get to Nashville, I gotta get my hogs. So we up early, and we walkin' all day and barely stoppin'. And all we're doin' is getting more and more wore out, and that means we fallin' farther and farther behind, and Jones, he's getting madder and madder, and says over and over, hurry up, we gotta get there. My hogs, my hogs."

"So we get to this stand here, but it starts up one of them bad storms, bad bad storm, with the wind blowin' everything around, and it rains, and it rains. We gotta stay here in this stand three or four days because it's rainin' so hard, and the wind is blowin' so hard. Finally, the rain stops, and the wind slacks off, but you know, the river's runnin' high after all that, high and muddy. But Jones, he wants to get along, so he gets us out on the road, and the road's just mud. Well, we get over to that side ford, there where the road goes down in the river." Brock pointed down the river about 200 yards, where a high ridge extended down to the river's edge. "But the water's way high, way too high. But Jones, he's all, move along, dammit, we gotta get there, I gotta get my hogs."

"So, he divides us up in two. He mixes some of the men in with some of the women and ties us all up together with a rope. And me and Cat are in the first bunch, and Jim in the second. Jones and one of the little White boys, Bobby, they make us get down into the water, Bobby's in front, and Master Jones comin' along behind. So we can barely stand, but we push our way down around that bluff there and finally come around out on the other side and get out of the water. We just pretty near drowned, but we all alive, at least. Believe me, we all saying Jesus, thank you, Jesus."

"So Master Jones leaves us there with Bobby, and Master Jones goes back in the water and gets back around the bluff, going up against the river, where the second bunch is waiting. I don't know how he done it with that water running so high, but he done it. He gets the other group down in the water, and that's where Jim is, and Jones is at the back, and the other little skinny White boy, Billy, in the front. And we watchin' them, 'cause the river bends there, so we can see up the river. We see it comin', a big old tree, the whole root and branches comin' down in the river. It musta been swept down somewhere way up the mountain, and it just comin' down like a hay wagon runnin' downhill. And God Almighty, they see it comin', but they can't do nothin', and that tree just grabbed a hold of that bunch, and they was gone. We barely saw them go by. And that's when we lost Jim."

Jefferson said nothing. Even in the dim light of the barn, he saw the tears on Brock's cheeks. Finally, he said, "I'm so sorry, Brock. I'm so so sorry."

The two men stood there facing each other in the dim light of the barn. Finally, Jefferson said, "Well, what happened after that, Brock? How did you get back here?"

"Well, we sittin' there, cold and wet and freezin' and hungry, for two days 'til the water goes down. The whole time little skinny Bobby, he don't even have his whip no more 'cause he lost it somewhere in the water. He's cryin' and beggin' for us not to kill him. He sayin' he'll let us all go free. All he wants to do is get home and see his mama."

"Finally, the river goes down low enough so we can get down in the water and come back around the bluff to this stand here. We come back up here, starvin' to death, and Bobby goes in, pretty soon they come out with some bacon and ash cake to feed us. Then a while later, Bobby comes out, goes around to this here barn, and next thing we see is him ridin' off, back up the river on some skinny ol' horse. The man comes out, Master Garnett, and he tells us all that he's our master now. Bobby sold us all to him. He's braggin', says he got the whole lot of us for a horse and fifty dollars. He was laughin' at that White boy, how he couldn't wait to get out of there and go back to his mama and all."

"So, we been here ever since. Master Garnett sellin' a few of us to travelers that come by. He says maybe he'll take us on down to Nashville and sell the rest of us. So in the meantime, he's got us workin' whatever way he can think of. And I guess he done saved our lives by buyin' us. So here we are."

There was again silence between the two men. Finally, Brock said, "Let me take that mare and get her took care of, Master Jefferson. She's a good old horse." And he went over and took the reins and led her to a stall and began pouring out some grain and water for her.

Jefferson said, "Brock, what would you think if I bought you and Cat back from Garnett and took you back to the farm?"

Brock came over and spoke to Jefferson. His eyes were hard again. "Master Jefferson, Master Garnett is my master and Cat's master now, and we do what he tells us. If you buy me and Cat, you'll be our master. And we do what you tell us. There ain't nothin' more to it than that.

What you askin' me about it for?"

"I don't know, Brock, I don't know. I'm just trying to find a better way. It just seems like there should be a better way than this."

Jefferson turned and headed through the open door. He stopped, turned back, and said, "Brock, I'm sorry to hear about Jim. Just so you know, when I left the farm, Kee and the rest were fine. I didn't tell anyone I was coming, so I didn't ask Kee about anything before I left. I'm sorry, I should have."

Brock looked over toward Jefferson. He still had the hard eyes, but he said, "Thank you, Master Jefferson, I'm real thankful for you tellin' me."

Jefferson walked back around to the front of the big building and went in the door. He found Mrs. Garnett and paid her a dollar and a half. He carried his saddlebag up the stairs to a room crowded with eight or ten coarse pallet beds.

He lay down across the bed and tried to figure it out. It wasn't too late. Maybe his father was telling him the truth about the new land. He could go back home, tell his father he was sorry, that he would go with him out to Mississippi. He still had the inheritance money, and he could give it to his father.

No, that wouldn't work. His father had lied to him. Jefferson couldn't tell how much of what his father told him was a lie. Maybe there really was new land to buy in Mississippi. Maybe there wasn't. It didn't matter. Wherever the truth lay, Jefferson knew it would all be to his father's benefit, not his. In the end, Jefferson's money would be gone. His father would take it and move on.

What else could he do? He could leave, head east alone, ride the mare back to the railway station, take the trains back to Chapel Hill, and finish his course work. Commencement was just weeks away. He could get his diploma. Go into business or read law, in Richmond or Raleigh, like his grandmother had imagined for him. Someday, maybe, he would come back home to the farm. Pay the back taxes, buy it back from the county. But the people, the ones he loved, would not be there. They would all be gone.

He heard a bell, the signal for supper. So he went back to the dining room, where the table was being laid out. He saw Cat setting out food on the table. He walked over and found a seat, and called out, "Hello, Cat." She turned, glanced at him, nodded slightly, and kept on with her work.

Jefferson saw the same hard look on her face as he had seen with Brock.

Only a few other travelers were boarding at the stand. Jefferson kept his head down while he ate. He finished his meal, drained his coffee cup, and headed back up to his room.

§

In the kitchen, Cat was continuing to work, cleaning up after the meal. As she worked, Brock came in. He nodded to her, and they moved into a corner. Brock spoke softly. "You see Master Jefferson at supper?" Cat nodded. "Did he speak to you?"

"He only said hello."

"You say anything back to him?"

"No, Pa, I just kept my mouth shut, like you said. Pa, what's he doin' here? What does he want?"

"Baby girl, I just don't know. He said somethin' about buyin' us back and takin' us back to the farm, but I don't know, I don't think he knows. I don't put much trust in him. For now, Baby girl, we gotta just do like we been, just go along. But if we see a way to make a move, we'll make it."

"Well, I don't put no trust in him, none at all," Cat said. "I don't trust him, and I don't like him comin' here. He's up to somethin'."

"Yes, but if he buys us, we gotta go along, at least 'til we see which way his head is turnin'."

"Yes, Pa, I know, you're right. I'm sorry, Pa, I just miss Ma so much. And Joe and Tim and Bell, I don't know what to do. I'm missin' them so bad."

"I know, Baby girl, I know, I miss them too. And Jim."

"Yes, Pa, Jim, too."

§

The next morning, Jefferson awoke. He was cold, and his shoulder was aching, the muscles stiff and cramped. He realized his choices had narrowed. He couldn't come this far only to give up and head back, his hands empty. There was still a chance for…what? He needed to find out.

He found Garnett at breakfast in the dining room. "Say, Mr. Garnett, I've been headed to Knoxville to buy a couple hands for our farm. Someone told me that sad story about Mr. Jones, how he, unfortunately, passed a few months back, and how you've got more hands now than you need. I wouldn't mind buying a couple of them off you, saving me from traveling over to Knoxville. Are you selling?"

Garnett looked over at Jefferson, appraising his prospects. "Who you got in mind?"

"That kitchen girl they call Cat, I could use her. And that old boy out in the barn, the one all scarred up on his back. They call him Brock. I could use him in my barn."

Garnett let his gaze linger on Jefferson. He could hear, could see, a hint of something, some bit of deception. At length, he replied, "Twenty-five hundred for the pair."

"Mr. Garnett, that sounds high. How about eighteen hundred?"

Garnett repeated, "Twenty-five hundred for the pair." He peered into Jefferson's eyes.

Jefferson looked away. "Fine, draw it up. I'd like to leave with them as soon as possible."

Garnett smiled. "That's fine, Mr. Adams. Let me get my ledger book and pen and paper, and I can write you up a bill of sale. Cash?"

Jefferson nodded. He left while Garnett began to write out the bills of sale. He went back to the room, loosened his pants, and took off the money belt. He counted out $2500 of bank notes. He drew the money belt back around his waist and fastened up his pants again. He walked back to the dining room, where Garnett was still at his table, the bill of sale laying beside him. Jefferson handed him the bank notes, Garnett counted, and they both signed. Garnett stuck out his hand, and Jefferson shook it. Garnett smiled broadly. He called out to one of the Black people who was still cleaning the tables. "Amy, go tell Cat and Brock to gather up whatever they got and come here. They both got a new master. Mr. Adams here."

In a few minutes, Brock and Cat appeared, carrying their tiny bundles of possessions. Jefferson was surprised to see Cat with a carved wooden bow slung on her back, and he saw what appeared to be the tips of several arrows protruding out the end of her blanket roll.

"Come on, I bought you both back," he announced, and he turned and walked out, headed to the barn. Brock and Cat followed. Silently, they helped Jefferson put the bridle, blanket, and saddle on the mare. Jefferson climbed up into the saddle.

"I'm sorry, I only have the one horse," Jefferson said to them.

"Master Jefferson, ain't no one gonna teach slaves to ride horses. It just make it easier for them to run away. We'll be fine walkin' along, right Cat?"

Cat said, "We be fine walkin'. We always walkin', 'less we chained up in a slave trader's wagon."

Jefferson turned the mare and headed towards the road. "Let's go, then."

Brock said, "That's fine, Master Jefferson, but if I can ask, where we goin'?"

"Home," Jefferson said.

Chapter 24—1861—44 years on the land— The journey back

Brock and Cat stepped onto the road and followed along after Jefferson, away from the stand. They were walking back now the way they had come six months earlier, on the same road, hard by the river. There had been three of them then, Jim was still alive. They had all been mixed in with other Black people, all force-marched along toward Nashville, fodder for the slave markets. But the hurricane struck and flooded the river, and they lost Jim, saw him swept away from them. Brock and Cat were left marooned here at this stand, like survivors from a shipwreck cast onto a foreign shore. Now they were headed back to…where? Home?

The three of them could only travel at the walking pace of Brock and Cat, and Jefferson quickly found it was easier to get off the mare and walk along with them, leading the mare with the reins. The road was mostly quiet, and they might walk along for a mile without seeing any other travelers. But there were occasional wagons, loaded down, carrying families headed west, bound for Tennessee or newer lands further on, Kansas, maybe, or Nebraska.

Jefferson looked over at Cat from time to time, but he never saw her look up. Her eyes stayed fixed forward on the road.

After a few hours, he said, "Cat, I didn't know that you used a bow. What do you get with it?"

Cat kept her eyes forward. "Possom and rabbit mostly. Master Thomas said I could."

There was silence. Brock filled the emptiness. "See, Master Jefferson, couple years ago, you was away in school, but we was havin' a bad time with squirrels. The trees didn't drop any nuts that year. So the squirrels, they was chewin' their way into the corn crib and stealin' all the corn. Master Thomas said we got to keep someone out there all night around the corn crib; try to keep them scared off. But they kept sneakin' away with the corn. Someone asked if maybe we could get a squirrel gun, just something little to shoot at 'em with. Master Thomas says no, damn it, no slave of his ain't never gonna have no damn gun. Then he says, hell, you all can make yourself some bows and arrows and see if you can shoot the damn squirrels with those. He was laughin' when he said it, but we done our best to make a couple bows. Toby got some leather from a harness that was wore out and made string for 'em. And we all took turns shootin' at the squirrels. Cat here, turns out she got right good using that bow. So now, if we ain't got bacon, we eat squirrel or rabbit or 'possum, whatever she can get. When Jones came and took us away, she brought along the bow and the arrows. Jones looked at it and laughed. But he let her carry it along."

The silence returned. After a few minutes, Jefferson said, "How close do you have to be to something to hit it?"

Cat said, "Depends on how big it is. And if it's movin'."

Jefferson said, "What about that beech tree?" There was a big beech tree just off the road about 60 feet in front of them.

Cat said nothing, but she paused in the road. She took the bow off her shoulder and strung it, opened up her blanket roll, and pulled out an arrow. She notched it, pulled back the string, aimed for a second, and let it fly. The arrow left the bow with a whoosh. There was a hard thunk as the point of the arrow hit the beech tree. Jefferson walked forward and saw that the arrow point, made from an old scrap of iron, had penetrated the trunk about an inch. He pulled back and forth and worked the arrow point out of the tree, walked back to where Cat was still standing, and handed it back to her. She already had the bow unstrung. She took the arrow wordlessly and wrapped it back up in her blanket roll. Her eyes were masked, revealing nothing.

Jefferson said, "All right then, that's good to know." Unconsciously, his hand dropped down and touched the hard barrel of the revolver through his jacket pocket.

The three continued walking along, mostly in silence, Jefferson leading the mare. The road became steeper, following the river toward Asheville. By early afternoon, they came to a spot where a small stream was running down into the river, and Jefferson stepped off the road. Jefferson let the horse drink and pulled some bacon and corn cake out of his saddlebags, and passed them around. They sat in the grass. Since they didn't have a cup, they all bent down and drank from the stream.

215~David Herington~ ~215~

"It took me 10 days of travel to find you. And that was mostly riding the mare. But I also was stopping at the stands, trying to find out information about Jones, so that slowed me down some. Plus, I took a long way around to start, just in case my father was going to try to come after me. So I think we can get home in a week."

Brock said, "Master Jefferson, sounds like Master Thomas didn't know you was comin' this way?"

"No, Brock, I left without telling him. I imagine he's not too happy with me right now."

"What about your grandmother, Missus Carrie. Did you tell her you were goin' to come looking for us?"

Jefferson felt his throat close up at the mention of his grandmother. "I forgot to tell you. Grandmother died about a month or two ago. You and Cat and Jim were already gone when she died. That's why my father's wanting to move away now. I guess with Grandmother gone he doesn't want to stay there. He wants to move on."

Brock said, "Missus Carrie passed. Master Jefferson, I'm sorry to hear that."

Cat looked at Jefferson. Her eyes were no longer stony. They were flashing in anger. "She sold off Granny Sarah and Granny Emma and the others. She lied about it, said they would all come back, but they didn't. She sold Elijah. I didn't even get to say goodbye. And she sold us, Jim and Pa and me, took us away from Ma and Joe and Tim and Bell. And now Jim's dead. Because of her."

Jefferson was not prepared for the words or the anger behind them. He tried to hold Cat's gaze, but he couldn't and looked down.

Brock said, "Cat, that's enough. She's dead. Let it lie. Plus, she's kin."

Jefferson's eyes came back up and fixed their gaze on Brock. "Kin? What do you mean?"

Brock could see now that Jefferson did not know the truth. He said, slowly and distinctly, "What I mean is, your grandmother Missus Carrie and my mama Sarah and Kee's mama Emma was all sisters. They all had the same Pa."

Jefferson stared back at Brock, his mouth open but no words forming.

Cat said, "How could you not know that? All the Black folk know. Missus Carrie knew. Master Thomas, he knows. You sayin' you didn't know that?"

Jefferson shut his eyes and said, "Let me just think for a minute." Jefferson sat in silence. Brock and Cat finished their food.

After a time, Jefferson raised his eyes and looked at Brock. "So, my grandmother was your aunt. And my father is your cousin."

Brock shrugged his shoulders a bit. "That sound 'bout right."

Jefferson turned to Cat. "And we're some kind of cousins, third cousins maybe."

Cat looked back at Jefferson but said nothing. The anger was still there.

The silence returned and lingered. Finally, Brock spoke. "Master Jefferson, how 'bout we get back on the road? We can still walk along a little farther today."

Jefferson turned to Brock. "Brock, I've got another question for you."

"That's fine, Master Jefferson. What is it?"

"When I came into the barn at the stand, I recognized you because you didn't have your shirt on. I recognized the scars on your back. Brock, I want to know how you got those scars. Did you try to run away?"

Now it was Brock's eyes that went from stony to angry. "That's all about your grandpa and your pa. And it ain't a good story on neither of 'em. You want to hear it?"

Jefferson nodded.

Brock began, telling the story of the musket, how Master Thomas tried to fire it and was caught. How Master Thomas lied to his father, and how Old Master George ordered his son to do the whipping on Brock. How Brock lay for days on the verge of dying. How, from that day on, Master Thomas always looked at Brock with hatred in his eyes, as if Brock had somehow been to blame for it all.

"Course, Master Jefferson, all that happened before you was born. I don't put any of that on you," Brock said.

"But now that you know, what you gonna do about it?" Cat asked.

Jefferson said nothing. He felt like he had been shot through.

Finally, Brock went over, grabbed the mare's reins, and pulled her towards the road. "Come on, Master Jefferson, we gotta put some more of this road behind us."

They moved back onto the road and continued to walk as before, Jefferson leading the mare. The road climbed, heading deeper into the High Country.

As he walked, Jefferson looked over at the river, sunlight sparkling off of ripples and eddies. A few days before, he had welcomed the sight of the river, and marveled at the way it cut through the mountain ridges. Now, he saw the river differently, like a raging frothy muddy beast. Like a killer, like a monster, like…who? His father? His grandmother? He moved his gaze back to the road.

As evening came on, they arrived at another stand. Jefferson went in and paid for their board, and came back out.

"I guess we can all go around to the kitchen and get some food. We can find a place to sleep in the barn, make sure the mare gets fed and watered," said Jefferson to the others.

"That wouldn't look right to folks," said Cat.

"She's right, Master Jefferson. You need to eat at the table and sleep indoors with the other White folks. You go sleepin' in the barn with the slaves, the man who owns this stand might think we're up to something, or maybe we're runaways. You go on inside, we'll take the mare to the barn and get her settled, and we can get something to eat in the kitchen. We'll be fine in the barn."

So Jefferson went back into the log building, where food was laid out on the big serving board and found a soft bed to sleep the night.

In the morning, Jefferson ate his breakfast and paid a little extra for some corncakes and bacon that would make a good snack for the three travelers around noon. He went around to the barn and met up with Brock and Cat, and set out again up the river.

Two days more, and they were back in Asheville. Dusk was settling in.

Jefferson now had a choice to make. They could take the same road he had traveled days before, following the smoother and easier Drovers Road down towards Rutherfordton. Or they could follow the post road, which ran more directly east, descending steeply down the face of the Blue Ridge. The post road was rougher, but it would make for a shorter trip, at least a whole day shorter, getting back to the farm. Jefferson decided faster was better.

The next morning, they headed out again, following the post road east for miles through a narrow valley until they were on the jagged lip of the Blue Ridge. They began the steep descent, following switch-backs, walking in the wagon ruts. Jefferson remembered standing up on the rocky knob back on the farm, looking out from there, and seeing the Blue Ridge in the distance. He wondered if he could see the farm from here. Looking out, he saw a sea of green dotted with lighter patches, cleared areas that he knew were farms and fields. Columns of smoke were rising from unseen chimney stacks. But he could not discern which of these smoky columns was arising from his home.

The roadside here held few signs of habitation, as the steepness of the land made it unsuitable for farming. Finally, as the sky began to darken again with dusk, the road leveled out, and cabins and small farms began to re appear. A signpost came into view declaring they were coming into Old Fort. Jefferson knew they were about a day's travel from the farm.

Jefferson decided to stay clear of Old Fort. This close to home, someone might recognize him and send word ahead to his father. His father might try to intervene somehow, maybe send the sheriff or the slave patrol out to pick them up, claiming that Brock and Cat were runaways.

Much better, Jefferson thought, to come upon his father unaware and have the advantage of surprise.

A small stream crossed the road, with woods for concealment, and Jefferson turned to Brock and Cat, "Let's camp there for the night." Jefferson left the road, guiding the mare into the woods, and out of sight, Brock and Cat following after him. Jefferson got matches from his saddlebag while Cat and Brock scoured around, gathering up dry sticks and tinder. In a little while, a small fire was going, comfort against the night air that, even this late in spring, would turn chilly once the sun set.

Jefferson dug in his saddlebag and pulled out the last of the corn cakes and bacon from breakfast, and passed portions around. The three travelers ate in a hush.

Jefferson broke the silence. "I am figuring we'll be home by tomorrow evening. I need to talk to you all about what happens after that."

Cat continued staring into the fire. She kept it going by adding sticks and branches whenever the flames began to falter.

Brock said, "That's fine, Master Jefferson. We'll be happy to listen."

Jefferson spoke. "So, I told you before: my father wants to leave the farm. He just wants to walk away from everything, the farm, the house, the land. He wants to move to some new land down in Mississippi and plant cotton, he says. So he's been planning how to do that and get the money for it. And as soon as my grandmother died, he told me it was time to move."

Jefferson paused.

Brock said, "Yes, sir, Master Jefferson?"

Jefferson continued, "After he told me what he was planning, I decided I didn't want to go. I don't want to leave the farm or the land. It's the only home I've ever known. I want to stay. I want to work the land. I think there's a lot more we could do to make the land pay for us."

Cat said, "Is that why you bought us back? So we could come back and work the land again like we done before? Work it for you?"

Jefferson said, "No, not work it for me. Work it with me. I want to be out there working every day. But I can't do it all by myself. I need help. That's why I bought you back because I know you, and I know Brock, and I know Kee and Joe and Tim and Bell. And I knew Jim. So this is what I'm asking, asking for all of you. You stay with me on the farm, don't try to run, give me five years of good hard work right alongside me. In five years, if it's what you want, I'll take you to a free state and make you all free, your whole family. That's the promise I want to make."

"What good is a promise from a White man to a slave?" asked Cat. "Ain't nobody gonna come along and make you keep your promise. Five years from now, you might be sayin' the same thing to us just five years more and you'll be free. A promise like that ain't worth nothin'?"

In the darkness, Jefferson couldn't see into Cat's eyes. But he knew they were flashing with anger.

Brock said, "What Cat's sayin' is true, Master Jefferson. There ain't no such thing as a White man makin' a promise to a slave and bein' bound to it. You still have us as slaves. No promise is gonna change that."

Jefferson said, "But that's all I can offer. What else could I do to prove it?"

Cat said, "You say you want to make us free. Well, go ahead and make us free. Why do we have to work for five more years when we already worked our whole lives for you? If you want to make us free, just make us free."

Jefferson said, "Cat, the law in North Carolina says that if I make you free, you have to leave the state in 90 days. And if you don't leave, you just get sold back into slavery again. The sheriff can come and put you in the jail and sell you. So, is that what you want? Because that's what will happen if I just set you free today."

Brock spoke up, "So you want us to work for you for five years, and then we'll be free? So, Master Jefferson, that's easy, just take us, all of us, me, Kee, Cat, the young ones, take us all with you to a free state. Do it now, not in five years. You get yourself a farm in a free state, and you make us free. We work for you, for wages, and I promise we all stay with you for five years and give you, every one of us, the very best work we could give to anyone, slave or free."

"But, what if I did that," Jefferson said, "we go to a free state; I set you free. You all could leave, and I've got nobody to help me. That wouldn't be fair, not to me. I put in all the money, and then it's gone."

"You makin' promises to us, Master Jefferson, and askin' us to trust you. I'm just askin' you to trust me, same way. Why ain't that fair?" Brock replied.

"Plus, Brock, going to a free state would just be like going to Mississippi with my father. I would have to leave the farm, leave my home, our home, the only home we have. You can't want to leave like that, leave the land behind."

"Master Jefferson, home for you ain't the same as home for us. You got a piece of land, a house, and your family graves, and that's your home. But for slaves, that ain't home. That's just the master's home. I ain't got no home, except for one thing. Kee and my young'uns, that's my home. And, Master Jefferson, excuse me, but you're wrong. Mississippi ain't like no free state, not for us. It's like sayin' dyin' and livin' is the same. No, Master Jefferson, you got that wrong; excuse me for sayin' so."

Jefferson was silent. He never had spoken like this with a Black person before, not even Cat, where he would listen and speak in turn.

Cat spoke again, "Master Jefferson, you take us all to a free state, make us free, let us work for wages. I promise I'll stay for five years, work as hard as I ever could for any master. After five years, I don't know, maybe I stay. Or maybe I go. Maybe I get married along the way. Maybe I got my own little ones. Then I do what's best for them, same as any woman, Black or White. That's fair. That's all I got to say."

After a while, Jefferson said, "I've got to get some sleep."

Brock said, "Yes, sir, Master Jefferson, ain't nobody decidin' nothing tonight. I got to talk to Kee about it all before I could tell you anything for sure."

Cat used a stick to push the coals together and put several more pieces of wood on top to burn down through the night. She lay down on her blanket and pulled it around her for warmth.

Chapter 25—1861—44 years on the land— Arrival

The next evening, the sun began to set, and shadows were stretching out in front of the travelers as they walked along the road. Finally, they crested a hill and looked ahead as the road cut a straight path through the trees toward the town. About a quarter mile further on, Jefferson saw the turnout for the cart path to the farm. The path back to his father, to the reckoning, the confrontation he knew would be coming. Jefferson could imagine his father, the perpetual sneer on his face, pulling on his cigarette, a glass of corn liquor in hand.

Jefferson stopped. He put his hand up onto the forehead of the mare. "Whoa, girl," he said to her. Brock and Cat stopped as well and looked at Jefferson questioningly.

Jefferson turned to the others and said, "That's the turnoff that leads up to the house. Now, this is what I think. If we just walk down there and go up the path, pretty soon the dogs will be barking, and some of the hands will come out to see what's going on. My father hears all the noise and comes down from the house. Then we're in a fix."

"So I think we need to go in quietly. We need to slip into the woods here and wait until it's dark. Once it's good and dark, I'm going to go down through the woods and go up to the house. My father usually stays up late in the library, smoking and drinking his liquor. If he's there, I'm going to talk to him, tell him what I want to do."

Cat said nothing. Brock said, "That's fine, Master Jefferson. What d'you want us to do? Stay back in the woods?"

Jefferson said, "Brock, I'm sorry, but yes, I think you and Cat need to stay here with the mare. I know you want to go down and see Kee and the others, but if you do that, things will get all stirred up, and I've lost my advantage over my father. So, I've got to have you stay here until morning, at least."

Cat said, "What are you plannin' to say to Master Thomas? Are you goin' to tell him about takin' all of us to a free state and makin' us free? That's what you promised to do."

Jefferson's face displayed irritation. "Cat, I never promised that, don't say I promised that. Look, I came and bought you back. If Jim had still been alive, I would've bought him too. But don't put those words in my mouth. When I make you a promise, I will keep it, but I haven't made that promise yet."

Damn, Jefferson thought to himself, I don't remember Cat being so uppity and insolent before. What's put all of that into her head? And why doesn't Brock say something to her about it? A flick or two with a hickory switch might do her some good.

Without another word, Jefferson turned off the road and into the woods, leading the mare through the trees. Cat looked at Brock, and he nodded his head towards the trees, and they followed after him into the woods. They found a small cleared-off area where some trees were cut for lumber in the past. The forest floor here was covered with ferns and grass. Jefferson sat down on a stump. Brock and Cat found stumps of their own. The three sat there in silence. The mare wandered around the clearing, nibbling and grazing on what she could find.

As he sat, Jefferson reflected on his day, the thoughts that swirled in him since the night before when he talked to Brock and Cat. Talked to them, listened to them like they were real people with real ideas, not just a couple of slaves he could command. Instead of welcoming his offer to them, his five-year plan to bring them to freedom, they pushed it back at him, practically calling it a lie, a ploy. And they made him their own offer. Take us to a free state. Make us free. Pay us wages. We promise you five years. Then we'll see, then we'll talk.

Jefferson saw it all clearly now, saw his world as he had never seen it before. Brock was right. Cat was right. They had been enslaved to him and his family their whole lives. Why five more years on just his word, a promise that he could break as easily as squashing a bug? They had earned freedom already, many times over.

He realized better now what he was looking for. When he started his search for Brock, Cat, and Jim, he was looking for a new way of life, not just his old life in a new place. He still wanted that. But his conception of what he wanted was changed now, and he was changed. A life undergirded by slavery, entwined with the enslavement of other people, could never be a good life, not for him. It would always be the same old life of bitter violence, with only a veneer of newness overlain.

He would make his father an offer. He would buy Kee and the others and pay a fair price. He would gather them together and head to a free state, maybe Illinois or Ohio. He would free them there. He would do it now, skip his Commencement. That would hardly matter to his father.

But first, he needed to get answers from his father about his grandmother. About her death. Did his father kill her, smother her in her sleep? He needed to know.

The darkness came on slowly, but as the sky lost its pink glow, Jefferson could look up through the treetops and see stars. He stood up and looked around the clearing. He could not even make out Brock or Cat in the dark. The utter darkness of nighttime in the woods enveloped him.

"All right, I'm going to go down through the woods, try to get up to the house without stirring up any noise. I'll see if my father is still up. After things are settled with him, I'll send someone back to get you."

Brock said, "Take care, Master Jefferson. We'll be waiting here for you. Just don't forget about us."

Jefferson felt the outline of the pocket revolver in his jacket pocket, which gave him a feeling of security. He stepped slowly and carefully, making a path through the dry leaves toward the creek. He put his hands out in front of him, feeling his way along, pushing branches away from his face.

In a few minutes, he saw beams of moonlight reflected off the creek ahead of him. He slid his way down the bluff to the edge of the stream, landing in soft sand. He cautiously stepped into the shallow rushing water and waded across. He did not pause to remove his boots, so he walked up out of the creek with his boots squishing and his feet cold and wet. He saw the slave shanties off to the right, softly outlined in the pale light of a quarter moon. He began to work his way around to the left, toward the barn.

§

Brock and Cat sat in the woods for about 10 minutes and listened as Jefferson slowly shuffled away from them over the carpet of decaying leaves and pine branches. When they heard the splashing of his feet in the creek, Brock stood up from his stump. He said to Cat, "Baby girl, I think we need to go down there and see how Master Jefferson gets along. He may need some help keepin' his spine stiff, goin' up against that pa of his. Come on, bring your bow."

Cat said, "Why we gotta go help him? They just two White men. Let them fight it out themselves. Whoever wins, it ain't gonna be nothing good for us to come out of it."

Brock said, "Cat, I know that Master Jefferson ain't no angel, but that pa of his is like the devil hisself. Wouldn't be nothin' worse for us than havin' Master Thomas be our master again. So we'll just go and see. We may not have to do nothing, only do somethin' if we need to."

Cat stood up and followed her father down through the woods, trying to trace along the pathway taken by Jefferson. They came down to the creek and waded through the cold water.

§

Jefferson stole stealthily behind the barn and, from there, made it to the kitchen cabin. He decided to go around to the front of the house to see if his father was awake, sitting in the library. He came around the side of the house and saw a dim patch of light shining out from the library onto the ground. The glass doors were swung open. He moved closer, and saw his father sitting at the desk, smoking a cigarette and sipping from a glass. The jug sat on the desk. Two oil lamps were sitting on the desk, throwing their soft pools of light into the room. He decided it was time.

"Father," Jefferson called through the open glass doors.

His father spun around, a big Colt Navy revolver in his hand. Jefferson heard the hammer cock, saw the barrel point at him.

"No, Father, it's me, Jefferson," Jefferson called out quickly.

"Jefferson? Is that you? Damn it, Son, I nearly shot you." Jefferson could tell that his father's voice was slurred. Thomas pulled the hammer back on the pistol to uncock it and let it down slowly. He laid the gun on the desk.

"Well, damn it, Son, come on in where I can see you."

Jefferson walked in through the glass doors. He walked around the desk and sat in the side chair. His grandmother's chair.

Jefferson began to speak, but his father cut him off. "Damn, Jefferson, I didn't expect to see you back. After I found out you grabbed all the money from the bank, I figured you were headed for California or somewhere. Where the hell you been?"

Jefferson tried to begin his speech, the one he rehearsed saying in his head. "So, Father, I just decided I didn't want to go to Mississippi, and I didn't want to use my inheritance money for that."

His father interrupted again, "Oh, hell, Jefferson, Mississippi, that whole damn thing fell apart. Turned out the land agent wasn't really a land agent. He was just a crook trying to get some money. But, Son, now I've got set up with a real land agent, and the bank says he's the real thing. And he's got some great land out in Texas that's going to be opened up, and he's offered us a good deal for that land. So, Jefferson, that was actually a good thing, locking up your money like that. We would've made a big mistake if we paid anything for that Mississippi land."

"No, Father, Texas is no good. I'm not going to give you my money to go to Texas any more than I was going to give it to you to go to Mississippi." Jefferson felt anger rising in him.

Thomas' eyes came into focus on his son, and his speech now seemed less slurred than it sounded a few seconds before. "Well, all right, Jefferson, you don't like Texas, and you don't like Mississippi. What do you like?"

Jefferson replied, "I don't know, Father. Maybe I'll just stay right here. Or, maybe Ohio, maybe Illinois, or someplace else. But wherever I go, I'll go with my money."

Jefferson could see his father's face grow dark, even by the dim light of the lamps.

"You damn greedy ungrateful son of a bitch," his father said, the venom rising in his voice. "So you're just gonna take your money and go off and leave me here on this little shit farm. After all the money I spent on you, sending you off to school, buying you clothes and books. Damn it, Jefferson, I knew you were lazy, but I never thought you would turn out to be such an ungrateful, greedy bastard."

His father's words bit into him. Jefferson felt his heart speed up and felt his face flushing.

"Father, that money is mine. You tried to steal it from me. You just said if you'd used it for the Mississippi land, it would've been lost. Now you still want to steal it from me. No, Father, that's my money. I'm not giving any of it to you for your stupid ideas."

Thomas was brought up short by Jefferson's response, the sharpness in Jefferson's words. He paused and looked at his son in the lamplight. Jefferson stared back, the two men squinting at each other across the desk.

§

Brock and Cat followed Jefferson's path behind the barns and up to the kitchen. From there, they crept silently to the front of the house. They saw the open glass doors to the library. A pool of light was shining out through the doorway onto the ground. They could hear the voices of the two men. Brock whispered to Cat, "Baby, I'm gonna walk up closer and see what I can see. I want you to stay back here in the dark, but watch me. You be ready if I give you the sign."

"Pa," Cat whispered back, "be careful. They got guns." Brock reached out and embraced Cat, then turned back toward the light.

Brock walked silently up to the open glass doors. Cat took her position, about 20 feet back in the darkness, where she could see through the doors into the room. She strung her bow. She put down her blanket and opened it up. She picked up one of the arrows and notched it. There were three more laying on the blanket.

§

Jefferson was thinking of what words to say next to his father, trying to keep his father off-balance. He opened his mouth to speak, but saw Brock standing in the lamplight just outside the open doors. For an instant, his face betrayed him as his eyes widened in surprise. Thomas saw the change of expression crossing Jefferson's face. He picked up his revolver and spun around in his chair, looking through the open doors to see what was there. Then he laughed and called out, "Brock, damn it, what the hell. Well, come on in here. I don't need you lurking around out there."

Brock stepped forward and walked into the room. Thomas waved his pistol at him, and Brock walked around the desk and stood next to the chair where Jefferson was seated.

Thomas said, "Well, Jefferson, I assume you did this somehow. What did you do, go find Jones and buy him back? Shit, Jefferson, we got plenty of slaves here now. I'm trying to get rid of them. What the hell are you thinking?"

Jefferson said, "I went after them to see if I could buy back Brock, Cat, and Jim. You sold them, Father, when I was at school. You sold them away from their family, Kee, and the other children. And now I find out we're all blood. We're all family. You and Brock are cousins. Grandmother and Sarah and Emma were sisters."

Thomas laughed again. "Jefferson, you're so full of shit. Is that what they teach you down at that school? Brock ain't my cousin any more than a monkey is my cousin. Brock and his people are slaves, and you and me are White. That's the only thing that matters. No one cares if some White man slept with his slaves back in the day. So, what, you got Jim and Cat round here somewhere too, I reckon?"

"No, Jim drowned in the river up on the other side of Asheville. So did half the slaves in the coffle. And don't look for Jones to be coming around. He drowned along with them."

"Huh," said Thomas. "Well, slave tradin' is a dirty damn business. But I reckon they'll be another trader come by. There always is. Maybe we ought to just sell the lot of them off before we head to Texas; it would make traveling a lot easier."

Jefferson stood up, put his hands on the edge of the desk, and leaned forward toward his father. "Dammit, father, I said I'm not going to Texas. I'm not going anywhere with you. I'm going to a free state. With Cat and the others. All you need to do is sell them to me, and we'll clear out."

Thomas leaned back in his chair, his face twisted in a sneer. "With Cat? So you did buy her back? All right, now it's starting to make sense. You've wanted that little gal since you was a kid yourself. Yeah, I see. Now it's all making good sense. You're wantin' to dip your pen in some black ink. Shit, Jefferson, there's plenty of ways to do that. Hell, you own the girl; just take her. Why I bet those big Black lips would feel fine, she'll do whatever you tell her to do. It's not like she can say no, you bein' her master now."

Now Jefferson leaned farther over the desk, pushed his face forward, and said to his father, "Shut your filthy dirty mouth! Shut your filthy dirty mouth! I'm sick of the way you talk to me. I'm sick of your filthy talk!"

Thomas saw his son's reaction and continued, "Why, I'm sure that girl can show you a lot of tricks. God knows how many White men and Black bucks have had her since she's been gone. Let's see, there was the slave trader, Jones, plus those two little boys he had tagging along with him in that coffle, and Lord knows how many there were along the way."

Jefferson screamed again at his father, "Shut your filthy mouth, shut your damn filthy mouth. I'm sick of hearing you talk like that!" Jefferson pulled his revolver out of his pocket and pointed it directly at his father, and continued to scream at him, "Damn it, I'm sick of you. I'm sick of your filthy talk! Shut up! Shut up! Shut up!" Jefferson pointed the revolver at his father's face, his hand shaking violently, his thumb pulling back the hammer.

Thomas said, "Just one thing, son. After you're done with her, maybe I can have her, you know, like Father, like Son."

Brock spoke up, "Master Jefferson, you just settle down, put that gun down. You ain't lookin' good, Master Jefferson."

Thomas smiled at Jefferson. "That's right, Jeff, listen to yo' good ol' uncle Brock there. Ol' Uncle Brock, he know good."

Jefferson was still quivering in rage. He screamed at his father, "Did you kill Grandmother? Tell me. You killed her, didn't you, you son of a bitch."

Thomas's face twitched. The sneer faded for a moment, then returned. "Jefferson, you ought to know you're only half-cocked."

Jefferson was still flushed and trembling with hatred, but he paused. He didn't understand what his father meant. "What?"

Thomas said, "Your pistol, Jefferson. You've got it half-cocked. It won't fire like that. You need to pull the hammer back to full cock before you can pull the trigger."

Jefferson's eyes had been focused fully on his father's face, his pistol pointed at his father's forehead. Now he looked down at his hand, at the revolver and the hammer. He looked back at his father and then back down at the gun. He put his thumb upon the hammer and began to pull back.

Thomas had his hands crossed in his lap, the big Colt Navy still held in his right hand. In one motion, he straightened his arm out, pointed the gun at his son, pulled back the hammer to full cock, and pulled the trigger. Fire flashed out of the barrel of the gun, and the noise of the exploding powder filled the room. The ball struck Jefferson just below the right collarbone. Brock saw Jefferson's jacket collar jump away from his chest at the impact and fall back. Jefferson's spine arched backward in reaction to being shot. Then he spun around to the right, dropping his pistol and falling hard to the floor.

His father stood up, pointed the pistol at the ceiling, and pulled the hammer back again to full cock. Shiny bits of brass, the remnants from the spent cap, fell onto the floor. Thomas looked over the desk at Jefferson. Brock looked down and could see that there was blood pooling on the floor underneath Jefferson. Jefferson's breathing was coming in gasps. His face had been florid with anger but was now pale white and covered in beads of sweat.

"He's done for," said his father impassively. "I should've done that when he was first born, after his mother died and I saw that crippled arm."

Thomas swung the pistol around and pointed it at Brock.

"Lift your hands, Brock, so I can see them," Thomas ordered. "Where's the money?"

Brock turned his eyes from Jefferson and looked at Thomas. "What money?"

"The money he took with him to buy you back. The bank said they gave him eight thousand. I know it didn't take that much just to buy you and Cat. Where's the rest of the money?"

Brock recalled seeing the money belt cinched around Jefferson's waist as they were camped along the road on their journey back to the farm. He realized it was still there, hidden beneath Jefferson's clothes. "Master Thomas, I don't know. He must've left it with the mare."

"All right, Brock, so where is the mare?"

"In the woods, over across the creek. Cat's over there too. Master Jefferson told her to stay there. He was thinkin' it might be too dangerous for her to come down here."

Thomas laughed. "Yeah, Jefferson was finally right about something." Thomas motioned with his gun. "All right, Brock, walk around the desk and keep your hands where I can see them. You're going to take me to the mare. Move, damn it."

Brock lifted his eyes and looked directly into Thomas' face. "No, sir, Master Thomas, I don't think so." And he raised his right arm over his head and waved. Immediately, Cat's first arrow came whistling through the open doors. It struck Thomas just to the right of his spine, level with his shoulder blade. Brock saw the tip of the arrow pop through the front of Thomas' shirt.

The shock of the arrow strike caused Thomas, like Jefferson, to arch his spine backward. As he did, he spun to his right, dropping his pistol. He teetered there, swaying back and forth but not yet falling, a scarlet patch blossoming on his shirt around the protruding arrowhead.

The second arrow struck Thomas's neck, just below the right ear, slicing through the vessels in his neck and severing his windpipe. It traveled through and embedded in the wall opposite the glass doors.

Thomas fell back across the desk chair. Blood poured out on the floor from the neck wounds.

Brock held up his hand to the glass door and called out, "That's enough, Baby girl."

Cat appeared at the open door and entered the room, her third arrow notched and ready to let fly. "Is he dead?" she asked.

Brock replied, "Yes, Baby girl, he's dead. You got him good. Let me check on Master Jefferson."

Brock knelt next to Jefferson. Jefferson was still gasping. He turned his head towards Brock. "Shoot him."

Brock said, "Master Jefferson, Cat got him with the bow."

Jefferson gasped out, "No, use my gun."

Brock understood. He grasped Jefferson's revolver from off of the floor. Brock had never fired a gun or even held one. But he had seen Master Thomas practicing with his pistols lots of times on whiskey bottles or pumpkins lined up on fence posts. A warning to the slaves about what would happen if they tried to run.

Brock took Jefferson's revolver in his right hand and pulled the hammer back, feeling it click. He grabbed the point of the arrow still protruding from Thomas' chest and pulled on it hard, pulling it forward out of Thomas' chest.

He aimed the pistol at the chest wound and fired, causing a powder burn on Thomas' blood-soaked shirt and skin. He fired another shot at the neck wound. He walked back over to Jefferson. Jefferson was no longer gasping; his chest was motionless. His face was blanched white, and the blood under him was set. Brock dropped the gun next to Jefferson's outstretched right hand. He walked over and grabbed the arrow shaft that was embedded in the wall. He couldn't pull it free, so he broke off the shaft. He held the first arrow and the broken shaft in his left hand.

"Come on, Baby girl, we gotta get outta here." He hurried around the desk, and he and Cat bounded out through the glass doors into the darkness. Cat grabbed the remaining arrow, and her blanket roll off the ground.

As soon as they were clear of the lamplight spilling out through the open doors, Brock grabbed Cat's arm. He whispered to her, "Baby girl, the overseer's gonna be up here in a few minutes, checkin' on those gunshots. And pretty soon, the Sheriff and a whole bunch of White men are gonna be all over this place, tryin' to figure out what happened.

Nobody knows we was here. Baby girl, we gotta go back up in the woods and lay up for a day. We can't let anyone know we been here."

Cat whispered back, "Pa, can't we at least go down and see Ma? I can't stand not seeing her."

"No, baby, not even Ma. We do that, someone will see us. We gotta get back up in the woods. Can't nobody know we was here. Come on; we gotta get down behind the barn."

They crept their way back behind the kitchen and headed down behind the barn. They could hear the dogs barking and the sound of voices down at the shanties. Over toward the overseer's cabin, they spotted a lantern moving toward the house in the darkness.

They crept slowly across the fields to the creek. They waded silently across it and went up into the woods on the other side, scaling the bluff, and getting as far back into the woods as they could in the darkness. Finally, they came back to the clearing. The mare nickered as they came through the trees.

"What do we do now, Pa?" Cat whispered.

"The Sheriff and White men will all be out there in the morning. They'll look at that mess and figure Master Thomas and Master Jefferson got in a big tussle and shot each other. So we gotta lay up here. Tomorrow night, we go down there, and we get Ma and Tim and Joe and Belle, and we get outta here."

"Where, Pa, where can we go? You thinkin' on goin' to one of those free states?"

"No, Baby girl, a free state ain't good enough. Even a free state, the slave catchers can come and take you back and make you a slave again. No, we gotta go farther. There's a place where the slave catchers can't come. A man was passin' by the stand that told me about it. He ran away from his master and got there and got free, but he was comin' back to try to get his wife."

"What place is that, Pa?"

"They call it Canada. It's far away, but it's free."

They sat in the darkness. After a while, Brock spoke in a whisper, "You know, Baby girl, Master Jefferson, he had it bad for you."

In the dark, Brock could not see Cat's face, but he could hear the acid in her voice. "Huh, seems to me he was just one more White man tryin' to use us, so he could get somethin' he wanted."

Brock said, "You may be right, Baby girl. Coulda' been some of both."

They both remained silent for several minutes.

"Pa…" Cat started.

"Baby girl, we need to stay quiet now. We can't let anyone hear us. You think you can get some sleep?"

"No, Pa, my whole insides are jumping and twitching."

"Me too."

They stayed seated in the darkness. They could hear faint voices, angry voices, shouting in the distance but could not make out the words.

Finally, as the moon set, the angry voices died away.

"Baby girl, I'm gonna lay down; try to get some sleep. You oughtta try to sleep some too."

"Alright, Pa, I'll try," Cat replied. They piled up dried leaves and lay down in them together, side by side, and covered up with their blankets for warmth.

Chapter 26—1861—44 years on the land—Reunion

C at suddenly realized that no one owned her. Sitting in the woods, watching the light fading and the darkness thickening around her, the thought came to her. Right now, in this tiny pinch of time, she was free. The two White men who might have claimed her as property, Master Jefferson and Master Thomas, were dead. She saw them the night before, their bodies ghostly white in death, their blood coating the floor.

Cat looked up through the trees toward the sky. Evening passed toward night, and she began to see a few stars. It had been just like this the evening before when they first sat down in this little clearing in the woods. She sat right here, sat on this very same stump next to Pa. But there were three of them then. Master Jefferson was still alive, sitting next to them.

No one owned her. She was free. The idea made her laugh inwardly. The only thing she was free to do was sit here in this clearing in the woods and die of hunger and thirst. Once she left here, she would be a slave again. She knew the sheriff and the other White men, who were at the house earlier in the day, wouldn't say she was free. They would say that she was still a slave. Master Jefferson had folks up in Richmond, and the White men would say she belonged to one of those people now. The White men would eventually figure out which one of those Richmond people was her new master. She would be sent to work for them. Or more likely, she would be sold off to a trader again.

Even worse, the sheriff might think she or Pa had done the killing. Of course, that part was true. She did kill Master Thomas. But only because Master Thomas was pointing his gun at Pa. She knew, though, that no one, neither the sheriff nor any of the other White men, would care about that.

Still, for just this moment, sitting in the woods, watching the stars come out, she was free.

She leaned forward on her stump and pulled her knees up to her chest, still as a stone in the dense forest that surround her. If she sat like this, she found she was bothered a little bit less by the emptiness in her stomach and the dryness in her mouth. Cat asked Pa earlier about going down to the creek for some water, but Pa said no. If the overseer or any of the slaves caught sight of her, they might tell the sheriff.

She looked upward again through the limbs and branches, watching the sky as a few more stars came out. She looked over at Pa, sitting a few feet away from her. He sat on his stump as still as her, still as a stone, his face impassive. Cat knew better than to ask him any questions. She knew he would say they had to wait longer for full darkness. Only then could they try to follow the path through the woods toward the creek. They would silently wade across and creep, unseen and unheard, toward the slave shanties. Toward the shanty where Ma, Joe, Tim, and Bell would be.

Now it was finally getting so dark that she could not make out her hand when she held it up in front of her. In a minute, Cat thought, Pa would finally decide it was dark enough so they could try moving through the woods, following the same track as they did the night before. Only this time, they would go toward the slave shanties. She would get to see Ma and the others and have hugs and kisses, but quietly. Ma and Pa would tell them what they would do next, how they could all escape to a free state or even to Canada, that faraway place Pa knew about, where they could all be free forever.

Cat heard a movement next to her and knew Pa was standing up. "Alright, baby girl, it's dark enough. Let's go down and try to get across the creek."

Cat stood up and followed along behind the sound of Pa's footsteps as he began to move slowly through the pitch-black space between the trees.

They came to the top of the bluff that descended to the creek. Pa sat down on the soft earth and began to inch his way down, feet first, toward the sound of the flowing water. Cat followed him down. In a minute, they were both sitting on the big broken boulders littering the stream bed. The rock faces were still warm with the warmth of the day. Cat bent down, and drank her fill of the cool water, and heard Pa doing the same. Having quenched their thirst, they inched their way farther into the water and stepped gingerly and carefully across the slippery submerged boulders until they came out on the other side, crawling their way onto the soft sandy bank on that side of the creek.

The slave shanties were set back only about twenty feet from the stream. Cat and Pa moved silently along until they stood just opposite their shanty, the rough wooden cabin where Cat was born twenty years before. The same patched-up cabin where Pa himself was born over twenty years before that.

Cat felt Pa leaning toward her and heard him whisper, "Baby girl, I'm just gonna toss a pebble against the wall, maybe get one of 'em to come out, so we can let 'em know we're here without making a big noise."

Pa leaned over, picked up a stone and tossed it lightly toward the shanty. There was a dull plunk as the stone struck. He waited a minute before tossing another stone, and there was another plunk.

In another few moments, the plank door to the shanty swung open, and Cat could just make out the profile of her baby brother Tim emerge from the inside. He looked around for a minute.

"I don't see nobody out here, Ma." A voice from within the shanty responded, "Well, go walk around some and look some more. I heard somethin', twice. It wasn't just my imaginin.'"

Tim walked slowly around the back of the shanty.

"Timmy-boy," Pa called out and moved quickly toward the figure of his son. He put his hand across Tim's open mouth, cutting short the cry of recognition that Tim was about to utter.

"Tim, it's Pa. Cat's over here behind me. Now, Tim, I'm gonna take my hand away, but you got to keep quiet. You can't say nothing out loud, just whisper. Alright?" Tim nodded, his eyes wide. Pa took his hand away.

"Pa, Pa, it really is you. Oh, Pa, we been missin' you so bad, you and Jim and Cat!! Oh, thank Jesus, you come back, Pa! Come in, Pa."

"No, Tim, now listen to me," Pa whispered. "I'm gonna wait here, me and Cat. You need to go in and go over to Ma and tell her real quiet that we are here, just like I told you. Don't let her say anything. Tell her she got to stay quiet. Tell the others, but, son, you got to tell 'em not to say anything, no yellin' or laughin'. After you told them that we're here, and told 'em to stay quiet, come to the door an' whistle a bit, and we'll come in. Alright?"

Tim nodded. He turned and headed back to the door and went in.

After a few long moments, they heard Tim's long low whistle from the doorway.

"Alright, baby girl, let's go, but slow, stay in back of me."

They moved toward the doorway through the darkness and peered into the even thicker darkness of the shanty. Brock called out softly, "Kee?"

Ma replied in a whisper, "I'm here. Oh, my Lord, it is you, Brock!" She stepped forward to embrace her husband. "And Cat!" She reached out her arm and brought Cat into her embrace. "Oh my God! Brock and Cat! How? That old trader Jones bring you back?"

"No, Kee, it was Master Jefferson who come and bought us and brought us back."

Ma's arms suddenly paused in their hugging, her embrace frozen in position. "What about Jim? Where's Jim? Did Master Jefferson buy him back?"

"Kee, we lost Jim."

"Sold away?"

"No, Kee. Gone. I'll tell you later. I'll tell all of it later."

Ma's embrace of Pa and Cat weakened, and her arms began to fall away. "Tim, get me the stool."

Tim, who was joining in the embrace with the others, moved back into the darkness of the shanty. In a second, he was back. "Here, Ma, I got the stool right behind you. Just sit down on it." In the dark stillness, Ma's heavy gasping was all they could hear.

"Kee, are you alright?"

After a few more moments, Ma quit panting enough to reply. "It's fine, Brock. You all hungry?"

"Yeah, a little bit."

"Bell, get 'em that ash cake."

Bell moved off, and in a second, she was back. "Hold out your hand Pa. You too, Cat."

Cat held out her hand and felt her sister touch it, then lay a small piece of something cold and rough onto her palm. Cat brought the piece of cornmeal cake to her mouth and swallowed it quickly. It barely touched her hunger.

Pa said, "Now, let me tell you what happened." Pa told the story about traveling in the coffle with the other Black people, driven along by Jones the slave trader. But he left out the part about the hurricane storm, how they lost Jim in the raging river.

Pa got to the end, where he and Cat and Master Jefferson arrived back at the farm, and how he and Cat waited in the woods while Master

Jefferson went to talk to his father. Again, he held back, not telling how he and Cat followed along behind Master Jefferson, what they saw, and what they did.

"So we was up in the woods across the creek," Pa said, reaching the end of his story, "where Master Jefferson told us to wait, and we heard guns firing. Master Jefferson never came back to get us, even though he said he would. So we came down to the creek and saw the sheriff and his men here, up at the house, so we just went back and waited in the woods til now."

There was silence. Ma sat on her stool. The others sat around her on the straw mattresses covered with old blankets spread out on the rough plank floor.

Finally, Cat spoke. "So what happened today?"

Ma answered, "Well, we all heard that shootin' last night. We was all outside the shanty, lookin' up at the house. We seen the overseer go over there, carryin' a lantern light. He yelled at us to all go into the shanties and stay put, so we did. So he come over here later 'bout midnight and told us all to stay in the shanties, not to go out to the fields today, or up to the house, or nothin', except he told Toby to take the wagon to town and get the sheriff to come out. So that's what we done."

Ma paused to catch her breath. "So this mornin', after the sheriff been there all night, the overseer comes down and calls us all to come up to the house, so we all go up there an' gather 'round the kitchen. The sheriff asks us what do we know about what happened last night? Course, nobody says nothin', 'cause none of us know nothin'."

Ma paused again to catch her breath. She continued. "So he sees that none of us ain't gonna say nothin' 'cause we don't know nothin', so he tells us that both Master Thomas and Master Jefferson are dead. Looks like they killed each other with their guns. They say Master Jefferson was carryin' a bunch of money with him and looked to have been off buyin' slaves. He says it ain't gonna make no difference for us. We still all slaves, but he'll have to find Master Thomas' people and find out what they want to do with the farm and with us. But we just gotta stay and work just like before, and the overseer is gonna be here just like before. And they say there's a war goin' on now, that we might hear about Lincoln comin' down here to make us free, but don't believe it, just keep workin' hard like we always do. So that's all."

"A war? What's he mean, a war?"

"I don't know, Brock. He just said there was a war startin', but not to pay no attention to nothin' we hear about it."

Silence settled over the shanty again.

Finally, Pa whispered again. "We gotta get out of here, Kee. All of us."

"What d'you mean, Brock?"

"Master Thomas' folks from up in Richmond ain't comin' here. I remember them from when they came a long time ago when we was just little. They came that one time and they ain't never come back since then, not once. They ain't gonna come down here just for us. They gonna tell the sheriff to sell us. He'll sell us to someone like Jones, an' we'll be sent all over. We'll be split up for good. We gotta go, we gotta run before they do that to us."

Ma paused a moment before replying to her husband. "Brock, I can't go nowhere. I surely can't run. I can't hardly walk."

"What're you talkin' 'bout?"

"It's my heart, Brock. It ain't no good. Come here, give me your hand. You too, Cat."

Pa and Cat came closer and extended their hands toward Ma's voice. When Ma felt their hands, she pulled them forward and placed their fingers on top of her breastbone.

Cat felt a fluttering and twitching in her fingertips and realized it came with every beat of her mother's heart. In a way, it felt like a purring kitten, except it was much stronger, causing her whole hand to quiver and shake. She pulled back her hand.

"My God! What is that, Kee?" Pa whispered, shock creeping into his voice.

"That's my heart, Brock. It did that some before you was gone, but now it been getting worse and worse. I just smother all the time now, and I stay all swollen up. Missus Carrie, before she passed, she told me not to come up to the house anymore, seein' as I couldn't even get up the hill and couldn't do nothing when I was there. So I just been stayin here in the shanty."

"We can carry you. We can take the wagon."

"Brock, use your head. A bunch of Black folks in a wagon? Without no pass? How far you gonna get before the patrol catch you?"

Silence returned to the shanty.

Finally, Ma spoke again. "Brock, I ain't got much time. I can't go an' you, and the young'uns can't stay. So, you all need to go."

"What about you?"

"Nothin' about me."

"What d'you mean?"

"Just that. You all go. I stay."

"No, Kee. Just no. That ain't happenin.'"

"We'll talk more."

Silence returned.

Ma spoke again. "Brock, you an' Cat need to get back up in the woods. You can't stay here. It ain't safe."

"Why? That overseer ain't coming down here."

"I ain't thinkin' 'bout the overseer. I'm thinkin' 'bout the Black folk. Someone sees you or Cat, they might go runnin' to the overseer. He starts wonderin' why you here; maybe you got somethin' to do with Master Thomas and Master Jefferson. Then we're in a fix. You two gotta stay hid. I can send Tim or Bell to bring you up some food tomorrow."

There was a long pause.

"Alright, Kee, you're right. We'll go back about half a mile where the blackberry thickets are. You whistle when you bring us the food. Come on, Cat."

Pa headed for the door, followed by Cat. They crept silently back to the creek, waded through the water, and climbed back up the bluff. At the top of the bluff, they paused and turned back, peering over at their shanty, barely visible in the moonlight. Cat lay her head against her father's shoulder.

"Pa, what are we gonna do?"

"I don't know, baby girl. I surely don't know."

Acknowledgements

First and foremost, I am indebted to my wife Karen for her tireless help in reading and rereading my drafts and her editing suggestions.

I also give my thanks to family and friends who, when prevailed upon to read my drafts, did so cheerfully and responded with valuable insights. In particular, I am grateful to Nancy Wood, Kurt Lindberg, Mary Lou and Lynn Blanton, Jennifer Herington and Kathy Tompkins.

I have drawn endless inspiration from the many Black authors, men and women, people who were born enslaved, emancipated themselves, and wrote accounts of their lives. Among those numerous authors, I would like to acknowledge in particular the works of Frederick Douglass, Harriet Jacobs, Josiah Henson, William and Ellen Craft, Solomon Northup, Lunsford Lane, and Charles Ball.

I also would like to thank the many contemporary historians and researchers whose work has helped to paint a nuanced picture of 19th Century western North Carolina. In particular, I am grateful to the late Edward W. Phifer, Jr. MD for his book and his published articles detailing the history of Burke County, NC. Likewise, John C. Inscoe, Ph.D. Professor of History, has produced numerous books and articles that help explain, to non-historians like myself, the diverse nature of life and thought in antebellum Appalachia. I extend my gratitude to these and many others who have labored hard to document that era.

I also give my heartfelt thanks to the team at Redhawk Publishing, who have labored with me on this project. In particular, I am grateful to Patty Thompson, Tim Peeler, Aurora King, Robert Canipe, and Richard Eller for their editing suggestions and for moving the project forward and, most especially, their patient encouragement of an "old dog" trying to learn a new trick.

About the Author

David Herington is a graduate of University of Maryland School of Medicine. He practiced Family Medicine for 36 years in Winston-Salem, Morganton and Rutherfordton, North Carolina. Currently retired, he and his wife Karen reside in eastern North Carolina. He is a proud father and an even prouder grandfather.